UNLESS
it's you

CHRISSY HOPEWELL

Content Note:

Unless It's You is a contemporary romance novel meant for mature readers and includes: death of loved one (off page before story begins), childhood abandonment, vague reference to addiction and alcoholism, swearing, and explicit sexual encounters between consenting adults.

Bonus Materials:

Sign up to Chrissy's newsletter for extra content, including bonus scenes for each book and a free novella! www.ChrissyHopewell.com

To my late great-aunt Eleanor, the inspiration behind Evelyn. I hope all of you have been lucky enough to have had someone in your lives who loves you to absolute pieces.

Unless: (conjunction): except if (used to introduce the case in which a statement being made is not yet true or valid).

1

ETHAN

Thursday, 04 July

The tattoo artist did a bollocks job inking the England Rugby rose on sixteen-year-old Leo's biceps, and I barely resist the urge to go and find the bloke to kick his arse for taking what little money this kid has.

"What do you think, Coach?" Leo's voice wavers, one arm stretched out for me to see, the other with a muddy rugby ball tucked underneath. He's so eager for my approval—for any adult's approval, really. That's what having no parental support will do to a kid. Makes them permanently insecure. *Ask me how I know.*

Kids like Leo are the reason I started volunteering as a coach at Sporting London—a charity in London for underprivileged teenagers—after leaving professional rugby five years ago. I spend weeknights training them to play, hoping to give them something else to focus on besides their depressing home life, something wholesome and healthy and hopeful. That's what rugby was to me. The game got me through a lot in life, and now I want to give back to the kids who are growing up like I did.

"I think you should've talked to me before letting some

untrained arse come at you with needles. And you should've waited till you were eighteen."

"I just wanted one like yours." He flinches when I gently touch the red skin with a finger.

And now I feel guilty for being a bad influence, when all I really want is to be a good one. Leo's mum's been gone for a decade, his dad doesn't provide, and he just got dropped in foster care as a teenager. He's had a rough go. Like most of them.

I glance down at my exposed sleeve tattoos, my right arm covered from shoulder to wrist with Celtic knotwork, spirals, crosses, and a shield and sword. My left forearm is inked with red roses to represent England Rugby, and my biceps is adorned with ivy, trees, and a mountain. Rugby and being outdoors are two of the three things that saved me when I was growing up with one parent: a mum who was never around, and when she was, never paid me much attention.

The third being Ben, my best friend, and his supportive, stable, and perfect parents. They're the reason I learned to play rugby in secondary school, and why I even got to university on a rugby scholarship, then showed enough promise that I got picked up to play pro after graduation. I was even better than Ben. It was the first time I was top choice at something.

But now Mum is *really* gone, and apparently, I can't handle it.

"We'll get it fixed. I know someone." I drop his forearm and wave at the group of teens jogging around one of the rugby pitches in Regent's Park, north London. "Now go do a lap, then pair up and throw with Callum."

Mum died three months ago, and after sleepwalking my way through my brand management job for a month, I applied for a six-month sabbatical. I'd just gotten passed over for a promotion, but that wasn't the real problem. I need time to process Mum's death, and the way her instability and neglect shaped my childhood. And, more urgently, I have to deal with the flat I grew up in outside of Newcastle. The flat which I've continued paying rent for since she passed.

It's too bad I can't even bring myself to *enter* her flat, let alone empty it.

Last time I tried—two weeks ago—I froze up outside the building, not even able to make it to her door. But I have to get this done. I clench my fist and try to find the strength.

Nothing's there.

I saw her a month before she died. She slammed the door in my face because her loser boyfriend was inside, and they were drunk or high. I'd walked away, ashamed that no matter how hard I tried, I'd always be second choice to my own mum. I'd tossed the two copies of a new romance novel I'd bought at the train station into the bin. It was a stupid habit I'd started five years ago, hoping to give us something to talk about. During quieter times of my childhood, when Mum was between boyfriends or benders, she'd curl up on the couch with a book, the covers always adorned with a bare-chested man embracing a woman in a flowing dress. I'd grab something from my library stack—Captain Underpants or Choose Your Own Adventure or, when I was a bit older, a fantasy novel— and snuggle next to her.

Once I was a teenager, I stopped.

And the romance novel thing never worked.

I'm taking the train up to Newcastle tomorrow to try going into her flat again. Maybe her ghost won't scare me away this time.

"Alright! Bring it in, lads." I wave the boys over to me. "Four of you there, and two of you as defenders." I arrange them into positions for a drill. "We're going to do a three-meter touch game. This is a decision-making passing drill. See how many points you can get. Move forward with each pass to pull defenders to you. Always try to move forward. Go!"

The boys in the row of four laugh and push and do their best to pass and move past the two defenders. Their throws are messy, but some hit their mark.

For all the good the organization does, Sporting London has been in trouble for the past few years, not bringing in enough donations to justify their overhead, so they're merging with another London charity, Mentor Me. They've gotten rid of a bunch of the Mentor Me staff already and are closing down their offices, with the hopes they can bring in the same amount of combined sponsorships and donations but with lower overhead. It all makes sense fundamentally as the specialties of mentoring and sports go together so well, but it's a shame people have to lose their jobs.

When the community relations lead at Sporting London told me what was going on, I offered to help in any way I could. I have free time during the sabbatical. And with my background in brand management, including working with ad agencies, they took me up on my offer of help. I'll be leading the development of a television campaign announcing the merger and asking for donations.

"Good," I call to the boys. "Remember, communication is key. Talk to each other. And use that space to drive where and when you pass. Right. Do it again." I run my hand over my beard, which is getting a bit out of hand since I've not had to go to an office every day.

Sporting London and Mentor Me chose Pepper Me Marketing —an advertising agency—to create the commercial. It all sounded good to me, something I'm comfortable doing. But then, a few days ago, I saw the name of the project lead at the ad agency.

Stella Hart.

I panicked for a moment, then attempted to calm down. There was no *way* it was the Stella Hart I knew, but I googled the agency anyway. A minute later, my stomach clenched with the confirmation.

I was wrong. It *was* my best friend's ex-girlfriend.

Stella and Ben broke up six months ago, after dating for a year. A whole damn year where I'd tried to avoid being around them. Why? Because of that one night, days before they got together.

It wasn't sex, but it was more intense than a simple one-night stand. We met at the birthday drinks of our mutual friend, Gemma, who Ben and I went to university with. Stella and I immediately clicked. We laughed and talked and played the people-watching game out loud that she'd been playing in her head for years—the Unless Game. We were watching Gemma take a second shot with a bloke at the bar, and when I mentioned it looked like they were getting along, she said something like, *Unless he makes the mistake of mentioning he doesn't like Taylor Swift.* And I said something like, *Unless he doesn't appreciate she needs a full week of birthday celebrations.* We both cackled and kept it going.

For some reason, I'd let myself relax with her. She was gorgeous, with shoulder-length blond hair and eyes as dark blue as a midnight sky, and wore tight skinny jeans and a form-fitting black tank top. And when I kissed her later that night, it was more than a random hookup.

My mobile vibrates in the pocket of my athletic shorts, startling me. I pull it out and check out the incoming call.

It's Ben, like the universe reminding me to keep my thoughts in line.

"Hello," I answer the call, keeping an eye on the boys.

"Alright, mate?"

"Yeah. Coaching right now."

"I won't keep you long. Just one question."

"Go on."

"Am I the only one severely suffering without rugby and football on the telly?"

I chuckle. "No, you're not. The offseason is brutal."

"I'm going to buy us tickets to the cricket at Lord's."

"Christ, we're desperate enough to watch cricket?"

"We might be, mate. We just might be."

Ben's always watching out for me, and since Mum died, he's checked in a lot more frequently. He and his parents were my only support and stability growing up. It's no different now.

I should tell him about seeing Stella tomorrow, but the words get stuck in my throat. It's not the time—I'm in the middle of practice. We end the call and I turn my attention back to the rugby drills, again lost in thoughts of Stella.

When we kissed back then, I'd been spending some time with Helen, my ex. But we weren't together, and right then, I'd decided I wouldn't get back with her. Being with someone like Stella . . . that was who I needed.

At least, that was what I thought at the time.

It shattered me when I found out Ben asked her out days after that night at Gemma's *second* birthday celebration of the week, the one I was late to. Stella said yes. And then they dated. For a *year*.

"Boys, that's great. Bring it in. Hey, toss me the ball." Leo sends an excellent spinning ball in my direction, and I easily catch it. "Let's recap today's practice, then I'll see you next week, alright?"

And now, I have to face Stella at the Pepper Me Marketing offices. *Tomorrow.* I wonder if she's as freaked out about the meeting as I am. Probably not. But I hope she's at least losing a bit of sleep over it.

But I'll get through it. *This* is important. Rugby. Sporting London. Helping these kids. I have to be able to handle facing Stella Hart.

2

STELLA

Friday, July 5

This meeting could've been a video call.

I should be napping off my jet lag from the overnight Newark-to-London flight in my flat, not struggling to function at my desk in the open-concept floor plan of Pepper Me Marketing, where I've worked for the last five years as advertising account director. After graduating from Rutgers and working in New York City for four years, I moved to London, earning my MBA before starting at Pepper Me.

I love London, but even though I try to get home at least twice a year to visit my family, it never feels like enough.

Especially after a funeral.

I drop my head in my hands and massage my temples, elbows resting on the desk. Maybe I can crawl under my cubicle and take the quickest snooze. I close my eyes, but visions of my great-aunt's memorial service in the urban park across from her apartment in northern New Jersey dance behind my lids. I picture her face, with deep crevices from a life well lived, and a dull ache squeezes my chest.

At ninety years old, Evelyn was ready, slowing down so much in the last few years that she just wasn't happy. How could her passing last month have been so surprising, then? I bite the inside of my cheek. No more calling her and hearing her voice. *Stel-LA!* she'd exclaim, singing my name with such happiness. *How ARE you, my darling?*

Ah. Shit. Evelyn's just gone.

Ever since my dad died when I was eleven, Evelyn and I have been close. Dad was always restless, seeming like he wanted something more than our quiet life. I would tuck myself under his arm and watch travel documentaries of unfamiliar places, wide-eyed at the world outside of Jersey. I wanted to see them, too. Settling down with a family probably wasn't the right choice for Dad.

My mom and two sisters didn't get him. I felt like I did. Evelyn did. The three of us were kindred spirits.

Evelyn took us to London after his death. A healing journey. I fell in love with London and got to see Evelyn in her element: traveling and sharing what she loved with us. One day during the trip, Mom took my sisters shopping at Harrods, and I went with Evelyn to London Zoo. I felt like the most important person in the world to her. She really had life figured out. No husband, no kids, just living to the fullest exactly as she wished.

Long ago, I decided I didn't want children, either. I wanted to live free and explore the world, like Evelyn.

I let out a rush of air and roll my shoulders back. I could've used a few more days in Jersey with my mom and my sisters. Just to hang out. I *would've* stayed a few more days so I could be there in person for Evelyn's will reading, which is now a video call on Monday, but I had to get back for this in-person meeting.

And again, which—like the will reading is—could've been a video call.

"Good morning!" Tessa, my boss, slows down as she approaches my cubicle. Tall and curvy, with gorgeous natural hair surrounding her round face like a halo, she figuratively and literally runs this place. Pepper Me Marketing is a holistic advertising agency. We produce creative pieces like traditional TV commercials, videos for digital use and social media platforms, and other creative work for clients in London and all over the world. I'm the liaison between the agency's creatives and clients, and I excel at making clients happy and ensuring we produce the best work possible.

Exhaustion aside, I'm pumped to be working on the Mentor Me and Sporting London merger. I volunteer with Mentor Me and see my teenaged mentee, Izzy, once a month for a coffee and a wander around London, or sometimes for day trips in nature outside the city, something Mentor Me likes to push as therapeutic for the kids. They're not wrong.

But since Pepper Me is doing this project pro bono, it's going to be on top of my already full workload.

Between Evelyn's death and the breakup with Ben that's been lingering over my head for the past six months, I've been distracted, so I'm hoping I can move forward and focus on work.

I'd have preferred to do it with a bit more sleep.

"Hey, Tessa."

She steps right into my cubicle and pulls me into an awkward hug from my chair, squishing my face into her shoulder blade.

"So sorry about your aunt," Tessa whispers in my ear, her lovely English accent making *aunt* sound a lot fancier.

"Thank you." My voice squeaks and the ache in my chest turns to tears in my eyes.

She leans away, her hands on my shoulders, staring intently at my face, as if checking that I'm really okay. "Well then. We'll get on with it, right?"

I nod and swallow away the lump in my throat.

"And apologies about the morning meeting, given your overnight flight." She stands straight and purses her lips. "I tried for the afternoon, but half eleven was the best I could do. It's a bit of chaos over at the charities. They've laid off a load of the

Mentor Me staff, and it's mostly just Sporting London people left."

"Oh no, really?"

"Yes, but I talked to the bloke leading the project on Wednesday—he's basically a volunteer but has extensive brand management experience—and he sounds like he'll be an excellent advocate for both charities."

She turns her palms up gracefully and grins at me. "Anyhoo, he was eager to get this kicked off A-S-A-P, and you were out of pocket, so here we are. See you in half an hour, hey?"

With that, she whisks herself away.

As bosses go, Tessa's not so bad. She puts up with me and mostly lets me do what I want around here, as long as I keep clients happy and get the advertising projects done on time. But she does like her in-person meetings with clients, especially early on.

I click my mouse and enter my laptop password, but get distracted by my vibrating cell phone as my desktop loads. A message pops up on my sisters' text chain. It's a text from my older sister, followed quickly by one from my younger sister, both up early back in the US.

REESE

How are you, Stella? Did you get in okay? It was so amazing being all together, even under the circumstances

MADDIE

Happy Friday, sisters! I hope you got some rest on your flight. I couldn't sleep last night. I'm curled up on my couch

REESE

Oliver just brought me a giant, steaming mug of coffee. I didn't sleep well either. Miss you already, Stella

MADDIE

I wish someone would bring me coffee!

After meeting in Scotland last summer and attempting to fake date, Reese and Oliver fell ridiculously in love. I witnessed their bliss first-hand this past week, and wasn't sure if I should vomit all over them or weep with envy.

Let's go with vomit.

I have no interest in being so in love that I lose all sense of who I am and what I want—and don't want—in life. As delightful as Oliver is, I still feel like Reese should have embraced being single for a lot longer, not let the first hot Scottish ex-professional soccer player who paid attention to her change the course of her life.

Wait . . . hmm. That doesn't sound quite right. Maybe she did okay.

An uninvited vision of my ex pops up in my brain. Tall, slender, wavy blond hair, baby blue eyes. Breaking up with Ben six months ago was the right thing to do. I don't even like my *boss* ordering me around, and having a man influence everything in my life, from what I eat for dinner to where I live or—like what happened before we split—having an opinion on my take on not having children.

He knew where I stood but thought he could change my mind. Doesn't matter that he was cute and perfect on paper, or seemed devastated by our breakup. Surely, I wasn't in love with him. I don't even know what that feels like. Honestly, I don't think I'm capable of being in love. Not anymore. Still, I feel that familiar twinge in my gut when I think of Ben. *Did* I do the right thing by walking away?

Better to walk away from him than get walked away from, which is what happened with Hunter before I moved to London seven years ago. That man broke me permanently, and while I've dated a few guys since—Ben most recently and for the longest—it always feels like I'm faking it. Like Reese and Oliver did last summer, except with a different ending.

Ben said it to me straight: I'm not girlfriend material. Not wife material. Not mother material. It was during our last fight, and the truth stung. He said I was a closed book, that he couldn't even talk to me.

I respond to the text chain with a GIF of a woman pouring an entire pot of coffee over her head.

ME

I'm at the office, counting down the minutes until I can crash at home. Love you both. Talk later xo

Now my meeting is in twenty minutes, but I'm officially in sloth mode. I click through my emails to find the message from Tessa with client information. I should know most of it because of the work I've already done with Mentor Me.

I skim the summary, focusing on the Sporting London information. Tessa pasted the contact's email into her message, and I let out a snort. What kind of monster agrees to come *into* an office and *get started right away*?

I'm good at my job managing the creative process with the agency and client, so this kind of initial meeting will be easy. I already know their objective is to announce the merger and ask for holiday donations. After the meeting, I'll get the brief written and approved, and then the creative team will work on concepts. There will be storyboard decisions, a director to choose, and talent to select. The client will be involved in each step. It should be a smooth process that I can do in my sleep, which is perfect as I might be actually asleep during the meeting.

"Who am I talking to today . . ." I mutter to myself and scroll down to the bottom of the email.

My hand freezes above the mouse and I gasp, as shocked as if a green ogre had popped over the cubicle wall, said *Cheerio!,* and handed me a triple mocha with whipped cream.

I squint my eyes and stare at the name of the client lead.

No. Can't be. Uh-uh.

The name dances in front of my suddenly alert eyes: *Ethan Fraser.*

There must be a million people in London with his name. A million ex-professional rugby players with tattoo sleeves and a full beard, who would make me want to hide with one withering, judgmental glance from his gorgeous dark eyes across the bar during the year I dated Ben. Wait, no, not gorgeous—angry. Brooding. Unfeeling. Mean.

Before that, he and I had such a fun night at Gemma's birthday drinks. Drinks, kisses, and I'd even shared the Unless Game with him, which he gleefully played along with. But the fun ended when he left me at the door to my flat. Gemma went to university with Ben and Ethan, so a few days later, when I met Ben at her birthday dinner, she'd insisted *he* was the one for me, *not* Ethan. She had the inside knowledge that Ethan was hanging out with his ex and was in the process of getting back together with her.

I was bummed, so when Ben asked me out, I said yes.

Ethan was such a dick to me during the time I was with Ben. Luckily, he wasn't around a lot, but when he was, he was always glaring at me from across the room. There was only one other night when he'd showed another side of him. I shake my head to get *that* weird memory out.

"No, no. No." I lean away from the screen. My heart races and I lay my hand on my chest to calm it.

Ten minutes until the meeting.

Nausea crashes over me. Why hadn't I read this email over the last few days, around drinking wine with my sisters, having coffee in my mom's bright yellow kitchen, or hanging out with my teenaged niece? I could've mentally prepared myself.

I could've avoided this absolute panic at the thought of my ex-boyfriend's best friend—who absolutely hates my guts—being my new client.

I can still feel his lips on mine from that night. Why do I remember the feel of Ethan's lips more than I remember Ben's?

Maybe there's another Ethan Fraser who happens to be the client lead for Sporting London. Maybe it's not *him*.

Guess I'm about to find out.

3

ETHAN

The wheels of the double-decker bus squeal as it screeches to a halt along the back edge of Regent's Park. A young mother and her toddler pad down the steps from the upper level, giving me something to look at for a few seconds other than the text that pinged in ten minutes ago.

PAUL (MUM'S LANDLORD)

Hello. I'm selling the flat. You've got thirty days
to empty it

Fuck me.

Thirty days? Three months hasn't been enough, so I'm sure as hell not going to figure things out in thirty days.

Maybe this will be the kick in the arse I need.

Mum's landlord isn't the nicest man. He certainly didn't think to sugar coat that text. But I haven't had direct contact with him in a long time, since I've continued to pay Mum's rent, just like I did the last years she was alive. And until now, he's quietly accepted my online payments without a word, not even a *my condolences* text message when she passed away. Did he wonder why I haven't stopped paying, even though she's gone? He certainly has no idea I'm unable to even enter Mum's flat. And sure as hell doesn't care.

I respond with a simple *okay*.

Two ladies in their sixties settle in across the aisle from me, chattering away. This is what Mum and her best friend, Suzanne, should be doing if Mum's life hadn't veered so badly off course.

Maybe I'll go visit Suzanne when I'm up in Newcastle this weekend, like I did last time. I keep thinking talking to someone who knew Mum will help me move past whatever barrier is keeping me frozen in place with the flat. Maybe this time will be the charm.

And since Helen still lives with Suzanne, her mum, I'd probably see her, too. Our mums were close friends while we grew up, and when we finally dated, I know at least Suzanne was hoping it'd last. She'd thought we were a good match, me and Helen. Ben was the odd one out, hanging out with us despite his golden, shiny family.

As usual, thoughts of Helen confuse me. I shift in my uncomfortable bus seat as we turn the corner around the park, Lord's Cricket Ground just visible on the right. We were close to getting back together before that night with Stella. Now Helen has made it clear she wants me. Again. But she's complicated. We were together, then she had a brief fling with Ben. She chose him.

But that's all ancient history.

Maybe going to see Helen and Suzanne is just another way for me to go all the way to Newcastle and still avoid the flat, just like the last time, when I stayed with Ben's parents. They kept giving me pitying looks—the same looks they gave me when I was a kid and Mum would disappear again and again, either physically or emotionally. Ben would bring me home to dinner five nights in a row, or hiking on the weekend followed by a week-long sleepover, during which his parents would force us to do schoolwork in between tossing a rugby ball. I don't know how I would have gotten to where I am today without Ben and his parents, Robin and Simon.

The bus pulls to a halt, and I trot down the steps and hop off at Baker Street. I dodge the London commuters and position myself against one of the tall buildings while I check my mobile for directions to Pepper Me Marketing.

Maybe I'll no longer think anything inappropriate when I'm face-to-face with Stella. It's been so long since I've seen her—long before she and Ben broke up. Maybe she'll have no effect on me and today will be completely professional.

Once inside the building and up a short ride on the lift, I tell the Pepper Me Marketing receptionist who I am, and the twenty-something woman smiles at me. I must have successfully put my professional face on.

"Ethan?" A tall, slender woman strides toward me from down the hall.

It's not Stella Hart.

"Yes." Maybe I'll get lucky and Stella will have quit between the time I got the invite on my calendar earlier this week—with her name so prominently at the top of the attendee list—and today.

"I'm Tessa Brown. Wonderful to meet you in person. Most of the team is already in the conference room, but we're still waiting for our account director." Tessa gestures for me to follow and glides away, confident I'll be behind her.

I adjust my rolled-up sleeves that display part of the tattoos covering my arms from wrist to shoulder, and trail Tessa around a corner and down a long hallway, leading to a big, open-plan work-space. Interconnected desks with low cubicle barriers fill the room.

"Thank you so much for coming out to see us in person today. We've found that when we have our clients with us on site for at least part of the project, we get so much more done. It's so collabo-rative, right? We can just talk things out, face-to-face. Brainstorm. Get our creative juices really flowing." Tessa flashes me a bright white smile. "I know you understand, given your experience with ad development."

"Yes, of course." She's not wrong, but this one time, I'd strongly prefer not facing this team in person.

"Here we are. Would you like coffee?" Tessa stops short in front of a cracked open door.

"No, thank you." My stomach's twisting into tight little knots. I don't think coffee would sit well.

"Right then. Come on in."

I breathe in and out through my nose.

How hard can it be to face Stella Hart?

HARD. It's fucking hard.

Especially with that look on her face. Shock? Dismay? Her jaw's hanging open so wide, she looks like a marionette doll.

Stella's as stunning as I remember, and I hate myself for thinking it.

Her shoulder-length blond hair shifts around her face as she looks at her laptop, then at me, then Tessa, who is introducing the team to me one-by-one. I smile and nod at each person as she explains their role. A pair of creatives named Graham and Luke, Chloe, the account manager, and then . . .

"And this is Stella Hart, your main contact and our very senior account director. You'll be in the best hands with her."

"Hello." I nod my head at Stella, and her eyes widen comically. She rubs her left thumb on her right wrist and my eyes flit down. A colorful blue-and-purple butterfly tattoo. I'd noticed it that night a year and a half ago. She's wearing a tight white tank top that swoops down to just over her breasts, and a blue fitted sweater that hangs past the waistline of her form-fitting jeans. And those damn red heels. I was already seated when she entered the room, a whoosh of sweet-scented air surrounding her and a spooked look on her face.

"Stella's been involved in Mentor Me, so she has all the background on that half of the merger. And I know you're an expert in the other half, right, Ethan?"

I nod and grab my beard, pulling and twisting the coarse hair in a nervous motion.

"I've been volunteering with Sporting London for five years," I say, because Tessa looks like she expects me to give a speech. "They're a fantastic organization that serves needy kids in Greater London. We want to make sure this merger between the two charities leaves us with one organization that still helps the same number of kids. More, really."

Stella's face softens slightly.

"Mmm, don't we all, Ethan?" Tessa coos. "And I think it means something personally to you, doesn't it?"

"Yes." I immediately regret telling Tessa about my past when we first talked, but we're in too deep now. "I wish there had been a group like this when I was growing up in Newcastle. I didn't have parental support during my childhood, just like many of the kids I coach. If it weren't for my best friend's family advising me, mentoring me, pushing me into rugby, helping me secure a scholarship to university, connecting me with the right people, everything . . . then I would be nowhere."

Why did I go and say all of that? Why did I mention Ben in front of Stella? I could've kept it much more surface level. But this isn't all about me. This is about Sporting London and the kids it helps. I need everyone to understand how important it is to me that we get this right.

Tessa nods and looks around the room at the other solemn-faced people. "Thanks for sharing that. It's so inspiring. You've come so far."

"Mentor Me is also a wonderful group," Stella says after a pause, running her hand along the back of her neck. "But they're not the most organized. After signing up to mentor Izzy, I never really heard from them. And they've not been great about driving donations. On top of that, they had an unnecessarily big office space in central London . . . still, I feel bad so many of them have lost their jobs. Anyway, I think we all have the same objective with this campaign."

"I know the board has been working with some of the displaced employees to help them find new positions." I'm not sure why I offer this information, other than the fact that I agree it's rough for the former Mentor Me employees.

Stella half smiles at me and I almost smile back, but I stiffen my spine and look at Tessa instead. I will not be making friends with that woman, even if she also spends time helping kids. I need to protect my mental health. Protect my heart, just like I did for the whole time she was dating Ben, when I spent way more time meeting my old rugby mates instead of accepting invitations to go out with Ben and Stella.

"Can we talk timelines? We'd like this on air by October. We have funding for two months of television, and since December spots are too expensive, we'll focus on October and November."

"Absolutely, that will work," Stella says. "We can do a sixty-day timeline from now until finished product, then it will take a few more weeks after that to get it approved by the networks and on air. October will work."

I keep my eyes fixed on Tessa, acting as if Stella hadn't said a word. Tessa blinks at me, eyes darting to Stella then back to me. I can see Stella shift in her chair out of the corner of my vision, waiting for me to look at her so she can continue speaking.

"We'll have to keep to a tight timeline, but, as Stella said, it'll work," Tessa finally says, after giving me plenty of time to acknowledge Stella. I do not. "You'll need to make quick decisions on storyboards, directors, and all the shoot details."

Stella lets out a huff of air and Tessa looks at her with concerned eyes.

I know I'm being an arse. I thought I'd be able to handle this. But how can I work with Stella? Even looking at her is painful.

The hurt comes rushing back. Ben pulling me aside the night of Gemma's birthday drinks, only a few days after Stella and I kissed, after I'd already broken things off with Helen. Him telling me he asked Stella out, having no idea what had happened between me and her days earlier.

That she said yes.

I wanted to tell him what had happened right then and there. I should've. I bet he wouldn't have gone out with her if I had.

Stella tried to talk to me later that night. She said *hey* at the bar, then had the audacity to say, *can we talk*? I fucking ignored her. I know I came off like an arse that night, too, but I didn't know what I'd possibly say to her. *Have fun with my best friend, who everyone prefers anyway?*

Ben's always been the ideal boyfriend—classic good looks, outgoing, makes everyone laugh, and has an aura of relaxed success that only comes with family support and money behind it.

I didn't say a thing to her. And I never told Ben about that night. A few months later, when we were out, after a few drinks, I caved and asked Gemma how Stella was doing. She gave me a funny look and pointed out how happy Ben and Stella were. She was right. They did seem happy.

Me? I was single, as usual. Most women want me for a one-night stand or a quick fling. I don't have that long-term boyfriend glow that Ben has.

"I'll get the schedule together and send out invites for the decision meetings we'll need you for, Ethan," Chloe says, giving Stella a side-eye.

"Thank you, Chloe." Stella regains her voice and composure. "And I will send you a draft brief later today."

She's talking directly to me now, and this time, there's no ignoring her. We lock eyes in some kind of to-the-death staring contest. First one to falter gets pushed in front of a London bus.

"I can write a brief. I've done it a million times." Shite, but I sound like a petulant child, insisting on my competence. I'm screwing this all up. I clench my jaw and breathe in deeply through my nose, trying to ground myself.

"I'm sure." Stella's gaze is unwavering, her voice calm, like I'm a toddler with a pair of scissors in one hand and a chunk of his sister's hair in another. "I'll get you a draft by the end of the day, then you let me know what you think. I'll integrate all your feedback before sharing the brief with our creative team." She nods her head to Graham and Luke.

"Great." I pull at my beard again, then force my hands down onto the table. There's a slight shake in them that makes my face heat.

Stella looks down at her laptop, breaking our staring contest with a flush in her cheeks. She bites her lower lip and types something.

Dammit, she's beautiful. I hate that I still find her attractive, after all this time, after all the rejection. I swallow and am sure the entire room hears it. Someone sighs, and I think it comes from Chloe.

I don't want Stella to ever find out how I really feel about her. I don't understand why her mere presence bothers me so much. Just like when they were dating, what I feel—*felt*—makes me a bad friend to Ben, an arsehole to her, and a terrible person overall.

I'd rather she thinks I hate her than know the truth.

4

STELLA

"Oh my god, Stella, Ethan is so fit!"

I lift my head to stare at Chloe, hoping she can read in my eyes how dead her words just made me.

Girl doesn't notice. Now that she has my attention, she dramatically drops her jaw and widens her eyes cartoonishly big, like the bottom of a venti Starbucks cup.

"Did you see those tattoos? Those muscles? They were, like, dying to escape from the confines of his clothing. And he used to be a professional rugby player, Tessa told me? He looks like one, doesn't he?" She draws out the words in her Aussie accent, each sentence ending as a dramatic question. "Holy smokes. He's like straight out of a movie."

"No." Make it stop. "No. I didn't see the tattoos or . . . whatever else you said." While I absolutely did *not* notice his rippling biceps or his romance-novel-hero-like presence, no one can convince me he didn't roll up the sleeves on his button-down shirt with the explicit purpose of showing off his gorgeous tattoos and distracting the entire freaking room. Not me, obviously. Chloe ignores me and chatters on.

"And the way he was staring at you, Stella, at the end there?"

She runs her hand through her hair and closes her eyes for a second, as if she's reveling in the thought of his gaze.

"What do you mean?" I narrow my eyes. Damn, but I know exactly what she means.

"He was, like, not just staring at you. More like *smoldering* at you." She extends the word smoldering. "I would have melted in a puddle on the floor." She fans herself with her hand.

I violently move my head from side to side. "Stop being dramatic. He wasn't smoldering at me. He was glaring at me."

"But . . . why?" She furrows her brow. "Why would he glare at you?"

Why does Ethan hate me? Because I kissed him and then got with his best friend. Not a great look, I know, but I also didn't realize Ethan had a kinda girlfriend the night we kissed.

And before today, I also didn't know what his past had been like. His childhood. The way he depended on Ben and his parents . . . Ben had never said much to me about him and Ethan growing up together. No wonder Ethan hated me so much when it looked like I wasn't being honest with his best friend.

My phone buzzes on the table and I flip it over. It's just Gemma checking to make sure I got back to London okay. This is all her fault. She's the one who introduced me to Ethan and Ben during her birthday week.

Gemma's my best friend in London, and we met during our MBA program, where I saved her ass in our Advanced Marketing Strategy class, and she saved mine in Advanced Corporate Finance. I still think I owe her a lot more than she owes me. And ever since we graduated five years ago, Gemma's bugged me to come out and meet her friends from university. That night, a year and a half ago, it finally happened.

Ethan and Ben.

"Ethan Fraser hates me." I shouldn't admit that to my direct report, but I let the words slip out. I suppose Ethan *really* hates me because I asked him to keep our night together a secret from Ben.

That conversation had been a disaster. It had been like talking to an angry dog, as I'd said the words—*can we not tell Ben what happened between us?*—and was met with a snarl. That was six months into dating Ben, and as far as I know, Ethan never told him.

Even worse, there was a second incident with Ethan.

Not long after I asked for secrecy, I was out on a Friday night with Ben and a couple of his coworkers and their girlfriends, trying to be social. Everyone was getting drunk. I think the girls and I were on our second or third bottle of wine. Ethan showed up. I remember dramatically rolling my eyes at him when he glared at me across the room. Ben was trying to get everyone to go to a club, and I'm not the clubbing type. Before I knew it, I was at the pub by myself after telling Ben I would call an Uber.

But I *wasn't* by myself. Ethan was still there, too.

I have a horrifying memory of actually hissing at Ethan when he approached me, like a cornered feral cat, then him helping me stand—turns out, I was absolutely trashed—and getting into an Uber with me. I woke up the next day in a t-shirt and pajama pants in my bed, alone, with memories of laying against Ethan's broad shoulder in the car, potentially rambling about how much I hated him and should never have kissed him.

I'll go to the grave with that story.

"Oooo, that sounds soooo dramatic! What happened?? How do you know him?" Chloe leans forward, elbows on the table, and plops her chin in her hands, waiting for some kind of amazing story that I'm absolutely not going to tell her.

And this is why the girl is going to ruin her life, as per the Unless Game. She shouldn't be excited about the new client hating her boss. She shouldn't be excited about drama at work. Unless she's determined to ruin her career by doing something stupid, like hooking up with one of the cameramen on the last London-based shoot we were on. Luckily, we'd kept the gossip down on that one, but it could've been much worse.

"It's not dramatic at all." Objectively, it is. I keep my face clear of emotions. "We have, um, mutual friends. He doesn't hate me. Well, not really. We just don't particularly get along."

I detest drama with men. Ever since Hunter.

He was a client at the ad agency I worked for out of college in New York City. A decade older than me, Hunter had a spectacular city apartment with stunning views of the Hudson, which I first saw after an agency Christmas party in Manhattan. He blew me away with how together he was. The job, the apartment . . . He was so different from every other boy I'd dated. Because he wasn't a boy. He was an adult. A man. I fell hard for Hunter, and when he asked me to move in a mere month later, I left my tiny shared apartment in Brooklyn and loaded three suitcases in the car he sent to bring me home to his place. It was a fairy tale, with a cleaner twice a week, prepared meals delivered every night, and enthusiastic sex.

Then, one Tuesday night, he came home extremely late and informed me he was getting back together with his estranged wife. Wife! They would try to work it out, and she was pregnant. Pregnant! I mean, what? I hadn't known he was seeing anyone else, let alone a wife I didn't know he had. I'd let myself fall for him, opening myself wide, without setting up any protections for my heart.

Devastated, I found an even crappier apartment with a microscopic room and shlepped my stuff back to Brooklyn.

Then Evelyn had showed up at my new place. Already in her early eighties, she took the train into the city and banged on my door, fully dressed up in a gold silk dress with her hair freshly done, announcing we would be going to see a Broadway show. She reminded me I didn't need a man, and that I could live a full, happy life all on my own. When I tried to resist, she merely said *pishposh!,* then pulled out the fanciest dress in my closet.

I can still hear her voice in my head. My stomach clenches. *I miss her.*

And Ethan? He totally detests me. Like, he'd shove me into the Thames to get rid of me if he had the chance.

"Sounds like the start of an enemies-to-lovers romance." Chloe twirls a chunk of her hair.

Enemies-to-lovers is my favorite romance trope, but only to read about, not to live through. It's not a real-life thing that happens.

"It's one hundred percent *not* an enemies-to-lovers romance, or any kind of romance at all." I ignore the queasy feeling in my belly. Jet lag is really catching up to me. "Let's focus on the actual work—I have an entire brief to create based on very little information. I'll catch up with you later about the meeting schedule." I stand and roll my neck.

"Bye!" Chloe calls when I slide out the door of the conference room. "Can't wait to hear more!"

"You won't," I mutter to myself as I stride down the hallway to my cubicle, clutching my laptop to my chest like a teenage girl grasping her folders in a high school hallway.

Fine. I admit it. Kissing Ethan wasn't torture. But it was a mistake. There was alcohol involved. A lot of alcohol. My heels pad quietly along the carpeted floor, and I concentrate on moving along, each step closer to the end of the day and the bed in my flat.

I have bigger problems to deal with than an ancient, ill-fated kiss.

5

———

STELLA

My phone buzzes with multiple incoming messages, jolting me out of my mini desk-nap. I sit up straight and arch my back, then rub my eyes, probably smearing mascara and winged eyeliner. My computer is snoozing, and before looking at my phone, I click my mouse to wake it up.

The creative brief stares back at me, almost done. Five o'clock on the longest Friday of my life. Actually, the brief's just . . . done, not almost done. I can't handle it anymore. I need to crash at home as soon as possible.

I type out a quick email and press send without re-reading.

To: Ethan Fraser
CC: Tessa Brown
From: Stella Hart
Date: 05 July 2024
Subject: Brief Approval
Message:

Here's the brief. Let me know your feedback and I'll get the creatives working on it Monday morning.

Best,
Stella

After pressing send, I breathe a sigh of relief. I open an email from Chloe, which has a proposed timeline. The first storyboard meeting will be next Thursday, which is aggressive timing. Usually, the creative team has two weeks to come up with ideas for a new TV commercial, and this is just four days starting Monday morning. But they've been warned. They're ready to start working as soon as we get the brief approved. As confident as I tried to sound in the meeting, it's a tight timeframe.

It'll also be a miracle if I can keep my shit together. I have multiple projects happening at the same time, and since Evelyn died, I've been so much less efficient.

Tessa pops up over my cubicle wall, like a boss-sized jack-in-the-box.

"Hi there. Can we have a quick chat?"

"Sure thing. I just emailed the client the brief, and I was about to head home and get some rest."

"Wonderful. About that email." Tessa holds up her phone and appears to scroll. "Can we, um, try to be a bit, um, more cordial? A bit warmer, perhaps?" She draws out the word *warmer*.

I flare my nostrils. "Was I not, uh, warm?" I click open my sent items and glance at the very short, somewhat curt email. Ah, okay, fine.

Tessa tilts her head. "Were you? Warm?" She shakes her phone in front of her chest, the screen facing me.

"Hmm. Yeah, you're right." I sigh and crinkle my forehead. "Sorry, Tessa. I'm just exhausted. I can send another email, if you'd like. Apologizing or something." *Please don't make me do that.*

She purses her lips, as if she's considering it. "Listen. I'm English. I understand being passive-aggressive in emails. But to Ethan? I don't really understand. There was a lot of confusing tension this morning in the meeting. Did I miss something?"

Well, shit.

"Sorry. No, you didn't miss anything. I think it's the jet lag." Nope. Not the jet lag. It's Ethan. I rub my forehead. "I promise I'll try harder."

"Right. But in the meantime, why don't you shoot him a quick text to let him know you're looking forward to getting his feedback? His mobile is in his email signature."

"But—" I pause, searching for a good excuse. "I really don't want to."

Tessa regards me with tired eyes and shrugs. "Have a lovely weekend, Stella." She wiggles her fingers at me and walks away.

I glance down at my inbox, which already has an unread email from Ethan.

To: Stella Hart
From: Ethan Fraser
CC: Tessa Brown
Date: 05 July 2024
Subject: Re: Brief Approval
Message:

Got it. I'm on a train now. Will read and get you feedback shortly.

-Ethan

A train? Where's he going?

None of my business, that's where.

And at the bottom of the email is his mobile number. Does Tessa really want me to be in a texting-level relationship with Ethan? Of course she does, and I often am with clients. It's usually the easiest way to get in touch. Damn. I tap his number into my contacts and press save, shivering a little as I do. My finger hovers over *send message*, but . . . I cannot text him. I just can't. Maybe in a bit.

I read the message that buzzed me out of my desk-nap. It's from Izzy, my mentee, and she's responding to a link I sent her earlier this week about a university scholarship competition I found on the still-functional charity website. Applicants must be high school kids involved in one of a list of charities, including Mentor Me. Their challenge is to come up with a launch plan for a new organic makeup line, sponsored by the corporation that owns the brand.

IZZY

OMG, this is amazing! I already have ideas.
Thank you!!!!!!!!

Good for her. I type back a quick response, suggesting she dump her ideas into a Google Doc so I can look them over. Izzy responds with a serious of emojis and then a GIF with a girl jumping up and down.

There are also several new messages in the text chain with Reese and Maddie. I scroll through to catch up on the chat with my sisters, then pause on the last three.

REESE

Did you guys see the video call invite from the lawyer for Monday?

MADDIE

Stuffy Richard? Yeah

REESE

The message was weird

Before responding, I check my personal email and yup, there it is, the expected invitation for Monday at one o'clock my time for Evelyn's will reading. But after reading the text of the invite, I scrunch my face.

Please join me for a reading of Evelyn Reynolds's last will and testament. Evelyn had some creative and very prescriptive conditions that need to be met before the contents of her estate are distributed amongst her great-nieces. I will reveal all the details on Monday.

What's that about? I immediately click back to the text chain, which has new messages.

> **MADDIE**
>
> I loved her so much, but Aunt Evelyn was kind of nuts
>
> **REESE**
>
> Stella, your brain is most like hers. What do you think?

Evelyn was a unique person. She didn't ever do things the way the world seemed to demand, and that's one of the reasons she and I connected so much. No marriage, no kids. Freedom. I swallow the lump in my throat.

> **ME**
>
> I have no idea, but I don't love the sound of it

When Ben started casually bringing up kids after dating for nine months, I shut down the conversation gently at first, especially when he looked so crestfallen. I think that's what really made me clam up with Ben. I should've ended it then.

Because if not wanting to have kids makes me not girlfriend material, then fine.

Thinking of the messy breakup reminds me I'm right to never let a man get close to me again. I'd even found myself considering marriage and children. Thinking that maybe something was wrong with me for not wanting kids. Wondering if I should try to get used to the idea.

I got out just in time.

Ethan's face pops up in my mind, an unwanted invasion. Even a simple kiss (or two, or ten) a long time ago is screwing with my job. Relationships are just not worth it.

REESE

I guess we'll find out on Monday

Evelyn is—was—an uncontrollable force. Her stories of traveling and exploring the world are what made me want to be like her. She was her own person. No one ever changed that. And as far as I know, she didn't regret one thing in her life.

But it's that adventurous attitude and no-regrets lifestyle that makes me nervous about her estate.

What were you up to, Aunt Evelyn?

6

ETHAN

I can't fucking do it.

I'm standing in front of Mum's flat. Frozen. Unable to follow through. Unable to face what's literally right in front of me. I can picture what's inside: an outdated kitchen with chipped black-and-white tiled floor, a beat-up sofa and mismatched loveseat, an old coffee table with a wobbly leg, and a dusty hallway leading to her bedroom and the tiny room that'd been mine. It's still shocking she'd managed to hold on to the same flat for that long.

Oh, right, because of the money I sent the landlord each month. A growl rumbles in my throat.

The only thing in the flat that doesn't scream desperation is a bookshelf in the corner, stacked with new and old romance novels, some of them from me, but she'd also go to library sales and hunt for good deals.

There's a key in my pocket. The landlord left it for me when I came up to Newcastle to deal with her cremation—no funeral, no memorial, just her ashes delivered to a mausoleum in an overgrown cemetery—and it feels like it's burning a hole in my jeans.

Why did I think this time would be different? I've come up

here a half dozen times since she died. Each time, I freeze up and can't go in. It's as if when I saw her last—when she refused to let me in—some kind of spell was placed on me. I can't do it. Even though I must, especially with the new thirty-day timeline.

"Fuck me." I back away and spin, trotting down the steps from her second-floor flat, my backpack shifting on my shoulders. Scuffed white paint peels off the walls on the stairwell, depressing gray cement glaring from the holes. There's trash on the steps. An old yellowing sock. A fast-food wrapper. Crumpled beer can. This place should be condemned. Who does the landlord think will buy Mum's flat?

And what'll happen if I don't empty it? He'll toss everything and keep the deposit, if there even was one from so long ago. Fine. Who cares?

But shouldn't I want to keep something to remember her by? Is there anything in there I should save? But Ben's parents took more pictures of me in my teenage years than Mum did. Robin and Simon handed me a box when I graduated university with Ben, before I moved to London to play rugby after getting drafted as an outside center with the London Stingers. Mum handed me nothing.

Rugby was the first thing in our lives that I was better at than Ben. I had to work so hard at university, having fallen behind at school due to my rubbish home situation. Rugby was the only reason I got into the same university as him. All of that came easily to my best mate. School, university, women, jobs, everything that followed. But he's never made me feel bad about any of it, and he was my biggest fan when I was playing pro.

Finally out of the decrepit building, I pull out my mobile and respond to Ben's text from half an hour ago asking me what I'm up to tonight, hoping to distract myself from the way my throat is being squeezed by Mum's ghost, as tight as the inside of a scrum.

ME

Hey, mate. Up in Newcastle

BEN

Again? What for?

I consider coming clean about my issues with Mum's flat. Explain why I keep coming up here and not getting my shite dealt with. But for this—I want to try to handle it on my own. Not always lean so heavily on Ben and his parents. So I tell a half truth.

ME

Tying up some loose ends with the flat

BEN

Let's grab a drink next week?

ME

Sure. How about after the boys' rugby practice next Friday? You still coming to help?

BEN

Right, of course, mate. Looking forward to showing the lads how to toss a rugby ball correctly since they have a rubbish coach

The last text makes me chuckle, and I jog down the footpath toward the bus stop, past a splintered wooden bench. I hop on a bus and put distance between me and the flat.

"ETHAN, COME IN." Suzanne waves me into her small, terraced house, and a mixture of emotions swirls inside me at the sight of Mum's best friend.

Both my mum and Helen's mum were troubled when we were young, but Suzanne pulled it together when we were around ten, and the two women had different paths from that point on.

Suzanne: steady job, neat house, involved in her daughter's and grandchild's lives. My mum: an addict, mostly unemployed, broke, and then gone.

"Hello." I let her wave of maternal warmth course through my body.

"It's so nice to see you again, love." She leans back and keeps her hands on my biceps for a beat longer, examining my face. "You okay?"

I nod and walk in when she steps back, wondering why I came, why I didn't go to the train station and straight back to London, head bowed between my legs.

But once the swirl of emotions settles, I decide seeing Helen's mum is nice. Comforting in some way. Ben's family was home to me growing up, but we were both friends with Helen, too, and her mum cared about all of us, despite her own troubles.

A screech echoes from further back in the house and a nappy-clad toddler waddles into the front room, a giant smile on his face, wispy blond curls sticking out from his head, and something resembling chocolate smeared all around his mouth.

Suzanne swoops him up and kisses him on the forehead. "Helen," she yells toward where the child came from. "Ethan's here!"

"What?" Helen rounds the corner, her long, dark hair in waves over her shoulders, a giant smile on her face before she even sees me. "Ethan! You're here again!" The small boy wiggles in his nan's arms and reaches for Helen, who grabs him and settles the child on her hip. "Come in, come sit."

Seeing Helen is weird, but good. I always had a huge thing for her. Which is why I was so fucking thrilled when we connected again five years ago, after I'd stopped playing rugby and gotten a brand management job in London. It finally happened. She was still up here in Borinwick, outside of Newcastle where we all grew up, and I was in London, but she'd been down visiting friends and met up with us at a pub one night. She came back to Ben and my place, and we hooked up. After that, she started coming to London once a month or so and stayed with me. And Ben. She and I were never anything defined, but I wanted to give us a chance.

Helen wraps an arm around my waist, and I pull her toward me in a half hug. She smiles up at me, as does her son, who I lean slightly away from as he leans toward me with his—admittedly cute—chocolate-covered face.

"Oh, sorry about that, Ethan. Henry, let's get you cleaned up and in a fresh nappy. And maybe to bed. Can you hang out? I'll be back in ten."

I nod, and Helen gives me a sweet smile and disappears down the hall with her son.

But back then, it wasn't long before it all fell apart. Helen confessed she was actually in love with Ben, not me. I was just some broken toy she was messing around with. She didn't say that, of course, and I pretended I didn't care. I told Ben to go for it. They hooked up a few times, then he lost interest. That was a bollocks time. I'd never told him how I was feeling about Helen—which I'm not even clear on—and my friendship with him was so much more important.

Helen and I got back in touch shortly after she had her son.

Suzanne waves me toward the couch, where I sink in.

"Everything settled with your mum?" Her brow furrows as she looks at me intently again, hands folded on her belly as she sits down on the other end of the couch.

"There's nothing to settle. There was no money, no anything, really." *Just a flat I can't enter.* But I don't say it. I can't even admit it to Suzanne or Helen.

"Mmm." A silence descends between us. "She loved you, you know. Even if you couldn't tell." A shimmer of tears fills her eyes.

I swallow. Have I even cried over Mum? I loved her. She was my mother. But do I miss her? No, not really. I miss the idea of her. But she didn't give a shite about me. *Suzanne* misses her, even though Mum was a disaster in the last years of her life. At least they had a friendship of sorts.

"It didn't feel like it."

"Mary—your mum—she had problems. I did, too."

"Yes, but you pulled it together. And kept it together." There's an edge to my voice and Suzanne leans back, as if I'd said something horrible. "You raised Helen. You provided for her. You're here now, helping with Henry, giving them a place to live." I make an effort to wipe any hostility off my face. It's not Suzanne's fault.

She sighs. "I know. I'm sorry. None of us had any money back then, and we both drank too much, partied too much, when we should have been raising our kids. I wish she could've figured things out. But she never did. She got so lost."

Anger wells up inside me. I'd made excuses for Mum my whole life. I'd enabled her by sending money even though she always treated me like rubbish. I'd tried to connect with her. But failed. Again and again. Sometimes talking to Mum's best friend helps. Sometimes it makes things worse, because *she* figured it out. She was a good mum to Helen.

Suzanne scoots closer to me and grabs a hand. "I know your mum hurt you . . . I know other people have as well . . ." Suzanne's eyes dart to the hallway where Helen disappeared. "But sometimes people do change. And sometimes it's worth it to take a chance, even when you've been hurt."

I don't even know what to say. Mum never changed, not in my whole life, but Helen might have. She pops back into the room, a bottle of beer in each hand.

"Hey," she says, her eyes locked on mine.

"I'm going to clean up the kitchen." Suzanne leaves me alone with Helen, with a meaningful nod to her daughter.

Helen slips next to me on the couch and tucks one leg beneath her, handing me a bottle. "I think I got Henry to go down for the night."

Just over a year and a half ago, I came up to Borinwick and

impulsively texted Helen. It was before I met Stella. Before that night. Helen and I met up for drinks, and after a handful of pints, ended up kissing. It was only at the end of the night she admitted she had a baby at home, so couldn't invite me back to hers.

I've never, not once in my life, thought of myself as a father figure. There are just too many ways to mess that up, and I'm not interested in figuring it out. I realized—after the night with Stella—that Helen's situation was too complicated for me. I told her I just wanted to be friends. We stayed in touch. But the last few times I've been up here—since Mum died—I sense that she wants more again.

It feels good to be wanted, especially by someone who once tossed me aside for Ben.

Even now, her knee is pressed up against my thigh, and she's looking at me warmly, her dark eyes open wide, her mouth turned up in a smile. She's always been so pretty.

"You okay?" she asks.

"Yeah."

"What are you doing up here? Not that I'm complaining. I love seeing you."

I swallow. I don't want to tell her anything about Mum's flat—I don't want to tell anyone about it—but it's like this terrible, shameful burden on my shoulders.

"A few more loose ends, that's all."

"Well, maybe text ahead next time and we can go out or something. I can ask Mum if she minds right now?"

I shake my head. "I'm not really up for it tonight."

"Okay, next time. But hey, let's do a quick selfie."

And before I can react, she snuggles under my arm and whips out her mobile. I manage something resembling a grin, or maybe a grimace. When she's done, she scoots back and faces me fully.

"Your beard got longer." Helen reaches out and touches my face, her hand running along my beard. "Where are you staying tonight?"

Not here. I can't. I don't know what it is. Sometimes I see Helen and her son and don't mind being with them, but other times, I think of how rough my childhood was, and wonder if her son's will be better, if Helen will keep it together, if the father—a bloke from our secondary school she dated for a few months but has only occasionally been around Henry—will step up for them. I don't know. But I can't sleep on this couch, and I can't sleep with Helen, and I can't face Ben's parents or Mum's flat.

Maybe I'm just scared. Maybe I should give Helen a shot. At least when I look at her, I don't want to scream, like when I see Stella Hart's face. Not that this has anything to do with Stella. *Fuck.* Why do I keep thinking about that infuriating woman? Now I can only picture those blue eyes and red high heels and the way her chest heaved when she stared at me earlier today . . .

And that text she sent while I was on the train. Something like: *just checking to make sure you'd be able to get me feedback, and if you had any questions.*

She added a smiley face at the end. What the fuck? I'd sent her feedback shortly after, having been working on it during the three-hour train ride.

Wasted train ride, as I'm already planning my escape back to London.

"I can't stay long. I'm catching the last train back to London." I chug my beer.

I have to get out of here.

7

———————

STELLA

Monday, July 8
BUCKET LIST DAY 1

Rushing from my weekly one-to-one meeting with Tessa, I log in to the video call from a small huddle room, exactly on time. Four tiles appear on my laptop screen, and my own image is the biggest, next to smaller ones of Reese, Maddie, and Richard Ramsey, Evelyn's lawyer.

"Hi, everyone."

"Hey, Stella," Reese says. "How was your week—"

The lawyer loudly clears his throat, cutting me off, and my older sister goes quiet, eyes wide. Maddie covers her mouth, presumably to stifle a laugh, even though she's muted.

"Shall we get started?" The older man taking up the fourth spot on the screen is in his late seventies or early eighties, with wispy white hair that barely covers his scalp, and age spots visible underneath to showcase how long he'd survived under the sun. "I'm Richard Ramsey, Evelyn's lawyer. I'm here to share the contents of her last will and testament." He shuffles some papers around and leans close to the laptop screen, lifting his glasses up and peering under them while clicking his mouse noisily. I can see right up his hairy nostrils.

I bite back a grin and gulp some coffee.

Richard proceeds to read a bunch of sentences from a printed piece of paper, legalese that I block out and reach for my phone instead.

ME

Couldn't this have been an email?

We could all use the money from Evelyn's estate, for different reasons and purposes. Reese is the oldest sister, and her divorce three years ago was rough. Luckily, she'd already had a solid career and means to support herself and her teenage daughter. Reese is the perfect example of someone who has thrived without her ex-husband. But this money will help her get through, as she'll have to pay college tuition soon.

Over the years, Reese has given me shit for not really opening myself up to the men I date, but I manage to avoid the drama that she's been through . . . mostly. It's my way of protecting who I am. I'll admit her hot Scottish boyfriend worships her and is appropriately humbled by her love. As he should be! Everything is going well with them . . . unless he screws it up somehow.

MADDIE

Stuffy Richard has no sense of humor. Best we
just suffer through this and laugh about it later

Maddie, the youngest of the three of us, could definitely use any monetary help she can get. She's unhappy in her current job as the manager of an Italian restaurant in New Jersey, but working in the hospitality sector is all she's done since dropping out of college a decade ago. Reese is constantly harping on her to go back to school, or find a better job with real benefits, or at least one that pays more so she can move out of her crappy apartment.

"Your great-aunt was my client, and she was also my close

friend." Richard adjusts his glasses and pauses for a beat. "As you know, she's never been . . . traditional. And two years ago, when she came to me with this idea, I tried very hard to talk her out of it." Richard tilts his chin down and leans even closer to the camera. "So very hard."

I crinkle my forehead and an uncomfortable seed of suspicion burrows in my belly. Idea? Two *years* ago? My fingers fly on my phone screen.

ME

What's he talking about?

MADDIE

No clue. She only told me that the three of us were the main people in her will. That's it

"When Evelyn would come to see me, she spoke about her life quite passionately. The things she did. The things she didn't do. Her regrets."

Regrets? I thought Evelyn didn't have any regrets. That's what's always made her such a role model for me. She lived her life her way, following her own rules, and didn't give a shit what anyone else thought.

Richard breathes in loudly through his nose.

"Deathbed regrets." He pauses for dramatic effect. "Your great-aunt watched an inappropriate number of YouTube videos and TED Talks for a ninety-year-old lady."

A bubble of laughter rolls around in my throat. Evelyn watched TED Talks? Yeah, okay, I could see that, I guess. She also had the iPad we'd FaceTime on, and was always downloading the newest social media apps so she could see what the younger generations were up to. Evelyn was Life Goals, doing whatever she wanted for her nine-plus decades. Nothing held her back. No husband, no kids. Just traveled the world, worked at a job she loved, and generally did exactly—and only—what she wanted.

"You are probably wondering what she regretted in her life." Richard plucks the question from my brain. "More importantly, at least to her in the end, how could she have avoided those regrets?" Richard pauses and I blink too many times, my throat feeling thick.

"Um, did you want us to answer that question?" Maddie runs her hands through her long, dark hair, pulling it over her shoulder and re-muting herself. I scratch the back of my head, wishing he'd get on with it.

"No. But you'd be surprised at how Evelyn tried to do so." One side of Richard's mouth turns up briefly. "Evelyn became fixated on bucket lists."

Bucket lists? I tilt my head and slide my hand off of my neck. I'm tired. Lounging in my flat all weekend and binge reading a new romance novel called *Don't Date Me* didn't shake my lingering jet lag. And now he's talking about bucket lists?

But it rings a bell in my brain.

Evelyn *did* mention a bucket list to me. I search my memory for her words. It was something simple, like: *just working on my bucket list, Stella darling*. I had no clue what she was talking about. A bucket list? In your nineties? But when I asked her what was on it, imagining skydiving or swimming with sharks, she chuckled and changed the subject.

And now that I think about it, had she said *my bucket list* or *the bucket lists*? I don't remember.

"Except for a token amount to her nephew's wife—your mother—Evelyn is leaving her complete estate to you three, divided evenly."

All of us stare silently into our screens, presumably at Richard's video square, waiting for him to continue. We all knew she would put us in her will. The three of us were the ones who loved her the most. Whom she loved the most. We knew this was coming, but to hear it spoken out loud, confirming how much we meant to Evelyn . . . there's a prickling of tears in my eyes.

"However, there's a rather unique catch."

I narrow my eyes. Of course, there's a catch. Evelyn never did things the normal way.

"While examining her life and her potential deathbed regrets, she thought about her great-nieces. She wanted only to help you three live long, fulfilled lives. So she thought: what are the things I think they should do to help achieve that goal? Your aunt Evelyn wrote each of *you* a bespoke bucket list, which you must complete in order to receive your inheritance."

Um, what now?

Maddie, with pink cheeks and wide eyes, appears to start talking, then finds the unmute button. "Can you explain that further, Stuf—uh, Richard?"

He holds up a finger and continues speaking. "And to convince you to actually complete the lists, she set a requirement that all three of you must do so within four weeks—that's twenty-eight days—or her entire estate will get donated to charity. Minus that small amount for your mother." Richard adjusts his glasses.

Reese audibly gasps and Maddie appears to choke on her own spit. My jaw drops open.

Oh, no. I can't do this. Not now.

Not with all my projects at work. I don't have the time or the strength. Tears sting my eyes, and I blink until they dissipate.

"One more detail."

"There's more?" Maddie groans.

"You may *not* talk to each other about your individual lists while completing them. I'll read a quick note she wrote on this topic." He clears his throat. "*Darlings, you must each complete your bucket list all on your own. The three of you have a beautiful sisterly bond, but I know you. Reese, you'll want to help everyone with their lists, especially Maddie. And Maddie, you'll listen to whatever Reese or Stella tell you to do. And Stella, you'll do it your own way anyway. The three of you can talk about this in four weeks.*"

"That's ridiculous." Reese shakes her head. "I just want to help."

Richard ignores her comment.

"I'm sending out an email to each of you right after we get off this call. There will be a document attached. The first page is a letter to all three of you, the second a letter to each of you individually, and third is a description of your bucket list items, including an explanation of why she chose it," Richard continues, like a damn robot we can't turn off. "I have the rather unfortunate role of judging whether you have completed the items in the spirit in which Evelyn intended, so I recommend touching base with me within a week with your plans so I can approve."

"Oh my god." Maddie blinks about a thousand times. "This is for real. Are you kidding me?"

"I wish I were." I swear Richard holds back a bit of a grin. "Not only did she give you each a handful of bucket list items, she added some colorful details on how they need to be executed. So read carefully."

Am I dreaming? Nightmaring? I dig one of my heels into the top of my other foot and wince. Nope. Definitely not asleep.

"Are there any questions?"

"Yes," all three of us say at once, but no one continues talking.

"Alright. Review your lists and let me know if you think of anything."

We end the call and I slam my laptop closed. Evelyn was certainly not a normal ninety-year-old. But I'm hoping she didn't do anything too ridiculous with this bucket list concept.

Suddenly, this small huddle room is suffocating, so I stand and gather my things.

Twenty-eight days. *Oh, Evelyn.*

THE HALLWAY IS empty and I'm thankful I don't run into Tessa or Chloe and have to pretend my mind isn't going a hundred miles an hour. I open my email and there's already a message waiting with the subject line *Stella's Bucket List*.

There's nothing in the body of the email, so I double click on the attached pdf. The document loads, and it's five pages long. There's a letter at the start, and I take a deep breath before reading.

Dear Beautiful Great-Nieces,

If you are reading this, I have passed away. Please know that I loved you three more than anyone else in the world. I hope that the wealth I accumulated over my lifetime serves you in some way. I hope it makes your life better, like you made my life better.

I'm lucky to have kept my wits about me in the end so I could put into place this wonderful project. It's not meant to be a burden, but to show you that every day of your life you make decisions, even if it doesn't feel like it. Every day you choose something over another thing. Those decisions to do or not do something influence your entire life.

Take care of each other, my girls. I will look after you if I can. Hey, maybe I'll come back to haunt you if you don't do as I ask in your lists. Haha, just kidding!

With much love,
Aunt Evelyn

P.S. Make sure you review the rules very carefully and provide evidence of each item completed. Richard will be the judge. I am one hundred percent serious about all of this. Do as I say. Love you!!!

The tears are still stuck in my eyes, and swallowing past the lump in my throat is difficult. I'm also not sure if I want to curse at Evelyn, laugh, or scream.

I am terrified to read my bucket list.

I quickly scroll past the page with the letter that starts *My Dearest Stella*. I can't do that one right now. I know I'll cry, and I have no intention of sobbing at my place of employment.

<u>Stella Hart's Bucket List, as written by Evelyn Reynolds</u>

1. Volunteer
2. Adopt an Animal
3. Adventure to the Isle of Skye in Scotland
4. Help Reese
5. Find the One that Got Away

You will need to choose someone as your advisor to guide you through this entire bucket list. Yes, let's repeat that: an advisor. They will need to 'sign off' on your list when completed. Talk to them about each item. Sometimes it's worth it to listen to what other people have to say. Yes, I can hear you screaming at me from wherever I am, but this is for your own good.

Literally everything on this page offends me.

An advisor? What am I, a high school kid choosing a college? What was she thinking?

I take a deep breath. Thankfully, the advisor part'll be easy. Gemma will one hundred percent do it. I unlock my phone and send her a text, ignoring the unread messages from my sisters for now.

I need to know more. I need to know *everything*, so I scroll to the more detailed bucket list descriptions. I bite my lip and squeeze my eyes shut, gathering strength.

Fuck, fuck, fuck. Okay. Here I go.

1. Volunteer

When I retired, the best thing I did was to volunteer at a hospital. I met wonderful people—doctors, nurses, patient care assistants, and the ones most don't appreciate enough like janitors and cafeteria workers. I wish I'd volunteered in my youth. I know it's hard to find the time, but I want you to go do something to help others. Do it with someone else, as that makes it even more meaningful.

2. Adopt an Animal

Stella, I know what you're going to say. No way, I'm not going to let an animal get in the way of me living my life exactly as I want to! Lol. I know you, dear! Here's the thing. I was the same. I never had children, and it was a choice I made. I'd never tell you to go have kids. However, having something to take care of grounded me. A being who loved me back unconditionally. I didn't do it until I was older. I kept putting it off, thinking it would get in the way of my life. Try it, my dear. Bring a friend with you to adopt.

I groan and scroll to number three. Only number three? Feels like a hundred.

3. Adventure to the Isle of Skye in Scotland

As you know, I traveled extensively with my job at Pan Am, often taking a long weekend to gallivant to faraway places. To have fish and chips in London, a fresh macaron in Paris, or authentic empanadas in Mexico. But the most magical place I've been to is the Isle of Skye, in Scotland. To me, it's a spiritual spot. It's where my true love proposed to me. The love I lost when I mistakenly said no. Go there and climb the

Old Man of Storr. Maybe there's some magic left. Maybe it'll be me, and I can speak to you. Take someone with you.

She had a true love? Who proposed to her? And she regretted saying no? I can't process all that new information.

And Skye . . . It might as well be on the other side of the planet from London. I don't have time to take planes, trains, and automobiles to the Isle of Skye, an inconvenient island off the northwest coast of Scotland. And those big, open spaces, with so much room to think, to feel, to . . . exist?

4. Help Reese

I had one cherished sister—your grandmother. Our lives ended up going in different directions. She had children and settled into a quiet, happy existence, and I went off on a different path, choosing travel and adventure. But her grandchildren ended up being the most important people in my life. I'm so lucky to have had you, Reese, and Maddie. You were my shining stars. My greatest joys.

My only regret with my own sister is that we weren't close in adulthood. I know you are close with Reese and Maddie, but make sure you never lose that. Sisterhood can be one of the strongest bonds you have. For this item, choose something to do for Reese. Something significant.

5. Find the One that Got Away

I alluded to this above, but I don't think I've ever told you about when I was thirty—only a handful of years younger than you—and lost the love of my life. I messed up and was too scared. He asked me to marry him on the top of the Old Man of Storr on the Isle of Skye. I would have had to give up my life in New Jersey, move to Scotland, and help him raise his kids. It terrified and overwhelmed me, so I said no. But I regretted it right away. I waited too long to fix my mistake, and by the time I tried to make things right, it was too late.

Go after that person and make sure you didn't make a mistake before he's a ghost haunting you for the rest of your life. Before that, talk to someone else about it. Get it straight in your head. Get it right.

Nausea washes over me and settles in the pit of my tummy, the smell of stale coffee mixing with a sense of dread. On the one hand, the knowledge that Evelyn lost someone who she thought of as her true love is disconcerting. She'd never said a thing about this man to me. And she . . . said no, then changed her mind, but it was too late? That's heartbreaking. A jarring confession from Evelyn.

But on the other hand, that's not my situation.

Ben's face flashes in my mind. *Oh shit.* I'm gonna have to talk to my ex-boyfriend.

I close the document and let out a half laugh, half cry. What on earth did I just read?

My phone vibrates, and I glance down at the screen. It's a text from Gemma.

GEMMA

CALLING YOU

Thank god. I need someone to help me through this. Someone to tell me how the hell to handle this list in only four weeks, how to get it done without losing my mind.

"Your great-aunt was unhinged," Gemma chirps.

"You should read this list, then you'll understand *just* how unhinged."

"While I can't wait to read it, unfortunately, I can't help."

"No! What? Why not?" And all at once, my confident plans for an advisor crumble.

"I'm going out of town for two weeks with Cercei starting

Friday, remember? I texted you last week. But I guess you were probably not paying attention to your messages in New Jersey."

That sounds about right. Ethan's face pops up in my mind.

"So that four-week deadline? It's not going to work."

"Can't I just cheat and have you sign off anyway?" But as soon as I say it, I feel sick. Cheating on Evelyn's bucket list would feel awful. "I might go off and have a breakdown now."

Gemma laughs. "How bad can the list be?"

"It's bad. What am I going to do?" I'm such a whiner. But honestly, who else is going to help me? It's so personal. It's not something I can ask a casual friend to do for me. Not that I have many casual friends. Or . . . any.

"Ask someone else to help?"

"Because I'm so good at that."

"What about that girl who works for you. Chloe, right?"

"Bite your tongue."

She laughs, too gleeful for my taste. "Well, who else do you talk to these days?"

"I dunno. You? Tessa? Oh, how about Graham, he's the creative director here. Does he count?"

"Jesus, your life is sad."

"Gemma!"

"Listen. You gotta let other people help you once in a while, okay? Find someone else at work. Or a stranger on the street. You obviously need more friends."

"Shut up."

"Ha. Go figure this out. Love you! Gotta run!"

She hangs up, and I realize I hadn't told her about working with Ethan. A story for another time, I guess.

Did Evelyn really think I can't make the right decisions for my life? That I don't know for sure I made the right choice breaking up with Ben? That I need to go on a hike in Scotland to prove something? Adopt an animal? Why didn't she trust me? I thought she and I were kindred spirits, like me and my dad. Strong, independent adventurers, even if my dad never got to experience all of that.

After he died, Reese stepped in as a mother figure for Maddie while Mom pulled herself together. And a father figure, I suppose. But I was determined not to need her, or anyone. Only Evelyn seemed to understand my fierce independence. She approved . . . just like my dad would've, I'm sure of it.

Now I feel like she thought I'm living my life wrong.

But I can't ignore the bucket list. I won't deny Reese and Maddie their inheritance.

I grab a sticky note and jot down a few names of people to consider for an advisor. After five minutes of thinking, all I have are three names: Tessa, Chloe, and Graham.

This is a disaster.

8

ETHAN

Wednesday, 10 July

Back at Pepper Me Marketing for a meeting on storyboard ideas, my heart does a funny flip when I see Stella huddled over her desk, her light hair fanned around her face. Something to do with the arch of her neck as it curves above the back of today's tank top makes my breath catch.

"Hart." A more polite and less awkward greeting might've gone something like: *Good morning, Stella,* but I can't bring myself to say her first name.

Her head turns sharply in my direction. She lifts a hand to me in a reluctant greeting.

"You asked Tessa already?" a voice projects from her mobile, set on the desk in front of her. It's the familiar voice of our mutual friend, Gemma.

"Yeah, and she said she's renovating her flat so can't spare any time outside work." Stella swoops up her mobile and takes Gemma off speaker.

"No. Chloe is not an option." Stella's whispering now, her body turned away from me, her voice wispy and higher than normal. She's panicked about something. "Gemma! Take this seriously." Her voice goes down a notch for the next words: "He is not an actual option for the bucket list, and I'm freaking out."

Bucket list? And who is he? I swallow and strain to hear Gemma's side of the conversation, but it's too muffled now that she's off speaker.

Another silence, and then Stella mutters something that sounds like *chaos monkey* before saying goodbye and tossing her mobile on the desk with a clunk.

"Everything okay?" Why did that come out sounding sarcastic? I'm still standing in the cubicle next to her, the one Tessa instructed I use during the project. I'm hovering, like a bystander watching the aftermath of a car accident.

Stella sighs deeply. "Yeah. It's fine. Just some . . . personal stuff."

Personal, but dealing with Chloe and Tessa as well? My interest is piqued.

"Bucket list related?" I settle into the black office chair and peek over the low partition. Stella's got her head in her hands, elbows on the desk.

"Yes." She huffs out with deep exhaustion. For a second, I think she's done talking, but she keeps going. "My great-aunt recently passed away and left me a bucket list to complete."

A wave of sympathy rushes over me. "I'm sorry to hear that."

Stella looks up and finally meets my gaze, as if assessing if I'm being sincere. "Thank you."

"It's kind of, um, unique, that she left you a bucket list." I try to picture my mum leaving me one. There's no way. She would never think of doing something that thoughtful. Not in life, and certainly not in death.

"Unique?" Stella lets out an annoyed breath. "She's completely unhinged. *Was,* anyway."

"Why?" I wish I would shut up and stop pushing Stella to talk to me. But I've not been able to get her out of my mind. I thought about her too much while I was in Newcastle, and even on Saturday, when I met up with my rugby mates to throw a ball in Regent's Park and go to the pub.

"My aunt Evelyn left me a personalized bucket list that she wrote just for me." She emphasizes each of the last three words. "And one for each of my sisters. And if we don't check everything off within a month, the whole estate goes to charity."

"Wow. That's savage." I can't stop the grin that crosses my face, and for a second, I think it'll piss Stella off, but she half-chuckles and smiles back.

"Yeah, she was." She takes a deep breath and rolls her shoulders back, then her neck, exposing the smooth skin of her throat.

Fuck. She has the same effect on me as she did the first night we met. I hate it. I can't be around her. It's . . . unsettling.

But I also want more of it.

"It might be fun to do something like that with your sisters. Maybe it'll help you, you know, feel better."

Another thing Mum had never given me—siblings. I'm thankful for that in some ways. It saved another kid from going through what I did. But I always wonder if it would have made my life easier to have someone else to suffer with. Someone who really understood.

Stella tilts her head and gives me a funny look. "We can't even talk about it with each other. She's got all these rules we have to follow. Or else, you know?"

Mum had no living siblings, either, and her parents had died young. There was never a great-aunt to give two shites about me. No one else to care. Only Ben and his parents.

She rolls her eyes to the ceiling, as if searching for strength from her late great-aunt. "And I need to find an advisor to, like, coach me through the list."

"What? Why?" Ah, that's what she was talking about to Gemma. I remind myself that I'm supposed to be acting like I hate her. But her voice is kind of hypnotic and sweet, and I want her to keep talking to me. *Ugh, sod off,* I order my inner voice.

Stella shakes her head, and it looks as if tears are in her eyes. There's definitely more to this story.

"Sorry for the overshare." She checks the time on her mobile. "Ready to head to the conference room?"

We grab our laptops and I follow her down the hallway toward the same room we met in last week.

While we're walking, before we join the rest of the team, I want to say more. Ask more. Share that I lost someone recently, too, someone who would never, ever have left me a bucket list.

Mum never left me anything at all.

I'm finding it hard to keep up the front that I hate Stella Hart, even though long ago, she proved that she's just like everyone else, choosing me second, preferring my best friend, knowing I'm broken and damaged and not worth her time.

Hating her is the best protection I have.

———

"I THINK that storyboard does a great job of communicating the merger and the donation drive."

"I'm happy you like it." Graham nods, clicking through the hand-drawn sequence of the winning idea. There's a rugby scene with a group of boys throwing a ball to an adult—their mentor— and then the same kids, plus several more, going on a hike together.

The Pepper Me creative team did an impressive job churning out three different commercial concepts in only a few days for me to review. This one is simple, but clearly shows the merger of Sporting London and Mentor Me to create Sporting UK Foundation, the new combined charity.

"Unless you think there's not enough about rugby in the spot?" Tessa says, looking at me intently. "It's just the one frame, probably only two or three seconds out of the fifteen-second commercial."

Unless.

The familiar word jars me. How many times have I thought about playing Stella's Unless Game? A lot. But it meant nothing to her, and I'm a total freak for even making that connection here in a meeting.

My traitorous eyes dart over to Stella. She's staring at me, sucking in her top lip, and I swear I can feel the connection between us buzzing.

Unless she is thinking about that night right now? Nah, definitely not. But . . .

"I like how it's balanced." I need to stay focused. "Makes it really clear there are two pillars of the new charity: sports and mentoring."

Tessa makes an agreeing murmur, then opens her mouth to say something. But Stella chimes in.

"Unless we have them tossing a rugby ball *during* the hike," Stella suggests. She emphasized the word *unless*. "Or kicking a soccer ball off the mountain." There are a few chuckles around the table.

"That might be a bit dangerous," Graham adds.

But I'm not chuckling with the rest of them. I'm staring at Stella, and she's staring at me.

"Unless we throw in a cricket bat along with the rugby and soccer balls," I add, my mouth involuntarily turned up in a smile. The group laughs.

Stella raises her eyebrows and throws a full-blown smile at me. Fucking hell. It's like being blinded by the sun.

"Best to stay focused on rugby for this spot, I'd think." Tessa gets us back on track and the group chats more about some of the adjustments to the storyboard, but everything goes smoothly. The creative team is going to revise the boards in record time, and I'll come in tomorrow late afternoon for a second meeting.

The rest of the team files out of the room, but I stay rooted to my chair. So does Stella.

"Coming, Stella? Ethan?" Tessa pauses at the door, glancing back and forth between us, an inquisitive look on her face.

"I just have another quick topic to discuss with Ethan," Stella says.

"Right. Let me know if you need me." With that, Tessa leaves the room, and it's just me and Stella.

Silence settles around us.

"Listen, Ethan, I know you've never quite liked me."

I blink about a billion times. That couldn't be farther from the truth.

"Hart. That's not true." But I'm clenching my jaw, and her gaze flits down to my mouth.

"Can we be honest with each other? Since we have to work together?"

We're on the verge of talking about that night, which is something I never want to do. My mind whirls and I try to come up with something to stop this conversation from happening.

"Unless we call a truce." It's all I can come up with.

The corner of her mouth twitches.

"A truce? Well, I suppose we can pretend to get along." She bites her lip, and my chest stirs. "Unless you can't handle being nice to me and you completely screw it up."

"Unless you can't handle my wit and charm . . ."

She cackles.

"What? You don't find me witty or charming?"

"I mean, not to me, anyway, not after . . ."

"Okay, okay. It's a truce."

I cut her off before she can talk about the first night we met, before the memory of pressing my lips against hers overwhelms me.

And with that, Stella Hart and I have a truce.

9

STELLA

BUCKET LIST DAY 3

I stride quickly away from the conference room, Ethan trailing behind me. I don't dare to look back at him. What was that? We had an actual inside joke when Tessa inadvertently used the word *unless*. Then I played along, and he stared at me . . . it was like he was peering into my soul, taking down my defenses with his intense stare.

I glance back over my shoulder, exactly like I was trying not to. *Damn!* He's peering at me with those dark-brown puppy dog eyes. Why did I even think he was glaring at me before? Shit. His sleeves are rolled up as usual, probably on purpose to seduce everyone with his gorgeous forearms and extensive ink, making him look, I dunno, dangerous and sexy.

Or is it just me who thinks that?

Ethan being here is too distracting. I have a hundred more meetings today, and I'm already on Day 3 of Evelyn's bucket list. But instead of seriously thinking about advisors and how I'm going to tackle each item, I'm thinking about Ethan Fraser's damn rose tattoos.

I did have one idea this morning on my way to work. It was a rainy London morning, so instead of the long walk from my flat in St John's Wood to our Baker Street offices, I jumped on a bus. There was an advertisement for London Zoo, which stated you could adopt an animal for a fifty quid donation. Clearly, the animal would stay at the zoo, but wouldn't that technically check the box for *Adopt an Animal*? I'm a little squirmy about it because it feels like a bit of cheating, and the last thing I want to do is skimp on Evelyn's last wishes, but what else am I gonna do? I don't have the time or the desire to adopt an actual animal.

I don't have the time for *any* of that bucket list. I have . . . twenty-five more days to get it done.

"Ethan," Tessa calls from her corner cubicle when we're halfway down the hall. We both stop, but I'm itching to run away. "Can you pop in here for a minute? I just need Ethan, Stella."

I nod and look at Ethan, who quickly glances at me before heading to Tessa's desk. I rush to my own cubicle, where Graham is waiting.

"Have a sec?" he says.

"I definitely do, for you, my favorite creative director." I give him what I'm hoping is a devastatingly charming smile and settle in my chair. He's my last hope for an advisor, because I'm sure not asking Chloe, desperate or not.

Then there's the person Gemma suggested this morning. The incredibly hot human who is currently with Tessa.

He's a last resort. Absolute last possible option. *Not* an option, not really.

Graham narrows his eyes. The two of us are work friends. We'll grab lunch together and the occasional happy hour. But asking him to be my advisor for Evelyn's bucket list is awkward as hell.

"You're doing that thing with your eyes where you squint and sort of smile, like you're about to make my timeline even more impossible."

"Ha, no timeline changes this morning. You go ahead, then I have a favor to ask. What do you need from me?"

Graham asks a quick question about the storyboards we're working on for a different client. I answer and when we're done with that topic, he patiently waits for me to continue speaking. I don't.

"You had something else?" he says after a minute.

I nod and can't help but fidget in my chair. "I have a favor to ask of you. A personal favor."

"For the last time, I only met that actor one time, and just because we're both from Essex, that doesn't mean I can get you his number."

I laugh. "It's not that again, and it was for a commercial! Not some creepy move to get him to sleep with me."

"Hmmm. Sure. Go on. I'm listening."

"It's about, uh, a bucket list. From my great-aunt."

Graham furrows his brow. "The one who just passed away?" A look of sympathy crosses his face.

"Yeah. She asked me to do this bucket list. I mean, she *needs* me to do it. Well, she didn't ask me, because she's dead, but she wrote a letter, before she died, presumably . . . "

Graham's eyes widen as I mumble my way through a completely incoherent explanation of the advisor thing. My hands are sweaty, my throat is dry, and I'm spewing absolute nonsense.

"Okay. You want me to do what?" He looks like I just asked him to sacrifice his cat.

I squint my eyes shut. "Give me a second." *Jesus. Pull it together.* I breathe in and out in an attempt to gather myself.

"Sure, and when you're done with whatever thing you're doing, can you summarize what you're asking? I got lost around the word *advisor.*"

I nod and concentrate on my breathing.

"Thanks for the work on the storyboards." Ethan's voice interrupts my one-minute meditation, and my eyes fly open.

Ethan's standing there talking to Graham. They chat for a minute about the storyboard idea, then Graham turns back to me.

"Stella? Advisor?"

Shit, shit, shit. Ethan's eyebrows raise and he watches me. He knows exactly what I was talking to Graham about. Heat warms my cheeks from pure embarrassment. Ethan and I might have had a little moment back there, but that doesn't mean I want to reveal my piles of dirty laundry to him.

"No, that's not what I said. Or meant to say, anyway." My brain whirls. What could I ask Graham for? I think about the list and when I get to the Skye item, my brain lights up. "Oh, I just need a quick photoshopping job in the next week or so, if you have a few minutes. No big deal if you can't, though."

The thing I really can't do in the next twenty-five days is go to the Isle of Skye. But Graham can help me with that. He's a Photoshop genius. That can be my evidence.

Guilt twists at me like a knife in the gut. *I'll go to Skye, Aunt Evelyn, I swear.* But I can't do it this month.

"Of course. What kind of photoshopping job?"

"I'll send you an email of what I need." Graham frowns, and I'm sure he's wondering why I didn't just do that to begin with. "Thank you!" I sound way too cheery.

Graham walks away with a lift of his hand.

I turn to Ethan, who is staring at me, leaning against his desk with his hands linked in front of him, a knowing smile on his face.

"What, are we friends now?" I cross my arms and try to appear confident and calm, not floundering and flustered like I feel. "I agreed to a truce, not being BFFs."

He presses his lips together.

I hate that I think he's so cute. As a male human being, Ethan Fraser does not disappoint. He reaches up and pulls at his beard. I bet if I kissed him, it would rub my chin raw. The crazy beard is a new thing. It was there, but much tidier a year and a half ago when we . . . no.

Inappropriate thoughts. And I'll never know how his crazy beard feels rubbing against my chin, because I have no intention of kissing this man ever again, and *oh Jesus, why am I even thinking of that?*

"So. Graham's not going to be your advisor?"

I shake my head.

"And you already asked Gemma. And Tessa."

A groan escapes my throat. "You are quite the eavesdropper." Why is there a smile creeping onto my face?

"Is there coffee in this place, Hart?"

"You want coffee?"

He nods.

"Yeah, okay. Come on." I open and close my hands and push back my chair, thinking too hard about the motions my body is going through to get from sitting at my desk to walking down the hall. Why does this man make me feel so self-conscious? I'm hyper aware of my four-inch heels and Ethan's large, muscular frame behind me. With the shoes, I reach a respectable five-foot-seven, but even then, Ethan's easily seven or eight inches taller than me.

He and Ben are an incredible contrast. My ex is tall, too, but not as tall as Ethan, and not nearly as muscular. Ben had never broken a bone playing rugby, and he told me it's because he ran so fast as a wing, nobody ever caught him. No tattoos. Clean shaven. Open, clear smile and bright blue eyes. Objectively attractive.

I have a brief flash from That Night of touching Ethan's chest and sliding my hands up to connect around his neck. Four-inch heels were no problem at all. They got me to just where I needed to be on his body.

And as much as I absolutely hate to admit it, I might enjoy doing that again. Climbing him like a tree.

Seriously? Someone save me from myself.

I pivot into the kitchen and gesture to the stack of cups next to the hulking coffee machine offering black coffee, lattes, cappuccinos, and various additives like flavored syrup and creamer.

Ethan presses the plain coffee button, and we stand awkwardly while London's slowest coffee machine spits out dark liquid.

"I have an offer to make you. A peace offering." Ethan crosses his arms and leans against the old linoleum counter.

"An offer?" I crinkle my forehead, summoning the most skeptical look I can.

"I can be your advisor for your great-aunt's bucket list."

I scoff, then see he is serious. "Really? That is maybe the worst idea anyone's ever had." I pretend I hadn't had the exact same thought moments ago.

But it *is* the worst idea. Which is why I was so aggravated at Gemma for suggesting it. Gemma, who found it gleefully entertaining when I told her I was working with Ethan on this project.

"Why?" He pretends to look offended. At least I *think* he's pretending. "Remember, we're friends now. And I would enjoy telling you what to do."

I sniff and really consider it. I need the help, and the days are ticking by, and I have nothing to show for them. What are my other options? I've literally run out of people in my life to ask. My sisters are a no-go, Gemma can't do it, and coworkers are all out of the running. Do I even have a choice here?

Side note: I need to get more people in my life.

"Fuck," I say, not meaning to speak aloud. "Sorry. I mean, okay, fine, you're my advisor."

He grins, showing his teeth to me. Is it a snarl? Nah, it's nice. I think.

"This will be fun."

"Sure. Fun." Hardly.

"Are you getting coffee?"

My eyes flit up to meet his gaze as he sips from his steaming black cup. I hadn't even noticed it was done.

Heat creeps up my neck. I throw a cup under the dispenser—I should've grabbed my mug from my desk, but Ethan's thrown *everything* off—and click vanilla latte. Today I could use extra sugar and wish I could pop out and get one of those whipped cream covered mochas from the coffee shop. I push my shoulders back and cross my arms, just like his were before. Am I exuding confidence? I better be.

"Your first task is to come with me to London Zoo in Regent's Park. Tomorrow." I make an immediate decision to go for the adopt-a-zoo-animal option. I've gotta get this moving.

He blinks. "Okay."

"You'll be here anyway for the follow-up storyboard meeting, so we'll go after work."

"It's a bucket list date."

"It's definitely not any kind of date, rugby dude."

"Rugby dude? Is that your nickname for me?" His eyebrow quirks up.

"Oh, shut up. I don't have a *nickname* for you."

As opposed to Ben's perfectly straight nose, Ethan's got a slight bump in his. I wonder how fast Ethan ran on the rugby pitch. I bet he was fast, too, but not afraid to get tackled.

Objectively, I shouldn't be thinking about any of this. And then I realize, because I called him *rugby dude*, he must know I'm picturing him in those tiny rugby shorts that would cling around his thick thighs, and a skin-tight jersey that would outline the muscles on his torso.

He grins at me. *Dammit! I knew it!*

A question pops up in my mind. I wonder what happened with the girl back home? The one he was getting back together with? The one who made it a clear choice for me to say yes to Ben when he asked me out, even with the memory of Ethan's kiss still on my mouth.

Ethan clears his throat and I startle. He raises both eyebrows and I blink five times in quick succession to get those images and questions out of my head.

"I had something else I wanted to show you. It was a commercial from another charity I thought was interesting," he says.

Now we're sharing interesting commercials with each other? At least it's work relevant. But I should cut off all further bonding. It's bad enough we're going to the zoo tomorrow. On a bucket list zoo date. Jesus.

Ethan slides his cup onto the small counter space between the coffee machine and the sink and reaches for his cell, sticking out of his side pocket.

"Actually, I have another meeting to run to. Can you send me the link?" I nod out the kitchen door and grab my coffee from the dispenser before he can even touch his phone.

But as I spin around and move toward the open doorway from the small kitchen to the hallway, one of my heels catches on the bump between the tiled floor and the rough carpet. My body starts to contort, surely in slow-motion, and I lurch forward, my vanilla latte flying out of my left hand into the hallway, and my torso involuntarily leaning forward to follow.

I'm screaming in my head as I picture the disastrous scene unfolding in front of Ethan. My arms flail and I prepare to land, sprawling, on the crappy corporate carpet. I shall never live this down. I'll ask Tessa to take me off the account. Hell, I'm just gonna quit and hide in my flat for the rest of my life.

But then strong hands wrap themselves around my body, one on my waist and one farther up, right under my breasts, stopping me mid-air. My hair swishes in front of my face, and I watch the vanilla latte as it crashes to the carpet and splashes everywhere, drops wetting the tops of my feet.

Instead of landing in a spot of old, soggy carpet, I'm pulled up to a standing position by Ethan, his other hand sliding down my torso to settle on my waist. For a century—or maybe seconds —the back of my body is pressed up against the front of his and this time my *body* screams, not just my head. I basically cease to breathe and can think of nothing but the feel of his hands around my waist and the hardness of his chest against my back. For a second, his beard is pressed to the top of my head and my hair embeds itself in the coarse hairs. I want to reach both my hands behind me and feel the sides of his hips with my fingers. I imagine spinning around and looking up into his eyes, so close to him.

I should be humiliated, not turned on. But for some reason I do not, under any circumstances, want Ethan Fraser to remove his hands from my body. I let myself lean back ever so slightly and I swear I hear him take a ragged breath.

We've been here before.

Ethan's hands shift and then he's gone, no longer touching me.

Fuck! What am I thinking? I step forward and spin around. Only five seconds have passed. But that's a lifetime longer than was appropriate to be pressed up against him.

"Are you okay?" Ethan's voice is off. Deeper. Scratchy.

Maybe he didn't notice any of the weirdness. Maybe it was all in my head. But Ethan's face is flushed, and his eyes have a weird glaze over them. *Fuck. He totally noticed.* His hands are spread, like they are trying to remember the shape of my body.

That's it. I totally have to resign.

"I'm so sorry. I'm usually not so clumsy." But I am today, in front of Ethan.

I scoop up the empty coffee cup from the ground, Ethan silently watching.

"I'm gonna get another. See you back there." I desperately try to dismiss him. He nods and walks away, and I waste a solid ten minutes lingering by the coffee machine, mindlessly scrolling my email and trying to get a hold of myself.

By the time I get back to my desk, Ethan's gone. I shove my noise-canceling headphones on in case he comes back.

My mind reels, trying to process what just happened. I gotta make sure Ethan and I never touch again. And that guy's my bucket list advisor?

Damn, but I don't trust our truce. I don't trust the way he's been looking at me, or the warm feeling in my core when my eyes lock with his warm brown ones.

But I don't have to trust him, right? And I definitely don't have to touch him again.

I hate that I want to.

10

ETHAN

Thursday, 11 July

"Are you ready to talk bucket list?" Stella and I walk side by side under the London Zoo entrance sign.

"Do I have to?"

"Well, if you'd like me to fulfill my advisor duties, then yes. Let me advise you."

"Ugh." Stella scans a code from her mobile at the entrance and shrugs off a light white sweater, revealing her sleeveless gray shirt. It's a rare hot London day, which basically means all the city emerges from their flats and offices and de-clothes. As she pushes through the entrance turnstile, my eyes drift over her sculpted shoulders and the outline of her bra beneath her shirt. She didn't have a sweater on when I stopped her from falling at the office yesterday. My hands were right there, on her sides, and I imagine them there again, running along the soft fabric, sliding them up her back, feeling that bra line with my fingers.

Fuuuuck. What am I supposed to do when I'm around her? This is unmanageable. And it's fucking hot out. I roll up my sleeves as far as they'll go, halfway up my biceps.

I don't understand a lot of things. Like why I'm attracted to this woman. I tried so hard to squash any feelings I had for her after she got with Ben. I tried to bury them with avoidance by having one-night stands with strangers I'd meet at the pub. It didn't work.

What's it about Stella Hart? Is it that she's off-limits? It must be.

"Come on." She waves for me to follow her. "There are five items on my bucket list."

"Go on."

"First one: *Volunteer*. Help somebody, or something."

"Okay, got it. And how will you do that?"

She sighs. "I mean, I'm sort of hoping that the Sporting UK Foundation commercial checks that box? We're doing the agency work pro bono. Think that counts?"

"No, not really, because *you* are literally getting paid to do it, even if the agency fees are waved."

"I dunno, it might be okay." Stella glances at me, biting her lip.

"No. And I think you're lucky you have me as an advisor. What's the next one?"

Stella scrunches her forehead and waves me toward a map behind a plastic surface. "Go to the Isle of Skye."

"What?"

"In Scotland."

"I know it's in Scotland." The memory of Mum taking me there when I was ten years old rushes at me. It's one of the few good memories I have of her from my childhood. It was a magic—

"Aunt Evelyn said it was a magical place."

I jolt and stare at Stella's profile as she drags a finger along the map of the animal habitats. It was the exact thing I was thinking. Skye is magical.

"When are you going to go to Skye?"

She glances at me nervously. "I'm not. I mean, I can't. I *can't* do it this month. There's too much happening, and Skye is, like, in the middle of nowhere."

"But you need to go for the list, right?" Then something dawns on me. A memory of a conversation I overheard yesterday. "Photoshop from Graham?"

She nods and her cheeks turn pink. "What's your favorite zoo animal?" Stella turns back to the zoo map.

"Don't change the subject. That is cheating. You can't cheat on this list."

"Oh god, I know." A quick glance at me, then she's back studying the map. "I feel awful even considering it. But I can't get it done. Not this month. I'm working on three commercials and the idea of taking a trip to bumfuck Scotland is too much for me to handle." She sounds like she's trying to convince herself.

"Hart, come on." I feel a stabbing of sympathy for her, but she can't cheat on this. She'll regret it, even if she gets away with it, even if she makes up for it later.

"Favorite animal?" she asks again.

"Monkey."

"Monkey? Don't they throw poop? Let's see the polar bears instead."

I follow her down a long pathway lined with a rainbow of flowers.

"Another bucket list item is to help one of my sisters. Reese. With what, you might ask?" She shrugs. "Aunt Evelyn wasn't very specific."

"Well, that's not helpful."

"Exactly. I have to think about that one more. I'm at a loss."

"Volunteer, go to Skye, help Reese. That's three."

"Adopt an animal." Stella's eyes dart to me briefly before she points down a different pathway.

"I can help with that one. I've got a litter of kittens at my flat. They're very cute."

"Um, what?" She turns her whole body to me and stops walking, a little grin on her face, spreading her pink lips and making my stomach flip over. "You have kittens at your flat?"

"Is that weird?" I cock my head. "My flatmate is a foster for an animal rescue, so we have a room in our flat that's just for kittens."

"You have a whole extra room in your London flat and you give it to kittens?" Stella puts her fists on her hips and tilts her head. "No one has an extra room in London."

"It's a very small room. More like a large closet. It doesn't even have a window. But we have a lamp that mimics the sun. They love to sleep under it."

She laughs, and it's this lovely melodic sound that's like sugar and spices and delicious Christmas puddings. Yeah, it was the laugh that got me the night we kissed. The laugh and that stupid game she had us playing. The way she didn't give a shite about what people thought. The way she didn't try to be something else that night, she wasn't flirting on purpose, she wasn't trying to seduce me, she wasn't blowing me off.

I know I have a goofy grin on my face, and I try to wipe it off and do my job as her advisor. When she stops laughing about the kitten room, she's still smiling at me, and she touches my arm with one hand and points to the signs again.

But her fingers on my bare skin are like fire.

Maybe we *can* survive this month, as long as we don't touch each other. I gently move my arm, but her hand remains.

Maybe we can be friends.

Or more than friends.

Then I remember Ben.

Fuck. Friends is a stretch. More than friends is not possible.

I fall into a comfortable step next to her. We walk together, perfectly natural, like we *are* friends. I don't hate it. It feels like we're balancing a glass ball on top of a bike basket and at any moment, a bump will cause it to pop off and shatter on the path. I glance down at her and have the urge to grab her hand and entwine our fingers together, maybe pull her around until our fronts are pressed together, then see what happens from there.

"So, is the fifth item to go to London Zoo? Is your great-aunt forcing you to face some deep fear of zoo animals?"

Stella scrunches her face at me. "Forget about the fifth item. I . . . . Let's not talk about it right now. Or ever."

"That's intriguing. I think you'll have to, and as your ad—"

"Hush. But I had an idea on the bus the other day of how to check off the adopt-an-animal item without adopting one for real."

"Wait, what?" Her words bring me back to reality and hang in the air like a cloud of body odor after a rugby game. I trail Stella around a curve toward the polar bear enclosure. We stop in front of a fenced-in habitat. Two polar bears sleep on a shaded rock across the wide moat, a long, clear body of water stretched out in front of them.

She's serious about cheating on this list.

"Cute little guys, aren't they?" Stella pulls out her mobile to snap a selfie of herself with the bears in the background.

"You're going to cheat on the whole thing?"

She pockets her mobile and turns to watch the bears, not making eye contact with me. "London Zoo lets you adopt an animal. Donate fifty quid and get an adoption certificate."

I let out a huff. "Seriously?" A ball of queasiness rolls around my stomach.

"I don't *want* to cheat on Aunt Evelyn's list. I really don't. But I also don't want to be tied down with a pet. Or a husband, or children, or anything like that. No matter what she or anyone else says." Stella's facing the enclosure and seems to be talking to herself, or someone else. Definitely not me.

Where did that all come from? I thought we were talking about pets, and she drops the fact that she's never going to have kids? Get married? All legitimate choices, and ones I don't disagree with, but it's intriguing for her to bring them up now. What kind of baggage is this girl carrying?

But I have a clue. Ben told me a bit about their fights in the end.

Still, *her* baggage can't be as bad as mine.

It almost distracts me from the fact that she's totally fucking up this bucket list. Not quite, though. The ball of queasiness turns to anger.

"I think you'll regret it, Hart."

She turns to me. "I'm a thirty-four-year-old woman. This bucket list is simply manipulative. She's taking out her own life regrets—ones I didn't even realize she had—on *me*. It's not fair."

Noted. There's something like hurt in Stella's face. Betrayal. Still, the way she's handling this doesn't sit right.

"You obviously loved your great-aunt, and she loved you enough to do this for you." I try to soften my voice.

"It was for her, not for me."

"What if this changes how you remember her? Won't you feel guilty? Regretful about cheating on something so important?"

What I would give to have had my mum care about me like this. I would never cheat on a bucket list from her. Stella will regret it forever.

"Why do you care so much if I cheat?" She spins toward me and crosses her arms across her chest. Girl is still wearing her high heels. Heels. At a zoo.

"Because someone loved you enough to write a bucket list for you." I clamp my mouth shut before I reveal too much, before the lump in my throat makes my voice squeaky.

Stella flinches but doesn't uncross her arms. Her eyes are filled with tears, and her expression softens at my words. "I know she loved me," Stella whispers.

"It's disrespectful to cheat. Just do the list. Take it seriously. I can help, Hart."

Her face contorts and her lips settle in a tight line, but her eyes are shining. Fuck, I don't want to make her cry, but she has to understand how fucked up this is. I can keep pushing. I can make her do things my way, can't I? But she's digging her heels in—figuratively—and the last thing I want to do is make Stella Hart hate me again, if she ever stopped. I swallow hard.

We engage in a staring contest, which lasts for thirty seconds, until her face falls and she sighs deeply. Stella opens her mouth to say something, then slams it shut again. Finally, she speaks.

"I've gotta stop back there to fill out the paperwork." She nods her head the way we came.

"Okay, let's do it." She'll regret it, but I'll be there for her.

"I can finish today on my own."

It's a punch to the gut. But if she doesn't want me there with her, I'm not going to force it. I nod. "I'll see you at the office sometime," I say, my tone far colder than I'd intended.

She nods her head once and strides away from me.

I don't know what I was thinking. I need to get my brain—and my body—under control when I'm around Stella.

11

—————

STELLA

BUCKET LIST DAY 4

The flat door slams behind me and I stand in my dimly lit kitchen. I hate how things went with Ethan at the zoo. As if I don't feel bad enough already about cheating on Evelyn's bucket list. I know it makes me a terrible person. I know my great-aunt would hate what I'm doing. I let out a small sob and cover my face with my hands. But him being so judgmental is making it even worse.

And why can't he call me by my freaking name? That *Hart* bullshit is driving me up a wall.

We had some . . . moments this week. Good moments. Between yesterday at the office with our unexpected bonding over the Unless Game, and then that touch in the kitchen. *Lord, that touch.* And today. I was looking forward to spending time with him, even though I'd dreaded telling him about the list. Sweet baby Jesus, I can NOT tell him about the *Find the One that Got Away* bucket list item.

It was a terrible idea for me to let him be my advisor.

A groan slips out of my throat, and I pour a glass of red wine from the open bottle on my counter. Alcohol would have made the zoo trip so much better. Why didn't I think of that? But the wine tastes stale and cheap. When did I open it, anyway? Last weekend, when I was recovering from jet lag? I push the glass away and splay my hands on the counter, tapping my pointer fingers on the linoleum.

I want to forget about the way his hard chest felt pressed against my back in the kitchen yesterday, how I wanted to lean back further into him. Definitely not thinking about how my hand felt resting on his arm at the zoo, before things went wrong. Not about the way he was actually kind to me. Smiled at me. The way he called it our *bucket list date*.

Absolutely not. I don't need that guy. I don't need anyone.

I *do* need to write an email to Stuffy Richard, to see if my plan to get this done in the required timeframe will get through his approvals. Screw the squirrelly feeling of guilt that's making the wine curdle in my stomach like spoiled milk. I open my laptop on the counter and type.

To: Richard Ramsey
From: Stella Hart
Date: 11 July 2024
Subject: Stella Hart Bucket List Update for Approval

Dear Richard,

I have a quick update for you on where I am with Aunt Evelyn's bucket list, as you'd said we should check in to make sure we're on the right track.

I've chosen my advisor. His name is Ethan Fraser, and he's an old friend and will help me and sign off on the list.

1. Volunteer
*I am leading a project to produce a commercial for a charity
that supports underprivileged kids in London. We will shoot
the spot just before the bucket list deadline.*

This is true. Ethan's voice rings in my head, telling me it
doesn't count if I'm getting paid to do it. *Shut up!*

2. Adopt an Animal
*I have already adopted an animal! Attached you'll find the
adoption certificate and a picture of me with my cuddly
polar bear, who will continue to live at London Zoo.*

3. Adventure to the Isle of Skye in Scotland
*I have it on my calendar to climb the Old Man of Storr on
Saturday, August 3, which is Day 27.*

That one's an utter lie and I hate myself for it. It's simply not
reasonable. I'll likely be on a TV shoot that week—the Sporting
UK Foundation one—and then suddenly will have to get my ass
up to the remote Isle of Skye and climb some dumb big rock.
Graham has won actual awards for his photoshopping skills, so
that's what's going to happen here. *I'll go in the fall, I promise,
Aunt Evelyn.*

4. Help Reese
*I'm going to invest in Reese's side business, which is creating
websites for artists and writers.*

I thought of this on the walk home from the zoo. Reese sent
me and Maddie a draft of her own website, which she's
launching soon to try to gather some clients. I admit, the way
I'm doing this one kind of sucks. Once she gets her share of
Evelyn's estate, Reese won't really need any financial help from

me. And her startup costs should be low. But it's all I can think of.

5. Find the One that Got Away
I'm going to send a message to my ex-boyfriend and connect with him. I don't think he's 'the one that got away,' but I will make sure I made the right decision to break up with him.

Thanks, and let me know if you see any problems with the above.

Best,
Stella Hart

Best? No, that's not my best, and I know it. Ethan knows it. And maybe even Stuffy Richard will know it.

Worse? Evelyn would know it.

I want to throw up the stale wine swirling in my belly, but instead I grab the half-full glass and slide onto one of my kitchen chairs, doubling down by taking a giant swig. Am I really going to send Ben a message? What, a text? A written letter? I shake my head violently and my hair whips into my eyeballs. This is the worst one. The nerve of Evelyn. I'd like to have a word with her.

I close my eyes and imagine Ethan reading that email. I'm sure he won't even sign off on the list as it is.

And that fifth item. I can't tell Ethan about it. It would remind him that I kissed him and then dated his *best friend*. As if he forgot. If I told Ethan, maybe he wouldn't even help with the list at all because it'd be a huge conflict of interest. Maybe he'd go tell Ben and they'd laugh at me together. And maybe then, Ben wouldn't even agree to talk to me.

I can't trust Ethan with that one.

I want to accept help from him. I really do. Let him save me from myself. But I can't. It's like my brain is at its emotional capacity and can't absorb one more thing. Being around Ethan even more, opening myself up to him, would push me over the edge. It would tip my carefully balanced life, one that's already been rocked by losing Evelyn.

I don't want to depend on anyone. Just like Evelyn and my dad, I'm better off on my own. Alone.

12

ETHAN

I've gotten nothing under control since Stella walked away from me at the zoo yesterday.

I feel terrible for snapping at her, and I'm walking under gray skies through Regent's Park to try to distract myself. The park is quieter during the day without sports. A woman pushing a stroller passes by with a giant coffee. A pair of university-age students jog along the paved path, chatting and seemingly carefree. I wish I could feel the same, but the idea of Stella cheating on her late great-aunt's bucket list still horrifies me. I remind myself that *I'm* not the one cheating, but it doesn't seem to help.

I let out a long, slow breath. Stella feels bad about it. That much was obvious. There was the hesitation when she told me her misguided plans, and the flinch when I noted how much her great-aunt must have loved her to write that list.

I felt sick all last night, even after settling on the couch and letting Colin's litter of tiny foster kittens crawl all over me, playfully biting my fingers and leaving tiny scratches on my arms. I wanted to text her. Tell her about losing Mum. What a mess I am.

I should do it.

Crossing the short pedestrian bridge over the pond, I hardly notice the rainbow of flowers and scattered ducks, the dreamy peace of this place. Before I realize it, I'm out of the park and on Baker Street, right in front of Pepper Me Marketing.

I have to talk to her.

ME

Do you have a few minutes? I'm down at street level

My heart pounds in my chest. What am I doing? Telling her about Mum? Because *that* feels a lot like letting this woman close to me. Too close.

But this is important. I want her to understand why I acted how I did at the zoo. Why I believe she shouldn't cheat on this bucket list. And she's grieving. I understand that—at least in my own way—too well. So I'm going to tell her.

She doesn't make me wait long.

STELLA

Coming

Three minutes later, Stella pushes out of the glass doors from the lobby of her building.

Fuck, but she's cute today—blond hair tucked behind her ears, dark-blue eyes wide and vulnerable, staring at me questioningly, temporarily without shields up. A tight black tank top with a V-neck dips in between her breasts, and a long sweater is slightly askew on her shoulders, showing just a sliver of skin. She rubs the colorful butterfly tattoo on her wrist.

I wonder what it'd be like to pull her into my arms and hug her. Not an accidental touch like yesterday when she tripped by the coffee machine. Not even a drunken kiss at a bar. Wrap my arms around her and protect her from the world.

But Stella Hart doesn't want protecting.

"Ethan? What's up?"

I'm frozen in place. I love my name on her lips. She's waiting for me to say something, but the way she's biting her lip disables my ability to voice cohesive thoughts.

"Hart." My voice is raspy, like I haven't used it in hours. And it's true. I've been stuck in my head, all alone. "I wanted to explain my behavior yesterday. At the zoo." I swallow, and surely, she can see my throat ripple.

"I get it. You think I suck. But, funny thing, I already think I suck, so I beat you to it." The words tumble out of her, and the muscles of my abdomen seize.

She has no idea how I feel about her. How I felt back then, how I feel now. The feeling that I'm having a really hard time fighting anymore. A big red bus stops at the curb three feet from us and commuters file off. Cars whiz by. Groups of people chatter to each other and on their mobiles.

But it all fades away.

"Truce or no truce, you've never liked me." Stella bites her bottom lip and her face crumples. "Why should it bother me now?" The last words come out as a whisper.

I flinch. How can she honestly think that I don't like her? How I acted toward her was pure self-protection—am I that good of an actor? I couldn't be friends with her. No way. It was all I could to do to avoid her, since she was dating my best friend.

I never hated her. Not for one second.

My mouth is dry. I should start talking. Or should I turn and leave? I pull on my beard, then shove my hands in my pockets and lock eyes with her.

"Three months ago, my mum died." My fucking voice cracks. I'm being so dramatic, but I suppose if there's anything it's okay to be dramatic about, it's losing someone you love. "We weren't close, but I wanted to be. My childhood was . . . not good. And she was troubled. She's always been."

"Oh, god, I'm so sorry." Stella steps forward and touches my forearms, which are stiff and anchored to my sides, my hands tucked securely in my jeans. She frowns, her forehead crinkling with sympathy. "And here I am, being such an ass about my great-aunt's bucket list." Her hands remain on my arms, warm and comforting.

"I would've done anything for Mum to have written me some kind of bucket list. Hell, a birthday card once in a while would have been enough, or a call, or returning my texts . . . or even letting me into her fucking flat, which I was paying for." I swallow, hard. "But she didn't do any of that. A bucket list? Never."

Stella tugs my hands out of my pockets and entwines her fingers with mine. The busy street around us has fallen away, and it's just me and her.

"My mum never gave me much thought at all. She never put me first. She never did things for me. I was always an inconvenience, someone she ignored completely most of the time. At her best, I was second choice. At her worst, I didn't even exist."

Stella makes a sweet squeak.

"Ethan. That's awful."

I shake my head. "Don't feel bad for me. I'm only telling you this so you understand. My arsehole behavior yesterday was not about you at all, but about all the baggage I carry from my mum."

Stella pauses for a beat before throwing her arms around my waist and pressing her body against mine. I'm shocked at the contact, frozen at the way she feels against me with this kind, intimate gesture.

"I'm sorry for what you went through," she murmurs. Her voice is muffled by my shirt, but I can feel the vibration of her against my chest. Her head fits perfectly beneath my chin, and I lean into the touch.

With horror, I realize my eyes are filling with water. Tears? Fuck, no. I blink a bunch of times to make them go away. I focus on an old bloke filing off a bus, behind an old lady who turns to grab his hand . . . oh, fuck.

"I like you, Hart." The words come out involuntarily. I didn't mean to say it out loud. But hearing them? It feels right.

She leans back and lets a smile settle on her lips. Something stirs in me. Something that's much more than like.

Is *this* pulling it together?

"You like me?" Her gaze flits briefly from my eyes down to my mouth and back up.

Fuck me. I nod.

"Okay. Let's start over from there. Forget the past. Forget the truce. You like me. And . . . I guess I like you."

Her words set off a flurry of emotion inside me. Forget the past? Unlikely. But I'll go along with Stella, as long as she keeps looking at me like this.

"Glad that's settled."

She steps back and I immediately mourn our lack of contact. "Everyone should feel like their mother chooses them first. Always. It's . . . what moms do."

"Not my mum." My voice is raspy. "And now I have to deal with—" I stop speaking. No. I don't need to tell Stella about any of the flat nonsense.

"Deal with what?"

I shake my head, regretting starting that sentence. "Nothing."

"Nope, sorry, that's not going to work for me. You've seen way more of my personal drama than I've seen of yours. Spill." She crosses her arms and taps a foot on the concrete.

"Fine. I have to clean out my mum's flat." I grab my beard and twist, pulling till it stings.

"It's been three months. You haven't done that?" She cocks her head to the side.

"No."

Stella stares at me. "Why not?"

"I just can't. It's too hard."

"Well, shit. Can I help?"

"No, no, please. I shouldn't have said anything. Sorry. Let's not talk about it anymore." Panic bubbles up inside me. She's literally the first person I've said a word to about the flat.

"Okay," she says after staring at me for a beat. Stella makes a zipping motion on her lips.

"But . . . your great-aunt chose *you*. You and your sisters. That's why I don't want you to cheat. You'll regret it."

Stella moans, running a hand through her hair. "I got an email back from the lawyer today. He did *not* like my suggestions for the way I want to complete the bucket list."

"Why am I not surprised?"

"I mean, Aunt Evelyn was a monster." She rolls her eyes but has a smile on her face.

I chuckle. "I think I would've enjoyed this great-aunt of yours. I'd like to have met her. Have a coffee, perhaps pick her brain about life."

Stella's cheeks flush. That was probably a comment that should have stayed in my head. She's staring at my face, examining, like she's trying to figure me out.

"I have a meeting in a few minutes. I gotta run back up." Stella's hands twitch by her sides.

I glance down at them. I miss her touch. I wish her fingers were still on my arm or wrapped around my waist.

"Right. See you around." I slowly turn to walk away from Stella Hart, but she calls me back.

"Hey, Ethan?"

I pause and wait intently.

"So sorry about your mom."

There's a softness and sincerity in her eyes that tightens my throat. I open my mouth to respond, but she disappears back into the building, leaving me on the street by myself, in a bustling crowd of midday Londoners.

13

STELLA

BUCKET LIST DAY 5

I don't head to the elevators to get to my meeting, but instead press my back against the cold marble wall of the lobby, my head turned to the door, mostly out of sight of Ethan. I watch him. He's frozen like one of the statues in Regent's Park. A rugby god, maybe, with his form-fitting t-shirt with the London Stingers club logo and jeans that hug his thick thighs. Something stirs inside me. Warm, like the glowing embers of a fire that could burst into flames if someone doesn't throw sand on top.

Ethan's confession about his mom passing away and how she treated him growing up clarifies so much about the way he's acted toward me. That vulnerability he showed just now, telling me about the flat he can't bring himself to deal with . . . it was like he was telling me something he's never told another soul.

"Oh, shit." I squint my eyes shut. I wish I could help. Don't I owe it to him? After me going on about missing my great-aunt, when he's the one missing his *mother*?

And I've been insisting on cheating on the list. The list my beloved great-aunt took the time to write, just for me. My stomach churns. How utterly insensitive. I *am* lucky, just like Ethan told me last night.

Evelyn loved me so much.

Even Stuffy Richard thinks I'm cheating. My eyes spring open and I pull my phone out of my back pocket, clicking on the email I skimmed earlier this morning.

To: Stella Hart
From: Richard Ramsey
Date: 12 July 2024
Subject: Re: Stella Hart Bucket List Update for Approval

Dear Stella,

If your Aunt Evelyn were in the room with you right now, would she approve of the plan you have? Evelyn directed me to judge your completion of the list by whether it was in the spirit in which she intended. Do you think your ideas are all in that spirit? If you tell me yes, then I'll certainly take that into consideration. But I urge you to carefully re-consider each item.

Best Regards,
Richard

Man, I am the absolute worst.

I haven't even read the letter she wrote me. The one that started *My Dearest Stella*, the one I scrolled past, disregarding a heartfelt last note from Evelyn as if it wasn't worth my attention. Yeah, it'll hurt to read. But I'm hurting anyway. I miss her. I want to call her, tell her about Ethan, tell her about the project with Sporting UK Foundation, hear her *pishposh* my troubles away.

I gotta read that letter.

I send a text to Chloe asking her to reschedule my meeting, and with a quick look outside confirming that Ethan's gone, I push back out the thick glass doors.

The sun is trying to peek through gray clouds, and I make the short walk to Regent's Park. Nestled in north London, the park is gorgeous in the spring and summer, the flowers and landscaping breathtaking around the walking trails, pond, and large open spaces. Brisk and fresh in the fall, cold but still beautiful in the winter, it's my favorite spot in London. Even without the sun.

It'd be better to read her letter there, in the rose gardens or sitting on a bench by the pond, than in some dark, sad conference room. Evelyn also loved London, and she's the one who first brought me here after Dad died. I know she was bummed that by the time I moved, she was in her mid-eighties and not up for traveling across the Atlantic to visit.

The towering, majestic white buildings of my MBA program stand to my left, and I dodge across the road onto the paved pathway into the park. Scattered people stroll the shaded trails, a pair of young adults lounges on a blanket in the grass, and a man and a young girl laugh and kick a soccer ball to each other.

I cross the pedestrian bridge and wander past a sea of colorful flowers, dodging the goose poop that covers the sidewalk and almost ruins the tranquility of the park, until I get to my favorite area: Queen Mary's Rose Gardens. I pass through the giant black gate adorned with golden decorations. The tall and short meticulously manicured shrubs make it feel like a maze, and each bed of thriving roses surely has secrets to reveal.

This is where I came after I found out Evelyn had passed. This is where I wanted to feel her, connect to her, before she was too far away. It was beautiful, but she just wasn't here.

I find an empty bench by the enormous fountain and sink down.

Why haven't I read this letter from Evelyn? I think it's partially because I miss her so badly, but I'm also mad at her. Mad that she felt the need to press her own life regrets onto her great-nieces after her death. Wouldn't it have been better if she were alive to see me do these things, and if I didn't have this timeframe that feels impossible to manage?

But it's time to face her words.

I breathe in until the warm summer air fills me deep into my core, and then tap my phone to pull up the full bucket list document. Her letter to me is on the second page.

My Dearest Stella,

Hello, my darling. I hope you are doing well, and my passing doesn't cause you too much pain. I wish I could have stuck around forever. You, sweet Stella, are the great-niece most like me. Most like your father, too. And as such, I think you'll be the one who resists this bucket list project the most. You like your independence, just like I do. I get it. You don't like being told what to do.

But . . . hear me out. I want to make sure you don't have blinders on to the joy and glory in the world around you. There are things I didn't get right in life. Not because I tried and failed, but because I was too scared. I didn't let people in at the right moments and I lived to regret that later.

Just give me four weeks. Do these five bucket list items, please? I know it won't be easy. I get it. Do it for yourself. Or do it for me. As a last resort, do it for Reese and Maddie, because as Richard explained, I'm quite serious about tossing my entire estate to charities, and I picked the ones I know you'd detest the most.

Remember:
Your life is your own.
Your decisions are your own.

And I love you so very much.

You've been everything to me. My shining light. My mini-me, in a lot of ways, and I wish I could be there to see how your life turns out.

Good luck with your bucket list.

All My Love,
Aunt Evelyn

My face crumbles and I can't stop tears from falling onto my cheeks. I wipe them away with the palms of my hands, and then rub the inside of my right wrist with my left thumb, tracing the lines of the butterfly tattoo shaded with different blues and purples. I got it when I first moved to London seven years ago. To me, it represented freedom and independence. I knew back then, still recovering from my relationship with Hunter, that I didn't want anything in my life that would hold me down or influence how I live.

But these days, I just feel lonely. Maybe it's Evelyn's passing. Maybe it's breaking up with Ben. Maybe it's working so much that I don't have time to foster new relationships in my life.

Grief ferments in the pit of my stomach. I lived across an ocean from Evelyn for the past seven years, but we talked at least once a week, and I saw her twice a year when I traveled back to New Jersey. I talked to her about my job, complained about Tessa and Chloe, shared with her why I was breaking up with Ben. We discussed how my student loans were still weighing on me. That I wasn't quite sure what I should be doing with the rest of my life, even though I was thirty-four and should have that sorted by now. Evelyn was the one I could really open up to, with never a bit of judgment. I love my sisters, but Evelyn understood me protecting myself from people I dated. I *thought* she was the same way.

But it turns out, she regretted it.

The pain in the center of my chest throbs and then fades. I give it a minute. I let myself feel the grief. It's there because I loved her so much, and the pulsing of it makes me feel her absence so intensely. Lets me mourn her. Love her, even in death.

I've got to try harder on this bucket list. But I simply can't finish all the items in the time I have. I know that. I'm away for a few days next week on a shoot for a different client, and by the time I get back, the twenty-eight-day clock will be halfway done. The fourth week of Evelyn's timeline is when we're trying to schedule the Sporting UK Foundation shoot, and that leaves just one week in the middle, and I have another shoot for a third client.

I'm going to struggle to even *cheat* my way through the list. Maybe if I can make a few of the items better, that will be enough. Enough to satisfy Richard, enough to ease the guilt in my soul, enough to make Ethan not think I'm a terrible person.

The first bucket list item is *Volunteer*. I look up from my phone as an exhausted-looking young mother walks by with a stroller covered in a thin blanket. Her eyes are bleary, and she might as well be sleepwalking. I look around the park, searching for inspiration in the rose bushes.

There must be some other way I can volunteer that would work.

A pair of women in their late teens or early twenties jog past me, and I catch a snippet of conversation about their upcoming university semester. Oh. OH. It hits me in the face just like that. I'm mentoring Izzy, and told her I'd help her with the scholarship competition application. That must be better than the Sporting UK Foundation campaign, since I'm not getting paid for mentoring. I hear Ethan's voice in my head reminding me that producing that commercial is my literal job, regardless of whether Pepper Me Marketing is waving agency fees.

I pull out my phone to text my mentee.

ME

Hey Izzy! How's that scholarship application going?

IZZY

So good! I was just gonna text you. Can you look at the Google Doc? I have some great ideas!

ME

Sure, I'll get back to you ASAP

I feel better for a split second, but when I tap back to the bucket list, number two practically shouts itself at me: *Adopt an Animal*.

I mean, this one is done, right? I adopted a polar bear and got a picture of myself with my new pet. I even have an adoption certificate. I can't let myself feel guilty about this. I live in central London. I can't get a pet. No way.

For number three, *Adventure to the Isle of Skye in Scotland*, I just can't fit it in. And I've already emailed Graham a picture of me —from when I went on a weekend walkabout with Gemma in Wales and we had on hiking gear—that can be photoshopped onto a stock image of the Old Man of Storr. I'll have to go some other time. After the estate is settled.

The fourth one, *Help Reese*, is awkward. I said I was going to invest in Reese's side hustle. But I suspect Richard wasn't impressed by that option, and honestly, I can see why. I roll my neck from side to side. What else can I do from so far away? I'll try to think of something else. If not . . . website business investment will have to do it.

It's the last one that gets me. *Find the One that Got Away*. I told Richard I'm going to send a message to Ben. Sounds like it checks the box to me. All I have to do is . . . actually do it. I've gotta rip the Band-Aid off on this one. I shudder, even though the sun is partially out from behind a cloud, warming my arms.

And how am I supposed to explain that to Ethan? Do I have to tell him about this one? Surely not. I look up as movement catches my eye. A couple appears around one of the tall shrubs, hands entwined, looking at each other lovingly as they stroll through the gardens. Ethan and I have bonded now. We're closer, even though that's hard to believe. I don't know how to deal with the swirling feelings I have about that man. I don't want to derail our fragile progress.

Eyes closed, I breathe deeply, in through my nose, letting the light fragrant rose scent fill my nostrils, this time not adding to my nausea. I've got this list covered. I let the breath out through my mouth.

Maybe Richard was being dramatic. Maybe this is almost good enough for the bucket list. But a wave of doubt hits from inside my chest, trying to drown me. *What if it's not?* What if Richard sees through me and knows I'm cheating my way through this?

"I'm not cheating on some of it," I say to the yellow, red, and pink rose bushes. I head back toward Baker Street.

An image manifests in my brain. Me meeting with Ben in person and having a real conversation about our relationship and how it ended. Looking into his pale-blue eyes and asking him to elaborate on his words that I'm not girlfriend or wife or mother material. Horror descends on me, and I freeze at the gate to the rose gardens. What would be the point?

I can't do that.

I can't do this list the way Evelyn wants me to. I'll do it my way, and that involves modifying some of the items so I can get through them without losing my mind. But I gotta start somewhere. And that should probably begin with the most painful task ahead of me: connecting with Ben.

14

ETHAN

It was raining and gray by the evening's practice. No excuse not to play rugby.

Ben joined us tonight to assist in showing the lads a few passing and catching techniques. Leo, Callum, and the other boys were immediately drawn to him. Everyone is, aren't they? They circled Ben like flies, almost innately understanding he is not like them, he is not like me. He didn't grow up broken.

"Thanks for coming out. The boys loved it." I pick up the cones and shove them down into the equipment duffel.

"No worries. It was fun. They're good lads. But it's been a bit since I tossed a rugby ball." Ben runs a hand through his light hair, wet from the rain. "Still good to grab a drink?"

"Yeah."

We head back toward Camden and duck into the first pub along the way, settling at a table with pints of lager, the equipment bag tucked by my feet.

"What's new?" I ask, eager to not talk about my own life.

"I have a Robin and Simon story for you." Ben smirks.

"Oh, do tell." Stories about Ben's wholesome parents are my

favorite. I keep in touch with them, but he's always got the latest gossip since they talk almost daily.

"They are now fixated on walking across the UK next summer."

I laugh. "Of course they are. Why?"

"I truly do not know. Now that Dad is retired, they want to do the Coast to Coast Walk, starting from the Irish Sea and all the way across northern England to the North Sea."

"Christ."

"I know. Mum's been doing all the research and thinks they can train for the next year and pull it off."

"They didn't mention that when I saw them last month. How far is it?"

"It's a brand-new obsession. The trail is over three hundred kilometers." Ben shakes his head. "There is absolutely no way. I'm going to have to make sure I'm free to go rescue them."

"Let me know, I can help."

"Thanks."

We both drink deeply from our pints. He sighs.

"What's wrong?" I furrow my brow at my usually cheery friend.

"They drive me nuts, but sometimes I look at my parents and wonder if I'll ever have what they have. You know what I mean?" He runs his hand through his drying blond locks. "I know you're not into the marriage or kids thing, but I'd always wanted to settle down by now. Maybe start a family. Do stupid things like plan an overly ambitious walk across the country with someone."

I swallow. Ben doesn't often get serious like this. He must be feeling like absolute rubbish.

"We're already mid-thirties, mate." Ben's face is stricken.

"You realize that's not old, right?"

"It feels old." He drinks from his now half-full pint.

"You'll find the right person eventually." It's all I can come up with.

"Is that your pep talk?" He groans. "Because it's shite."

I grunt. "You know pep talks really aren't my thing."

"I dunno. Maybe wanting to settle down is too much. I really fucked it up with Stella Hart when I pushed her on the kids thing. I think about that all the time, mate."

Fuuuuck. My eyes practically pop out of my head at his mention of Stella, but thankfully, he doesn't notice and keeps talking.

"Maybe I can live without kids? Maybe marriage—or even a serious relationship—would be enough."

He keeps talking, but I'm stuck back on the Stella comment. I *have* to bring up working with her. Now. I haven't been intentionally lying to him so far . . . but now it feels like I would be.

"Thanks for listening." Finally, he takes a breath.

I nod. "Of course, mate. And since you mentioned Stella . . ."

He blinks rapidly at me. "Yeah?"

"You know how I'm doing that commercial for Sporting London, soon to be Sporting UK Foundation? About the merger?"

Ben nods. "Yeah, you texted me about that."

I'm not sure why I feel such dread, and almost guilt.

But I *do* know. It's the feelings for Stella that I've always tried to hold back. The ones that are stronger than ever.

"Well, guess who is the lead at the advertising agency?"

Ben stares at me blankly, then his eyes widen.

"No. Stella?"

I nod. "Yes."

"Holy shite." He lets out a huff and swirls his pint, then drinks deeply. "I miss that girl. How is she?"

"Fine, I guess." He *misses* her? Dammit.

"Is she single, do you know?"

I chug my entire pint as he watches me, waiting for a response. There is no way I'm going to tell him I'm helping with her great-aunt's bucket list. No way I'll tell him about the lingering touches we've shared—in the office kitchen, outside her building this morning.

About how I want more. I want *her*.

I'm a traitor. Here is my best friend, telling me about how he wants a wholesome marriage and family like his parents, and I'm lusting after his ex-girlfriend. Who he's clearly got lingering feelings for.

"I'm not sure. I haven't asked."

"I should text her. Maybe she'd see me again."

My gut squeezes in horror. I know she's Ben's, not mine, but the idea of them texting, calling, talking . . . kissing. It makes me want to hurl.

"You're still hung up on her?" I attempt to sound as casual as possible.

He tilts his head and stares vacantly past me.

"I don't know. She's kind of like my one who got away, you know?"

I swallow loudly and am thankful for the low roar of the busy pub.

Ben's reaction gives me pause. *Is* he still hung up on Stella? I thought he'd quickly moved on since he'd dated multiple women after their breakup, including a cute German university student he'd met within weeks.

"Have you heard from Ulrike lately?"

"She's another one who got away! I'm on a bad streak. First Stella breaks it off, then Ulrike a few months later." Ben rubs his jaw. "I'm actually not sure if Ulrike dumped me, or just headed back to Germany for a month and then forgot all about us when she got back. I should text her, too."

Ben's so casual about everything. Dating Stella, losing Stella, moving on to the German girl, moving on *from* the German girl . . .

Does he still want Stella, though? Maybe. I need to be more

careful. No more touching. No more flirting. She's off-limits, like she's always been.

"Stella was so hot with those high heels and aloof attitude. I was never sure she really liked me, you know? And now, well, I guess she didn't." He lets out a chuckle, but hearing him talk about her like this makes me squirm.

I was right to avoid them when they were dating. There's no way I would've been able to handle it.

And for all his talk now, Ben didn't appreciate her. There was that one night when he left her drunk in the pub and went clubbing with the rest of the group they were with. I got her home safe. She leaned against my shoulder in the Uber and drunkenly told me she never should've kissed me, then went on to recap that whole night we spent together in excruciating detail.

As if I'd forgotten any of it.

And when we got to her flat, she asked me to stay with her.

I said no, of course. But I would never have left her alone at that pub, if she'd been mine. Which she wasn't. She isn't.

I need to change the subject.

"I saw Helen back home on Friday."

"Did you now?" Ben raises his eyebrows. "You didn't tell me that when we texted."

"It was a last-minute decision."

"Did you spend the night with her?" He leans forward with interest.

"Nah. Just hung out for a bit. Talked to Suzanne about Mum."

"Lost opportunity. Helen's always wanted you."

"Except when she wanted you." Ben's got so many women who want him, he literally forgets about that time when I was hooking up with Helen and then she confessed her love for him instead.

"Oh, yeah, there was that." Ben laughs, and I join in, even though it's not really funny. "So, nothing happening there?"

I shrug. "I don't know, probably not." I do know. There's nothing between me and Helen.

But between me and Stella?

Fuck if I know what's going on there.

What I do know is that I told her about my mum passing away. I told her about Mum's flat, which isn't something I've shared with another person. And right now, my fingers are itching to text her. See how she is. See her.

But I shouldn't do it.

15

STELLA

I'm finally home, on my couch with a glass of fresh red wine, ready to deal with bucket list item number five: *Find the One that Got Away.*

I detest social media and do everything I can to avoid it, but because I work in advertising, I need to be on all the hellish platforms occasionally to check out what's trending with brands and advertising.

And tonight, to investigate what my ex-boyfriend's been up to.

After going through my personal email inbox and deleting a ton of messages, including a bunch of spam and one from an MBA classmate soliciting funding for his business expansion, I open Facebook on my phone and click through to Ben's page.

He's got the same profile picture from when we were dating—him standing on the top of a snowy mountain in Austria, reflective sunglasses on, leaning on his ski poles, a giant, white-toothed grin on his face. My finger hovers over the send message button, but I hesitate. I'm not quite ready yet.

Scrolling down to his recent posts, I stop at the top one, which is a month-old happy birthday message to his best friend.

Ethan Fraser.

Don't click on Ethan's profile. Don't click. Whatever you do, you psychopath, don't do that. Seriously. It would be invasive and inappropriate and—

I click Ethan's name and his profile loads. I haven't thought about what I'll write to Ben, so this is another way to put off starting that task.

Yup. That's it.

Ethan's profile picture is a close-up of one of his tattoos. The swirling Celtic circles are mesmerizing, and I wish he'd zoomed out just a bit so I could see the full view of his biceps. Scrolling down, he's not posted anything in a long time, but someone else has tagged him in photos. A woman.

Helen Jones.

Snuggled next to Ethan on a couch, it's an obvious selfie, her cheek pressed against his chest. She's tilted her head so she's staring at the camera with lips stuck out, cheeks raised in a subtle smile. Helen's pretty, with long dark hair, a delicate face, and a smattering of freckles across her nose and cheekbones. Ethan's not outright smiling, but has a subtle, closed-mouth grin, and his right arm drapes around her shoulders, tattoos of roses and trees and a mountain visible.

Helen's caption: *Love spending time with this guy.*

She posted it last weekend, and last Friday night he was on a train. Shit, does he have a girlfriend? Damn. I want to pluck this girl out of the picture and throw her into the cold North Sea.

Her name rings a bell.

Helen.

My brain spins. Oh, no. I remember. Isn't she the girl he was getting back together with when we had our one night together? Are they *still* together? That was over a year and a half ago. The bottom of my stomach drops out.

I don't like how I feel about this. Of course, he has a girlfriend. He's objectively gorgeous and yeah, a little dark and broody, but I'd seen more than a few glimpses of his humanity. And those fucking shoulders? Wide hands? Beard I'd like to drag him down to me with?

I shake my head to get the physical thoughts of him out. He's a real person in there, not just a glaring, hunky, hot-as-hell beast.

Wait, what? I groan. But I can't stop scrolling. Helen posted a bunch of pictures of her and Ethan over the past few months, but not much before that.

On a park bench one month ago, Ethan's arms across the back of the wooden seat, Helen snuggled up close to him with her hand on his knee, head tilted into the crook of his shoulder like the couch picture. *Summer in Newcastle with one of my favorites,* the caption says.

In a backyard on a metal chair two months ago. In this one, she's on his freaking *lap,* her arm looped around his neck. He's got a beer in his right hand, and I imagine his left is wrapped around her waist. Yuck. He's looking at her, she's looking at him, and I hate the intensity that's obvious between them. Her caption on this one is: *Drowning our sorrows together. So happy I can be here for him.*

I shudder. Ethan doesn't seem like a Facebook picture kind of guy, but I guess he doesn't mind. I click through to the comments and likes on the post like a true stalker, but he hasn't engaged at all.

And finally, one from a short time before that, in a pub. *Can't believe I ever let this one get away.* There's no more of her and Ethan. I scroll back up, and Helen's status is *it's complicated.*

They weren't together, and now . . . they might be?

"Ugh!" What am I doing? This isn't why I logged on to Facebook, but it's a great example of why I try never to do so. I don't want to be thinking about Ethan and Helen. A jealous snake twists inside my body and I squirm, hating the feeling of it slithering around.

I should be thinking about Evelyn's bucket list and sending a message to Ben.

I click a few times until I'm back on Ben's page. I don't even bother scrolling down to see if there're pictures of him and a new woman. Knowing that wouldn't do anything for my situation. Instead, I find the message button and type in the window that pops up.

Ben—I hope you're doing well. I need to talk to you about something. Remember my great-aunt? Aunt Evelyn? Well, she passed away last month.

Tears spring to my eyes, and I blink them away. Ben will remember Evelyn. I talked about her all the time. He knows how much she meant to me. Ben and I might not have been right for each other—at least in my mind—but he was a good person, even though he said some not-so-nice things to me at the end. I could tell him about the bucket list. Maybe he'd care, like Ethan does. I bet it would at least open up a conversation, a connection, and make it easier for me to do what Evelyn asked.

She left me a bucket list.

I pause and don't press send. The words don't seem right. Why? I roll my neck and squint my eyes at the screen, then tap-tap-tap until the sentence is gone. I really don't want to talk to him about the bucket list.

Ethan's voice echoes in my head: *I like her. I like your aunt Evelyn very much.*

Hmm.

Realization dawns on me. I don't want to be telling Ben about the bucket list. I want to be talking to Ethan about it. Even with his judgment. It's probably because I know I have to talk to him about it, since he's my advisor.

I fill my lungs with air and continue typing my message to Ben.

She wanted me to do a few things. A bucket list. And one of those things is to talk to you.

I hesitate and frown. How honest should I be?

Aunt Evelyn was happy when you and I were together. I think she thinks—thought—I made some kind of mistake breaking up with you. I'm not trying to get back together, and I'm sure you've moved on . . .

Damn, what if he thinks I do want to get back together? But does it matter? I just need him to talk to me. Hopefully, in this message chain. It really doesn't make a difference what he thinks about me, as long as I check the bucket list item off.

. . . but I was hoping to have an honest conversation about why we broke up, and why it was the right thing to do.

I know this is a lot to ask. We can do it here, over email, or text. It's awkward as hell. But maybe the last six months have let us see everything more clearly.

-Stella

I press send without proofreading. Then I remember how Evelyn wanted me to talk to someone else first, so I open a new email.

To: Gemma Clark
From: Stella Hart
Date: 12 July 2024
Subject: Why Ben and I Broke Up (for Evelyn's bucket list)
Message:

Gemma,
As you might be able to guess, Aunt Evelyn is making me
write this email. It's a list of reasons why Ben and I broke up.

- *He is too classically good looking (boring)*
- *He likes dogs (I'm allergic)*
- *His flat was too messy (I like things organized)*
- *He laughed too much (didn't let me act sad)*
- *He was always losing things, like his keys or his phone*
  (and he'd have too much fun while we looked)

Hmm, this list isn't turning out quite as convincing as I'd hoped. I'm basically writing his online dating profile. Why did we really break up? Really really?

I think of a few more.

- *When we were out in a group, sometimes I'd still feel*
  like I was all alone
- *He didn't make me feel like myself*

I don't know exactly how to explain these. It's just a feeling I had. Have. Which is why our breakup went so badly, with him asking me, upset and exasperated, *what more do you want? How can you want more than we have?* I just kind of shrugged and repeated the same thing, then eventually walked away from the situation.

The questions he asked brought up painful memories of a fight I overheard between my parents before Dad passed away.

I keep typing.

- *He started talking about kids, even though I'd always*
  said no
- *He started talking about marriage, even though I'd*
  always said probably not

These two felt like a betrayal. They made me feel like something was wrong with me for not wanting what so many others wanted. I questioned my reasons and almost ignored my gut.

Remember, Gemma?

There was always something missing. It wasn't anything obvious. No big problem. But when he asked me to move in with him and started talking about kids? That was my tipping point. I've never wanted kids, and I thought Ben accepted that, but he didn't, not really, because why else would he bring it up again and again?

That sucked. Him asking me to move in—which might've been okay, even though I was immediately freaked out—was one thing, but the kid thing was another. He started trying to convince me. Like that's something that I would change my mind about? In my mid-thirties? The whole thing made me feel like he had never really listened to me. That he didn't really know me.

Maybe that was my fault for not letting him in, like I do with all the guys I date, according to Reese.

I don't want to see Ben in person. I don't want to face him and explain everything all over again. *Please, make this easy on me, Ben.*

Without thinking, I click through to Ethan's profile, staring at that tagged picture of him and Helen.

Who is Helen Jones, to have snagged Ethan Fraser? The snake stirs again. The word *lucky* floats in my mind.

What if I had ignored Gemma telling me about Ethan and Helen, and gone for Ethan instead? Would things have turned out differently for everyone involved? I picture it for a moment. Me, wrapped in Ethan's arms instead of Ben's. Sleeping in his bed. Kissing his mouth. Undressing him to see what he looks like underneath those button-down shirts . . .

Shit. I cannot keep thinking about my client like this.

But he's more than that already, and I know it.

Hopefully, Ben responds to me right away so I can check another item off the list. I don't like losing myself down memory lane. I don't like questioning my past decisions, wondering if I'm really as strong a person as I thought I was.

It's Friday night, I'm exhausted, and I can't wait to spend another weekend relaxing and hopefully not thinking about Ben Hughes.

Or Ethan Fraser.

But I can't get that guy out of my head. I think about him telling me about his mom dying and her flat, and how he can't even go in. I unlock my phone again and go to my deleted email folder.

Yeah, there it is. That email from an MBA classmate raising funds to expand his business. He's got a packing and moving company that started in London but is now expanding to the whole of the UK. I bet he could help Ethan with his mom's flat.

Not that he asked for my help. Not that it's any of my business, really. But I move the email out of my trash folder anyway.

I toss my phone on the coffee table and head to the kitchen to refill my wine.

16

ETHAN

Monday, 15 July

I push open the door to the coffee shop two blocks from Pepper Me Marketing, intending to grab a giant one before heading to the office for a meeting to talk final storyboards and directors for the Sporting UK Foundation commercial.

And there she is. Stella Hart.

The woman I can't get out of my head is right in front of me, like she stepped out of my daydreams and into line for coffee.

But she's not quite in the line, standing off to the side facing me, staring down at her mobile. Tight jeans cling to her hips, a pink sleeveless silky shirt with a scooping neckline exposing a hint of skin above her breasts, her blond hair sweeping down on either side of her face like a shield. She bites her lip and furrows her eyebrows. One hand runs through her hair, pushing it back from her face, just to have it fall where it was.

I breathe in and out noisily. *Bloody hell.* What's going on? Something with her great-aunt's will? I rumble in my throat. My thoughts go to exactly the wrong place, and I imagine bringing her into my arms. No. I should leave before she notices me. I should step back outside and see her at the office, in an actual meeting, not here.

"Hart." I approach her instead, and her name comes out of my mouth like a raspy statement. I can't leave her here with that distressed look on her face.

Stella looks up, eyes wide. "Oh, hey."

"You okay?" Unable to keep my distance, I stop too close to her. Close enough that I could lean over and kiss her forehead or push her hair behind her ear.

"Yeah." Her eyes blink a few times rapidly, like I pulled her out of a trance. "I mean, I don't know, actually. My sister just texted me saying she urgently needs to talk." Stella lifts her mobile in the air like it's evidence. "But now she's not answering her phone. Who does that? Who sends an urgent text, then is completely unavailable? Why wouldn't she wait to text me until she can text back? Or just call?"

Tears fill Stella's gorgeous dark-blue eyes.

"Hey." I reach my hand out and touch her bare upper arm, rubbing up and down slowly. Her skin is smooth and warm, and she leans into my hand. "I'm sure everything's fine. She'll call back when she can."

The vulnerability in Stella's eyes is too much for me to handle. Her gaze darts down to my hand moving on her body and then back up to me, our eyes locking. She takes a half a step closer.

"Last time she had something urgent to tell me, Aunt Evelyn had died." Her words come out as a whisper. A tear escapes from her right eye and I lift my free hand and wipe it away with a finger, letting my touch linger. "But I know it's worse for you. You just lost your mom. I'm sorry it's always about me." She shakes her head.

"Come here." Before I can stop myself, I pull her gently against my chest, wrapping my arms around her and running my palms up her back, just like I wanted to when I first walked in. After a soft, surprised sound, Stella lets her body melt against me, pressing her hands against my chest and moving the one without the mobile ever-so-slowly, driving me crazy. I let my face drop down and press my mouth against the top of her head, wanting to plant a kiss there, but stopping myself. I love the feeling of her cheek pressed against my chest.

A wave of warmth drowns me, coming from the center of my body. Fuck. This feels so good. And not just the stirring in my groin that makes me wonder what it'd be like if we were skin-to-skin, but her in my arms feels . . . right.

Stella's mobile vibrates against my chest, and she jumps back a step. I reluctantly let her go, but she's still close to me, and her cheeks are as flushed as mine feel.

"Is it your sister?"

"Damn." She glares down at the screen. "A text from my mentee. I'm supposed to get her feedback on her submission for a scholarship competition." Stella shuts her eyes and I drink in her plump pink lips and the skin of her neck. What I would do to touch her freely.

"Why don't you grab a table, and I can stay while you wait for your sister to call back? I'll get us coffees. Vanilla latte?"

She opens her eyes, and they smile before her mouth does. "Thanks for paying attention, but today I need something more. Can I have a triple mocha with extra whip?"

A tingle runs up my spine when she smiles at me. I shrug like it's no big deal. "Sure thing. And I can tuck you in for a nap under the conference room table later when you crash."

She chuckles before turning to stalk a pair of women with laptop bags gathering trash from their table.

I accidentally order two triple mochas with extra whipped cream, probably because I'm distracted by the thought of crawling under a conference room table *with* Stella. The fit barista's eyes roam over my tattoos, visible on my forearms because of my usual rolled-up sleeves, and she smiles softly at me. Normally I'd smile back and consider flirting, maybe even asking her out for what would inevitably be a one-night stand.

"Nice ink," she says, but I have no interest in the barista.

When I get to the table, Stella reaches for the coffee and wiggles the top off. She swipes a finger in the whipped cream and licks it off, her mouth closing over her finger.

I'm dead. I can no longer survive in this world. In this coffee shop. Across from Stella sucking her finger. She must be doing that on purpose.

"Is that how you're supposed to drink this monstrosity?" I manage to squeak out as I carefully remove my own coffee lid.

"You got one too? Mr. Black Coffee?"

"Thought I'd try something new. I'm an adventurous guy." I'm not the only one who has been paying attention.

"You play rugby, hike, and what else? Do you skydive or gamble or snowboard off cliffs?" She takes a gulp of her drink, eyes trained on me, then licks a glob of whipped cream off her upper lip.

Fuck me.

"Nah. Besides the rugby, I'm solidly risk adverse." I shrug. "I try to be a stable human being. Coaching rugby has helped me stay focused. It's what the boys need, not just on the pitch, but in mentors overall. They get . . . attached. More than normal kids do, with a normal coach. Because I show up for them every time. Like tonight's practice."

Stella makes an agreeing sound, her eyes locked on mine, a hint of whipped cream still on her upper lip.

"And when the season ends—in a few weeks—I always feel dreadful, because I don't see them three times a week for a while. I worry about them. Are they okay? Getting what they need? Do they have a place to sleep?"

Fuuuuck. Shut up! I'm oversharing. Please stop.

But Stella nods. "It's amazing that you care so much about

them. It makes sense, though. They must remind you of yourself as a kid."

In her pause, I lean forward, unable to stop staring at her mouth. "You just have a . . ."

"What?"

I reach over and wipe my thumb across her top lip, getting the last bit of whipped cream and letting my thumb linger a beat longer than necessary.

". . . a little something."

"Thanks." She presses her lips together in a smile, then creases her forehead. "You deserved more. You deserved someone you could depend on. Someone to check your homework, or make you a snack, or give you a hug."

I laugh, and it comes out joyless. "Mum was never there. She had no interest in my education. I'd be lucky if there was a box of biscuits in the house. And she was *not* a hugger." My aversion to risk comes from nurture—or lack thereof—not nature. I'm protective of the boys I coach, but my fucked-up childhood is why I never want to be a father myself. It's too risky. Too much responsibility. I can do more good as a mentor.

"I seem to have a habit of spilling my guts around you." I swill a gulp of the disgustingly sweet beverage.

"Ethan . . ." Now she's got a look of pity on her face. I hate pity.

"Hey, what you said before," I say, remembering where the conversation veered off the path earlier. "About how it's so much worse with my mum than your great-aunt. That's not true. You're allowed to feel however you need to about her passing, and you shouldn't feel bad about being sad around me, just because it's your great-aunt versus my mum. Grief is not a competition."

Some of the color drains from her cheeks. I reach over and cover her hand with mine. Her eyes widen and dart down to where our bodies are now connected. She moves her hand. At first, I think she's pulling away—and maybe that was her intention—but she turns her hand palm up. Another tingle runs up my spine. Her eyes dance over my inked forearms.

"What do your tattoos mean?" Her voice is low. Soft.

I swallow and move my left arm, the one with roses swirling from my wrist to my elbow, then ivy, trees, and mountains to my shoulder.

"The roses are all for England Rugby."

"You got your arm covered in tattoos for rugby?" She cracks a grin and tension drains from her shoulders.

"It's really important to me. Rugby saved me. In secondary school, and at university. And after. It was my anchor."

"Sorry, I didn't intend to make it seem not important." Her brow furrows, and she moves her hand under mine, our palms rubbing together slowly, heat building like two sticks sparking a campfire.

"It's not just rugby tattoos." I rotate my biceps, where the trees and mountains are inked, covered by my shirt. "Also, how I love the mountains. Hiking. Being outside." I move my other arm— covered with Celtic knotwork, spirals, crosses, and a shield and sword—but only slightly, so as not to disrupt our connected hands. "And this is my Celtic heritage. I was young and impulsive when I got it done."

She glances back up at me, another smile, and then her mobile vibrates on the table. Stella yanks her hand from mine and grabs it.

"It's Reese!" She leaps up and darts away from the table, with a worried glance back at me.

I take a deep breath. What am I doing? Why did I tell her all those things, thoughts that should stay firmly within the confines of my own mind?

Why is Stella Hart making me act like this?

17

———————

STELLA

BUCKET LIST DAY 8

"Reese! What's wrong?" My heart races and the calm I was feeling with Ethan seconds ago has vanished. My stomach twists in anticipation of something horrible. I push the door to the coffee shop open and step outside onto the busy sidewalk, dodging a man on his cell phone. Inside is too crowded for this conversation, too dense with people sitting around tiny tables, and not with Ethan right there.

"Oh no, nothing's wrong. I'm sorry to worry you! Everything is so great, Stella!" Reese's voice is gleeful. High pitched. Light with happiness.

"You scared the shit out of me." The panic gripping my insides loosens. I lean up against the glass window of the coffee shop, my knees shaky.

"I have good news—the best news. Oliver and I are engaged. We're getting married!" she screams, rattling my brain.

"Oh, congratulations! That's amazing." A rush of relief washes away the rest of the stress, leaving my legs feeling like putty. "Tell me all about it."

I concentrate on Reese's joyful words and can't help but grin at her storytelling of how her Scottish boyfriend proposed at the tattoo parlor where he works. I'm happy for her. Her relationship with the man she met in Scotland a year ago sounds, well, just perfect. I hope it is.

Reese is definitely wife material. Girlfriend material. Mother material. And she settled into her fairy-tale romance with Oliver seamlessly. Something I've never been able to do, not since Hunter screwed me up a decade ago.

"We're thinking that we'll get married next summer in Scotland."

"Really? Wow, that'll be so beautiful." Scotland, one of the places I should be going to this month to satisfy Evelyn's bucket list instead of cheating with Graham's advanced Photoshop skills. My insides churn. I wonder what crazy things Evelyn put on Reese's list?

"Have you been, Stella?"

"Not yet, but it sounds like next summer I will." I cringe. That'll be much too late for the bucket list.

Then it occurs to me. What will I tell my sisters when we all come clean about our lists after everything is settled? Will I have to lie to them and say I'd actually gone to Skye? Shit, this is getting so complicated. I guess I can google pictures and read travel blogs until I know everything about it.

"I have an important question for you." Reese's voice is lower, more serious.

"I hope it's not about the bucket list."

She laughs breathlessly, more like an excited teenager who just got asked to prom than an almost forty-year-old soccer mom.

"Nope. I would love for you and Maddie—and Chelsea, obviously, my daughter would kill me if I didn't include her—to be my co-maids of honor. I'm not going to make a big deal of it, and I know you hate marriage and weddings and, like, love," she rushes through her speech like a nervous bridesmaid.

"Reese, I don't hate love! Or weddings or marriage. That would make me an absolute grinch. I just don't want it for me."

"Wow." Reese pauses. "I have thoughts on what you just admitted out loud."

"You know what I mean. I promise I don't hate those things. I just don't want to get hurt. And that's what letting a guy I date close to me would lead to."

"Way to bring the mood down, little sister."

I laugh. "I'm sorry. Ignore everything I said."

"Okay . . . but I wish you'd let someone in for real. You deserve so much more than you've gotten."

I groan. "Seriously, can we get back to your engagement? And of course I'll be your co-maid of honor."

"Thanks, Stella, I'm so happy." Luckily, she lets it go. For now.

Joyous tears spring to my eyes. Then something occurs to me.

I push back from the glass of the coffee shop. Bucket list item number four. *Help Reese.* Doing something for the wedding would be perfect.

"Hey, why don't I plan the bachelorette party? I can put together a fun night in London or Edinburgh a few days before the wedding. We have time to figure out the details."

She gasps. "Yes! That would be wonderful. Edinburgh would be best. Then Oliver's son's mother could easily come as well."

After we hang up, the sides of my mouth are still lifted. Being Reese's maid of honor and planning her bachelorette party checks off number four. It's not some lame contribution to her side hustle that she won't even need after Evelyn's estate gets sorted.

I re-enter the coffee shop and immediately meet Ethan's eyes. His eyebrows are raised, and he stares at me intensely as I slide back into the chair across from him. Dark-brown eyes are locked on mine, so damn deep and gorgeous.

"Everything okay?"

"Yes, she's engaged. Jesus. I was so freaked out." I flash back to a heartbeat ago when I was wrapped in Ethan's arms, my face against his chest. My cheeks grow warm. He did not hesitate to comfort me. To pull me into his strong, capable arms.

"I'm so glad for you."

"And this checks off another bucket list item. To help Reese with something. I'm one of her maids of honor, plus I'm planning her bachelorette party."

"Hen do."

I laugh. "Right. Seven years living in London, and I still think that sounds weird. But anyway, that'll be a better *Help Reese* item than I'd planned."

"Nice work, Hart." Ethan leans back and assesses me. A sip of his coffee leaves a blob of whipped cream in his beard, just like I had a few minutes ago.

"Um . . ." I gesture to his face, and he blinks at me.

"What?"

"Hold on . . ." I reach over to wipe the blob of whipped cream from just below his lip. It's a tiny amount, but it stands out against his dark facial hair. My hand swipes under his lip slowly, and I swear he leans into my touch.

"Whipped cream," I say. What am I thinking? Doing? But I know, and it involves crawling on Ethan's lap and wrapping my arms around his neck. I can picture precisely what would come after that as well. A wave of unexpected desire pulls me in, threatening to swallow me whole.

Whipped cream is doing this to me? *Pull it together,* I order myself.

"Thanks." His voice is husky.

I slowly lower my hand. The tension between us crackles and sparks like a live electric wire. Too many emotions have coursed through my veins in the past ten minutes. Too many confusing thoughts in my head. The way he's looking at me . . . It's overwhelming.

A crashing sound from behind the register shocks us out of whatever spell we're under. I startle and rack my brain for some topic of conversation that won't involve me thinking about sitting on Ethan Fraser's lap.

Instead, I tilt my head toward the door. "Want to go to the office? We've got a storyboard meeting in thirty minutes."

He stands and grabs my empty coffee cup, dumping it with his in the trash on the way to the door. Maybe I'll have time to douse my whole head in cold water before sitting next to him in the conference room.

I might've liked it better when we hated each other.

"Tell me about your mentee?" He reaches to push the door open ahead of me and we join the rush of people outside. "What's the competition she's in?"

"Izzy." I turn to Ethan and smile. "I got her to enter this scholarship competition. She's got to come up with a launch plan for an organic makeup line. But the document she shared with me on Friday was exclusively based around organic social media."

"Might need a bit of beefing up."

I nod and hold eye contact, ignoring the people streaming around us on the narrow sidewalk.

"Hey." Ethan pulls me toward his chest with an arm around my shoulders, saving me from a giant dude looking at his phone and barreling forward. We don't miss a step.

"You saved me."

"I think that bloke plays rugby for England."

I laugh, expecting Ethan to remove his arm, but he doesn't. I fit exactly right against him. But when we stop at a traffic light, he drops it from my body.

"Izzy's document also has zero numbers in it."

The walking signal turns green, and we join the pedestrians pouring across the road. Ethan puts his hand on the small of my back, as if he's escorting me into a formal event. We're less than a block from Pepper Me Marketing, where we'll be around everyone else.

But I want more time with him alone.

"Want help?"

"Help?"

"You want help with Izzy's competition submission?"

"Oh . . . you want to help me?"

"I want to help *you* help *her*. Remember how I have a soft spot for kids like Izzy?"

More time with Ethan. That's what I just asked for, and the universe is presenting it to me.

"Yeah, help would be good. Thank you."

"Also, this is a much better option for your *Volunteer* bucket list item."

"Yup." I swipe my card to enter the building, biting back a grin.

"You're making such progress."

"I know. It's because I have an amazing advisor."

"Damn straight you do." Then Ethan Fraser *winks* at me. He's charming as fuck when he wants to be.

"I can send you what Izzy has so far."

"Why don't we look at it over a drink? I have rugby practice with the lads tonight, but tomorrow?"

We stand in front of the bank of elevators. Something has changed between us.

"Sure. Tomorrow after work we can get a drink."

As I admitted on Friday, I like him.

And as *he* admitted . . . he likes me, too. And the way he's looking at me right now, with those huge dark eyes, pulling at his beard, maybe there's more than that here.

18

ETHAN

Tuesday, 16 July

The bartender pushes a pint to me and a glass of red wine to Stella. We're at the Windsor Castle pub up the street from Pepper Me Marketing. It's a small, cozy bar that smells like Thai food and old wooden furniture.

"Tell me about your mentee." I'm determined to avoid deeply personal confessions today. I've been a total disaster with her since we've been working together. I've confessed too much.

Stella leans her side against the bar and sips from her glass. "Izzy is exactly the kid who needs help from Mentor Me, or Sporting UK Foundation, or any kind of organization like that. She lives in a rough neighborhood and has an unstable home life with her mom, who's always disappearing on her for days at a time, doesn't provide for her . . ." She trails off, her eyes open wide.

"Sounds familiar." I squeeze my ab muscles, my core aching from the long run I took around Regent's Park yesterday after rugby practice. I tried to sweat out the growing feelings I have for Stella.

I don't think it worked.

"Sorry. Yeah. I guess it would be familiar to you."

"No worries." I nod my head away from the bar. "Let's sit. Tell me more." I choose a table along the back wall with a soft bench on one side and a couple of chairs on the other, hoping she'll sit next to me on the bench. She doesn't.

"Her mom disappeared a few days ago, then got back in the middle of last night. Meanwhile, she's trying to enter this scholarship competition, which could be life-changing, but I can't help but wonder what's the point? She doesn't have the support. What can I really do to help her in the long term?" Stella's face crumples, but she keeps her eyes locked on mine, searching for an answer that I might just have.

I shake my head twice. "Don't think like that. You are doing it. Just being there for her is helping. Having someone to text. To call. Someone who will support her. That's what Ben's family was to me." I flinch when I say his name, hoping she doesn't notice my physical reaction. "His parents helped me get to university. If it weren't for Robin and Simon, I don't know where I would be today. These kids need someone to believe in them."

I lean forward on the table, forearms crossed and hands tucked in the nooks of my elbows. Images of my childhood flash through my brain. Days on end without my mum when she disappeared with a boyfriend or went on a bender with a friend, Helen's mum more than once. Ben would tell his parents and they would come pick me up, a pitying look in their eyes. A shadow descends on my shoulders as I start to slip down that well of bad memories.

"And look at what a wild success you are now," Stella says, deadpan, but the corners of her eyes crinkle.

I snort, then laugh, a rolling chuckle. It feels good. I don't want to spiral down into the mess of my childhood. I'm years beyond that now. Stella laughs with me, her eyes wide, her face smoothed out.

"I'm fucking amazing."

"Jesus, don't get a big head about it. I never said that." She twists her face in mock disgust.

"You thought it, though."

She rolls her eyes dramatically. "Can we get back to Izzy, please?" But she's still smiling, and so am I, and that shadow inside me, beckoning me to the edge of the black hole, has completely disappeared and been replaced with a bright, warm sun, the one that occasionally shines on London.

Fuck, she's gorgeous.

I think it before I can stop myself, and now I'm on a lust-filled roll. Those full pink lips, the ones she's pressing together, and . . . damn, licking with a quick flick of her tongue.

"Hello? Why are you looking at me like that?" But she's blushing, and I bet she knows what I'm thinking. Cause I'm thinking about kissing her. I'm thinking about that night I got to run my hands up her back and press her mouth to mine. I'm thinking about more.

My center feels warm and alive, like something's growing, a feeling I'm not familiar with. I want to trace her jaw with my fingers and pull her toward me. I desperately want to kiss her and see if I can make the feeling change, evolve.

Fuck. I *really* like her. From the way she's furiously independent, to how she's focused on helping her mentee—even before the bucket list—and the way she's offended by her great-aunt's demands.

I more than like her.

It doesn't matter how off-limits she is. I'm not sure if I've ever had this feeling for a woman before.

What a beautiful disaster. I can't let it happen, of course, not as we talk about how what she's doing for Izzy is like what Ben's family did for me. I can't betray my best friend like that. He still has a thing for her, I know it, and it's not like she's into me.

Or is she?

But even if she did want to take this further, I shouldn't let it happen. There are so many women out there. Helen wants to be with me. Hell, I can go back to the coffee shop and ask the barista out. I've never had a problem getting women to talk to me. Choosing me day after day? That's another story.

But not *this* woman. I can't with her.

I swallow hard.

"Let's look at that launch plan." I need to change direction before things get out of hand.

Stella blinks. "Right. Yeah, of course. I texted you the Google Docs link."

We both grab our mobiles and scroll through the document.

"I like her stuff. When I read it again, I realized it's got some good thought to it, a bit of strategy I didn't know she had in her. But the plan needs more meat and a clear structure." Stella narrows her eyes and scrunches one side of her mouth. I have to remind myself to look at the document, not her lips.

"She's really into influencers, huh?"

Stella nods. "But that's such a huge thing now. Everyone under the age of twenty-five treats social media platforms like their search engine."

I shake my head. "I go on Facebook about once a year, and I only occasionally check out the other ones for marketing purposes. But in my job, we have whole departments that specialize in that, so I don't have to know it all."

When I look back up, she's giving me a funny look. "Facebook's not my favorite either."

"But I think she could use a Year One profit-and-loss statement."

"You're right." She's now intently staring down at her mobile, her brow creased, blond hair falling at either side of her head like a smooth waterfall, looking fucking adorable.

"I can create a simplified spreadsheet for her to complete. I'll make it really basic."

"That would be amazing," Stella murmurs. "And I'm thinking

we get her to translate this into five or six impactful slides instead of a multi-page document."

We. I swallow. "Does she have any paid advertising in here?"

"Not clear. I'm not sure she really understands how much brands pay to advertise on social platforms. Her plan needs a balance of paid and unpaid media for sure."

I nod. "I'll send you that template and will be happy to look at it when she's done."

Stella locks her mobile and lays it on the table. "Thank you."

"Here to help. So, am I earning my money as your advisor?"

Color rises to her cheeks. "Yes, I'd say you are."

"This is definitely not cheating."

"It's not."

"But about the other ones—"

"Let's not go there, okay?" Her eyes flutter shut.

What's going on in her head? Bloody hell, I wish I knew.

"Hart. I think you need help," I say. "Actual help. Not just some bullshit signature saying you did the things your aunt Evelyn wanted you to do. Let me really help you where I can." My voice is low and raspy. Her eyes are still closed, and I lean forward. If I slipped my hand behind her head, I could pull her close to me and bring our lips together. We're that close. My heart races.

Her eyes fly open and focus on mine, then flit down to my mouth. She's thinking it, too. I know it.

But instead of leaning forward and kissing me, she pushes her chair back abruptly and stands.

"I need to use the restroom."

And she bolts away from the table.

Away from me.

19

STELLA

BUCKET LIST DAY 9

In the empty pub bathroom, I lean on the cold porcelain sink and stare at myself in the smudged mirror. My heart is pounding and my cheeks are flushed, like I've had a handful of pints, not one glass of wine. I'm disheveled, my hair tousled from running my hands through it on the way here, thinking about meeting up with Ethan.

Do I want to let Ethan closer to me? Let him help me—like *really* help me—with Evelyn's bucket list? Do I want *anyone's* help, ever?

No, I never do. That's the easy answer. I do things on my own. I live alone. I make all the decisions. I don't let people close—especially men. Because the thing is, I know they'll just leave me eventually, one way or the other. Like my dad did when I was eleven. Like Hunter did a decade ago. So I shut them out instead. I leave *them*. I do it to every guy I date, including Ben.

I'm not *romantic relationship* material.

I don't think my dad was either. One night, during a whispered fight that I listened to from the landing of our stairs, I heard him ask my mother a single, pained question: *don't you want more?* It was like Ben said to me at the end, which is why it was so triggering: *how can you want more than we have?*

Dad wasn't romantic relationship material. Neither was Evelyn.

But maybe she *was*. Or maybe she wanted to be, could've been, and spent her life regretting not trying when she had the chance.

I squeeze my eyes shut. I've been in the bathroom for ages, but I feel like I'm on the verge of some great revelation.

What if I had let Ben convince me to get married and have kids? That's not who I am. Thank god I didn't. Even though we dated for a year, and I thought I was letting him in, I wasn't. He didn't know me. If he had, he would never have asked for those things.

But *Ethan* knows me better than that, the good and the bad. He knows that I'm the kind of person who would cheat on a bucket list, but also feel terrible about it. And he still wants to help.

I shudder. I should tell Ethan I can get it done—done enough, anyway—without his help. Then in a few weeks, our forced time together will all be over. The bucket list, the commercial . . . He can walk back out of my life.

But . . . do I want to live the rest of my life not letting anyone in, like Evelyn did?

I groan and rub my eyes with my palms. I have a vision of laughing with Ethan *that* night. Playing the Unless Game together, staring at strangers, giggling, pointing, judging, gazing into each other's eyes, and then eventually, feeling his lips on mine. My breath snags at the mere thought of it.

More recently, though, he's been there for me, like when I was freaking out about the bucket list, or the panic attack I had when I got that text from Reese before I knew it was good news. And he's opened up to me. About his mom and her flat. How he's struggling with that.

He needs help, too, not just me, and I get the feeling he also would never ask for it. I open my eyes.

"I don't want to live my life not letting anyone in." I say it out loud, trying it on for size. Then I nod at myself in the mirror like a crazy person. I don't want to live the next thirty-four years the way I've lived the last ones. I want to get close to someone.

Someone like Ethan.

Tell him you want his help, you idiot. My reflection cringes back at me. *And then tell him that you want to help him with his mom's flat.*

That feels right. I'm gonna go back out there and be completely vulnerable with Ethan. That'll come as easily to me as stripping naked and dancing in front of the tube station.

I wish I'd brought in my bag so I could roll on some lip gloss or fill in my eyeliner, which I appear to have partially rubbed away with all my indecision.

He had been so close to me just now, near enough to kiss. He wouldn't have done that, would he?

I don't know. I'd bet he doesn't either.

Maybe I should find out.

———

"I WANT your help with the bucket list. Like, for real help." I settle back in my chair and drain the tiny sip left in my wine glass.

He raises his eyebrows. It should be illegal for a face to be so gloriously sculpted.

"Good. Because, to start with, I have a new plan for at least one of the items." His gaze flits down to my lips for a split second.

My breath catches in my throat. "That was fast."

"I've been thinking about it."

Did I imagine that quick glance to my mouth? He's been thinking about my bucket list. About me. What is this between us that makes me want to trust him?

"Come to my flat. I have kittens."

I burst out laughing and he grins wider at me. "Yeah, you've told me that before. But I'm not adopting a kitten. I don't want a pet, just like I don't want kids."

"Woah." Ethan raises his eyebrows. "That was quite the jump." He leans forward and touches my hand, just his left thumb, with a gentle stroke on top of mine. Our faces are incredibly close once again. A shot of electricity skitters up my arm and into my shoulder. *What is that?* Some kind of malfunctioning nerve, that's all. Maybe I should get to a doctor.

Sure, I decided back in front of the pub bathroom mirror to let him closer to me, but I'd appreciate it if my body didn't betray me each time we happen to make physical contact.

"I don't want kids either. It's okay. But this isn't a human child I'm forcing on you. Just come pet some cats, okay?"

I catch a whiff of the mint gum he must have been chewing before we met up, mixed with a hint of a musky cologne that makes me want to bury my head in his neck and breathe deeply. It smells like leather and woods and something spicy.

The room spins lazily. Shit. I must look like a bloodhound, sniffing around him.

"You don't want kids?" I'm distracted by the way his throat moves as he chugs the last half of his pint and the overall . . . *Ethanness* of him. So rough on the outside, but I'm now ninety-nine percent sure there's a soft, maybe even sweet inside to him. I pick up my empty wine glass, wishing there were more in there.

He shakes his head. "No. And that's not something anyone should try to talk you into."

"I agree."

Ethan's eyes bore into mine. He must know about what happened with Ben at the end.

"Hart, what's the fifth item on your bucket list?"

Oh, no, I can't tell him about Ben now. It'll ruin whatever moment is happening between us. Last night, Ben responded, saying he wants to meet up. I haven't responded back yet, because the truth is, I have no desire to see Ben, or even talk to him. I push thoughts of my ex aside.

"I . . . really don't want to talk about it. Just know that I'm not cheating on that one, okay? I'll tell you, eventually. Before the end of the month." Or never, if I can manage it.

Ethan opens his mouth to respond, but I speak before he can.

"I was thinking about your mom's flat."

He startles with a slight movement of his head, and blinks slowly. "What? Why?"

"You're here trying to convince me I need help with Aunt Evelyn's bucket list, but I think you could use some help, too."

"I'd rather focus on you."

"Listen, if I'm going to go meet kittens at your flat, at least let me do something for you. I thought I could message an MBA classmate of mine to see if I could arrange for his company to pack and empty her flat for you. Okay? It's no big deal. It's what they do."

Ethan visibly swallows and clenches his fists. "Fine." The word is short and tense, but the look—the hint of relief—on his face tells me it is a big deal. And all of a sudden, something warm and sweet radiates from my chest.

"I'll do it tonight," I say, and he nods once.

"Let's go meet kittens." Ethan stands and gestures to the pub door, waiting for me to move.

I grab my laptop bag and push back my chair.

It's just kittens. In his flat. Where we'll be all alone.

What can it hurt?

20

STELLA

I stand awkwardly inside Ethan's silent, dark flat. There's a table right off the entranceway, leading to a small, tidy kitchen. It's open to the living room, with bookshelves, a couch, and a coffee table.

"Roommate not home?" I look down the dark hallway past the kitchen.

"Guess not." Ethan throws his keys on the side table by the front door, flicks the light on, and slips his backpack down off his shoulders. His incredibly broad shoulders.

He turns to me, and we stare at each other.

Ethan waves at the couch, breaking eye contact. "Make yourself at home. I'll be right back." He disappears down the hallway.

Ethan's flat is in Camden, a half-hour walk from the pub cutting through Regent's Park, which would've been lovely, but not in my heels. Instead, we grabbed an Uber and rode in silence, me questioning all my life decisions in the back seat of that car.

I look around and a high-pitched giggle escapes my throat. What am I doing alone with Ethan Fraser in his flat? Did I really come here to meet kittens?

I let my laptop bag slip from my arm onto the floor next to

Ethan's backpack and wander toward the bookshelf, my heels clicking on the hard flooring. A bunch of nonfiction titles are on the bottom shelves, with labels like *History of Britain* and *The British Conquerors*. One of the two men who live here is obviously a history buff. But the top two shelves are filled with bright, happy, pink and blue and purple kissing books. Exactly the kind I love. Just because I haven't had my own happily ever after doesn't mean I don't like to read about other people's. It's all made up, anyway.

I half snort and glance down the hallway. No way do the romance books belong to Ethan, but I adore the fact that his roommate reads them. I drag my finger along the spines and pause at *Love to Hate You*, the same book I picked up at Waterstones the other day, currently sitting on my nightstand. Ironically, it's an enemies-to-lovers romance, which I scoffed at because of what Chloe had said early on about me and Ethan.

Before he finds me snooping, I wander back to the comfortable gray couch and sit on the edge, low-level panic heating my core. I want to slip off my heels, but that feels way too comfortable. Too personal. What am I doing here? I shouldn't be in this flat, right?

Ethan's a *client*.

Ethan's my *ex-boyfriend's best friend*.

Ethan might be *seeing someone else*.

I want nothing to do with any of that mess. Right?

Suddenly, a small, furry, black ball lands on the couch next to me. A meow squeaks out of the little creature.

"This is Nessie."

I gasp. "Oh my god." I've never seen such a tiny cat. Her face is the most adorable little floof. "Awww."

"She's six weeks old." Ethan comes around and squats on the floor next to the couch, tossing his phone screen side up on the coffee table.

Nessie taps my thigh with her paw and immediately gets her nails stuck in my jeans. Mewing, she looks up at me accusingly.

I hesitate before gently lifting her, detaching her sharp kitten claws from the fabric. "Don't get your nails stuck on my leg, silly." She squirms in my hand and swipes at me, so I lift her right in front of my face—out of eyeball-gouging distance—and give her an understanding nod. "I get it, Nessie. You don't want to be told what to do."

Ethan snorts, and I put her back down on the couch. She stretches her body before creeping toward Ethan and the edge of the couch.

My heart swells just a bit at the sight. Of Nessie? Or Ethan? Hard to tell.

"The others are sleeping in a big pile, and she was the only one who acknowledged my presence." Nessie hops right to the edge of the couch, not seeming to understand the danger of a fall to the hardwood floor, but Ethan picks her up and deposits her farther back, one of his big hands easily encompassing the kitten's entire body. "She's my favorite."

"Why?"

He appears to think for a minute, staring at Nessie, who is attacking a string stuck to the couch cushion.

"Maybe because she's dark and kind of grumpy." He shrugs and looks up at me, his chocolate eyes beckoning, serious and deep. "Maybe a bit like me?"

I smile and press my lips together. "Sounds about right." But I have the urge to try to convince him that dark isn't always a bad thing. Maybe it's just a cover for being strong. After what he's been through? To get where he is today? He's gotta be.

"They'll be ready for adoption in about two weeks."

Some kind of look must've crossed my face, because he holds up one hand.

"I know, I know, you're not a pet person. But we *could* place a kitten with you temporarily, in a foster situation." Ethan has his hand out to Nessie and she's biting his fingers, her teeth not digging in too deep. "We can't keep all of them here."

And all at once, I know why *I'm* here. Not to meet kittens or adopt Nessie or talk about the bucket list.

I'm here to kiss Ethan.

Whether I like it or not, that's why I got in an Uber to his flat. To feel his lips on mine. I want to see what it's like, again. I want to remember how his beard feels against my chin. I want to touch our lips together and know how soft his are, find out if they feel the same as they did that last time, so long ago.

When I don't respond, Ethan keeps talking, but his voice sounds muffled, far away. "This is a better answer to *Adopt an Animal*, even though you're already the proud owner of a polar bear." He eases up from his squat and scoots onto the couch, the kitten trapped in the space between our thighs, climbing on me, then climbing on him, then finally sitting between us in the narrow space, licking a paw.

My eyes flick down to Ethan's lips, then his inked arms, one of which is draped across the back of the couch, the other on his far knee, presumably ready to save Nessie from throwing herself off the edge. I want nothing more than to run my hands over his forearms and up his biceps, to touch his tattoos with my fingers. A fire sparks in my belly and burns away all the legitimate excuses as they pop up, like thin sheets of dry paper in a bonfire.

Client? Ex-boyfriend's best friend? Seeing someone else?

I'm overthinking all of this.

And as I know from my current read, people in romance novels—like the brightly colored rose pink and sky blue and light green ones over on that bookshelf—sometimes make out with people who they once thought hated them.

Ethan notices my silence, and now he's staring at me, too, scratching Nessie's head without even looking at her. The air is thick, and the silence is heavy. I feel like I'm breathing too loud. I lick my lips unintentionally, and his gaze darts down and back up quickly.

I'm not going for a happily ever after, but I'm going to check this off the bucket list I didn't know I had. My own bucket list. Before I can stop myself, I lunge forward and crash our mouths together, his beard tickling my chin, his lips soft and giving. I put my hands on his chest and quiver at the hard muscles beneath his shirt. Time freezes as our bodies connect and those damn sparks have moved from my arms to my center, running up my spine, guiding me to move closer to him. We're connected, but neither of us moves our lips. They're simply touching, softly, but burning and sparking at the contact. I could stay here a hundred years, but I want more.

A desperate sound escapes his throat and I lean into him further, our lips molding together perfectly, his soft and gentle. He slides a hand into my hair and opens his mouth slightly, moving his other hand down my arm and onto my waist, settling on the top of my hip. There's an ache between my legs and I want his hands all over me. I want to be as close to this man as possible. My hand clenches around his shirt, pulling him closer.

My head is empty, except for one thought: *I'm kissing Ethan Fraser.* He slips his tongue into my mouth, exploring, testing, and I breathe into him. I shift instinctively on the couch, planning to straddle him to try to soothe the ache, when a searing pain in my hand shocks my system.

I gasp and fly back from the kiss to find Nessie with her teeth buried in my thumb, front paws leaning against Ethan's chest. "Holy shit!"

"Christ, Nessie." Ethan lets out a fast breath and gently pries the kitten off of me, staring down at the prick of blood on my thumb. "You're bleeding. She's never actually broken skin. Let me put her away."

Ethan disappears down the hall for thirty seconds and returns to the couch without a cat, but with a tissue. He gingerly takes my hand and presses the tiny wound, which has already stopped bleeding.

"She did not like that." My heart is racing a hundred miles an hour. I want to tell him that even if Nessie didn't like us kissing, I did.

Ethan looks up at me, gazing into my eyes, then looking down at my lips, still pulsing from his kiss.

"Stella . . ." he starts, but his phone vibrates loudly on the coffee table. The name Helen dances across the screen.

Reality crashes down on me. This happened last time. We kissed and had an amazing night, but then I found out he was getting back with Helen. Then I dated Ben.

I know he's seeing Helen again. That he saw her last weekend when he was up in Newcastle. And we've kissed, and now I'm going to see Ben again.

It's déjà vu. I hate it.

This is a horrible mistake. I brace myself for whatever he's about to say, then realize I don't want to hear it at all. The pleasant tingles up my spine are replaced with a grip on my digestive system that makes me want to throw up. I wish I could disappear out of this flat and away from my humiliation.

"Shit," I say, my voice small and shaky. "I'm so sorry I did that."

But am I?

Yes. Definitely. I just made things so much more complicated in every part of my life. Work, Evelyn's bucket list, my personal life. *Damn!*

"No. Stella. Let's talk about this." His voice is almost sharp, and I wait for him to continue, dreading what he's going to say, but his cell phone starts vibrating again and voices ring out in the hallway outside the flat, followed immediately by key sounds at the front door.

Someone curses, and another person laughs. *Thank god, an interruption.* To let me escape this mistake.

This is my out.

"Bloody hell." Ethan's eyes dart from the front door to the

phone vibrating its way to the edge of the table. "Fucking worst timing."

"Well, hello." A voice booms from the now-open door.

Ethan briefly glances at the new arrivals, then returns his gaze to me. "Colin. This is . . ." He pauses, like he forgot my name, which is ridiculous, but maybe he's trying to figure out who the hell I really am. "Stella. Stella, this is Colin, my roommate, and our friend, Sam."

Then Ethan's expression changes, as if he's just thought of something, or figured something out. Probably what a mistake I am.

"We're playing poker tonight, mate. Didn't you remember?" Colin strides over to the kitchen, loading drinks into the fridge.

I need to get out of here.

"I was just leaving. Ethan, see you later." I leap up, dart around the couch, and grab my bag from where it rests by Ethan's at the open door. Colin watches me with a confused grin.

"I'll walk you out of the building." Ethan stands and moves toward me. He's staring at me intently, all broad shoulders and tattoos and . . . he's just untouchable. And I tried to touch him.

"No!" I practically shout, needing to wallow in regret alone. "I'm good. Bye."

I dart out the open door and slam it behind me, practically running down the hall and out of his building. I cannot believe I kissed him. That I took a chance on an impulsive feeling and a stupid attraction. It doesn't matter that it feels like he's genuinely accepting of me as I am, that he listens to the words that come out of my mouth, that he's helping me with Evelyn's bucket list.

I shouldn't have kissed him. I shouldn't be letting myself develop any feelings for him.

It's still light out, a long London summer evening still stretching ahead, so I walk back through the park to clear my head instead of jumping on a red bus or into an Uber, high heels or not. Once I'm far enough away, striding along the edge of Regent's

Park toward St John's Wood, the reality of what I just thought overwhelms me.

I'm not just attracted to Ethan. I have real feelings for him.

And I acted on those feelings, right in the middle of an important project at work and not even halfway through the bucket list month. I've probably ruined everything. At work. With Ethan.

Thankfully, I'm heading out of town tomorrow for another client's commercial shoot a few hours outside of London, and there are no more meetings with Ethan this week.

It's only when I get to the front door of my flat that I realize he called me Stella.

21

ETHAN

Monday, 22 July

It's been almost a week since Stella kissed me and Nessie interrupted us by digging her inconveniently sharp kitten teeth into Stella's thumb.

We could've laughed it off, but then it all went wrong. The call from Helen, the look on Stella's face . . . and I froze, like a real arsehole, then thought of Ben, and how wrong it was to have my mouth on her.

I was thinking of *Ben* at that moment. Ben! Fuck me.

And then Stella fled. I should've chased after her.

I've texted her every day. She's responded back with curt responses.

She was out of town on a commercial shoot.

She had to go out with the client for dinner.

She was *so* busy.

And then on Saturday, she was exhausted.

After that, she just didn't respond.

I shouldn't have let her walk out the door last week without telling her . . . what, exactly? That kissing her filled my soul? That I wanted to keep going, that I think about her every day?

I'm so mad at myself for fucking that up. For letting her freak out. For letting her think *I* was freaking out, even though I was.

Each morning, I've gone to the gym and lifted weights for an hour, followed by a long run, thinking about how Stella was sitting on my couch. Opening up to me, revealing a little more of herself.

But yesterday, while I was jogging along the canal back toward Camden, past London Zoo on the edge of Regent's Park, I had an idea. I made a call to set it in motion.

Maybe it's just a distraction from the fact that I'm about ten days away from the contents of Mum's flat being dumped in the bin. At this point? I'm going to let it happen, and I'm not going to think about Stella emailing her classmate about helping. I can't think about it for one more minute. I'd rather focus on Stella, her bucket list, and getting the Sporting UK Foundation commercial finished.

I shower and trim my beard, humming with excess energy. Colin's out of town for the night, which is a relief as he's given me a lot of shite since sort of meeting Stella last week. I was so distracted during our poker night that Colin and the others kicked my arse.

I'm acting weird as fuck, he said. Weirder than normal.

Stella's not at her desk when I get to Pepper Me Marketing, so I throw my bag down and slide into my chair for five minutes. Today we're discussing final storyboards, shoot location, and talent. It's perfect. It's fate. It's all falling into place.

My mobile buzzes with an incoming text.

BEN

If you don't respond to this text, mate, I'm sending out a search party

Damn. Up until the point Stella kissed me last week, I could pretend that nothing was happening between us. I can't deny it any longer. But talking to Ben and not telling him everything? It would feel like even more of a betrayal. I bailed on drinks last Friday night, and haven't responded to his texts immediately like I usually do. What kind of friend does that make me? Especially after he opened up about feeling like he'll never find someone to share his life with.

ME

Sorry for being MIA. Drinks on Wednesday?

BEN

There he is! No worries, mate

BEN

And yeah on drinks, but no bailing last minute. Last Friday you left me to drink with my wanker coworkers. What'd you get up to?

ME

Nothing, I just felt like rubbish

I turn my mobile over and groan. I need to compartmentalize my friendship with Ben, otherwise I won't be able to work on things with Stella. I won't be able to do what I'm about to do. I grab my laptop and head to the conference room.

"Good morning," Tessa coos when I push open the door. She's perched on the edge of her chair next to Stella, who pales when our eyes meet.

My heart squeezes at the sight of her. *Hell, she's so pretty sitting there.*

Stella's wearing a sleeveless, semi see-through white shirt, jeans, and I'd bet a hundred quid another pair of those unreasonable, towering high heels.

"Morning." I attempt to hold her gaze, but she can't do it and looks down.

"Have a seat." Tessa gestures to the empty chair next to Chloe, right across from Stella. "Did you have a nice weekend?"

I nod. "I did."

No, I didn't. I avoided my best friend, stressed about Stella, ran until my legs were too weak to hold me up, and beat myself up for even feeling this way about Ben's ex-girlfriend. His history with Stella makes every bit of what I'm feeling so much more complicated.

"Excellent. Good." Tessa is watching me with narrowed eyes, then glances over at Stella. It's a weird vibe in the room, isn't it? Shite.

"Well, shall we get started?" Tessa says. "Today, we have three things to finalize: storyboards, location, and talent. Why don't we start with storyboards, as they should be close to final as we've incorporated all previous feedback."

A silence falls on the room as Tessa looks expectantly at Stella, who is still staring at me like a blond, beautiful zombie.

"Graham?" Tessa says, sighing subtly. "Why don't you take us through?"

"Absolutely. As we discussed before," Graham says, "we'll start off with this rugby scene. Two boys tossing a ball back and forth, with a coach off to the side." He gestures to the big screen on the wall. "Then we'll cut to a five-second clip of the interview with rugby boy number one talking about what the team means to him."

I nod, temporarily distracted from thinking about Stella. I've gotten official approval from Leo's guardian to let him be in the commercial. Both he *and* Callum. It'll be a fantastic opportunity for them.

"Next, a group of four kids—the two rugby boys and two girls —will be seen walking toward a crop of trees with a pair of mentors," Graham continues. "One more cut to a five-second interview with girl number one, then finally a shot of the group of six at a scenic overlook. Your team approved the script last week, Ethan."

"It's perfect." I turn my hands palms up. "It's a clear

announcement of the merger and call for donations. Exactly what Sporting UK Foundation is looking for."

"That's wonderful to hear." Tessa clasps her hands together.

"We can move on to locations then." Stella breaks her trance and clicks her mouse a few times to project her laptop onto the screen. "Here are the final options. Oh, and Gerald, our director, is on video call with us."

"This sure is a tight one." Tessa grins, cheery as always.

I watch Stella, memorizing every angle and line of her face, waiting for her to continue talking. Remembering how it felt to bury my hand in her hair. Wondering how it would feel to maybe tug her head back so I could get to her neck. I shift in my chair and swallow, sure the whole room can hear my thoughts.

"As you know, we identified several location options." Stella glances at me and holds eye contact, even though I suspect by her restless fingers tapping on the table that she's just as unsettled.

She keeps talking, but I'm so distracted by her lips, and her neck, and her hands . . . I love being the center of her attention. I feel special, even though it's her literal job to present to the client, which is me. I nod to indicate I hear her, even though I'm waiting to interrupt and tell her what I've already decided.

"Obviously, we need a forest and mountain type setting, so our team identified a location in Wales to the north of Cardiff." Stella's cheeks pinken and she breaks eye contact and looks back at the computer to the video call. "As a second option, a pseudo-mountain about an hour's drive from London, more like a rolling hill really, but we could make it look legit."

"Well," the director interrupts. "There's another location the client's interested in. Sorry we didn't have time to connect before this meeting, Stella."

Stella cocks her head and crinkles her forehead, clearly confused, and looking more than a little annoyed. "Another location? I don't think we have time to add another—"

"Ethan and I had a conversation late last night with the producer."

"Ohhh-kay." Stella glances at me, then Tessa, who looks just as surprised.

Uh-oh. Hope I didn't screw this up. Maybe going behind her back wasn't the best idea? Well. Too late to change things now.

"We're going to shoot the commercial on the Isle of Skye," I jump in.

We lock eyes. The room falls away.

"The Cuillin ranges are a favorite hiking area, a place to reconnect with nature and the rugged beauty of Scotland. Of the entire United Kingdom, really." Somehow, I sound steady and confident. What's she thinking? She kind of looks like she's going to cry. Or scream. Hard to tell. "We want the commercial to be impactful, but also have a good story behind it, not cheat with a pseudo-mountain." I soften the word cheat. It's not an accusation, it's a reminder.

Was this a mistake? Too personal at her place of work? The woman doesn't even want my help, not really, and now I'm forcing her to go to the place her great-aunt was also trying to force her to go to?

But this isn't just about Stella. It's about me, too. Ever since she told me about the Skye bucket list item, I've had a reel of memories running through my head from when my mum took me there. Maybe it'd be a magical place for me, too. Maybe I'd find some peace around my mum's death and my whole fucked-up childhood. Some closure.

Stella nods once. "Okay. But I'm not sure it's in the budget." Her voice is soft, breathless.

"I ran the numbers. We can do it." One of the corporate sponsors made an additional contribution last week that would cover the increased costs. *Fate.*

I keep talking before I chicken out, or forget important details, or pass out from the tension in the air between me and Stella.

"Two of the kids I coach, Leo and Callum, are going to be the rugby players in the commercial. And if you think it's a good idea, we can have Izzy be one of the girls. The one we interview."

She gasps softly, her shoulders raising with the breath. "I think that'd be amazing for her." Stella's eyes are still locked with mine.

"Wonderful. It's decided then. The shoot will be on the Isle of Skye next week. I won't be able to attend myself, but Stella will represent the account team." Tessa smiles like we just solved world hunger. "Chloe's going to take you through the adult talent options next."

I wish I knew what Stella was thinking. She looks so far away right now. *I did that.* Is it good? Bad? Did I overstep incredibly? I don't think Stella hears any of the conversation that's happening around us. I'm nodding and giving my alignment. But Stella? She's in another world.

My mind fixates on the way it felt to have Stella in my arms. I imagine a world where I can kiss her whenever I want and there's no Ben complication. A world where I don't have to pull back from the warm feelings that fill my body every time I'm around her.

I'm getting in too deep, and I know it.

22

STELLA

BUCKET LIST DAY 15

I can't remember the last time a person did something like this for me. Maybe it was back in my twenties when Aunt Evelyn showed up in New York City for that Broadway show to comfort me after Hunter broke my heart.

The door clicks shut behind Tessa and Chloe. Alone with Ethan, I keep my eyes trained on the exit. I can't look at him yet. Ethan, who seems to understand Evelyn and her intentions with the list. Who is concerned about me getting it done in a way that I can live with myself. Who wants me to succeed, because he thinks Evelyn saw the best version of me, one I didn't even know was there, and he wishes his mom had seen that in him.

Warmth creeps up from my core to my neck, burning my cheeks. I shift in my chair, feeling like it's on fire, like I'm on fire. There's so much swirling inside me right now, dynamite being thrown at a campfire, about to explode. I hate it. I love it. It's the worst feeling. The best feeling? Dammit.

I'm not falling for Ethan Fraser, am I?

But I am. I know it.

I will myself to look over to him, terrified of what I'll see. The expression on his face blows me away. His stare is so intense I feel it in my toes, and *for fuck's sake*—his lips are parted slightly, his eyes wide, and he's breathing deeply, just like I am.

"Ethan." But there's a lump in my throat and I have to stop speaking or I'm certain I'll cry.

"Don't think I did that only for you." He leans forward and his face is soft and open.

My stomach drops like a two-story dip on a rollercoaster that feels awful at the same time as exhilarating. I concentrate on relaxing my body, pushing my shoulders down and trying to dissipate the feeling of vertigo.

"You didn't? Then . . . Why?" My throat is dry. Where's my coffee?

Ethan stares at me, his brown eyes burning through mine, pulling me into his deep sea. He cocks his head to the side.

"Fine. Shooting in Skye was *partially* about you. And your aunt Evelyn's bucket list." He pauses, and a corner of his mouth twitches. "Maybe even mostly."

I note the easy way my great-aunt's name comes out of his mouth. Like he knew her.

"I have one good memory with my mum from my childhood, and it happens to have taken place on the Isle of Skye." He swallows. "So I was thinking this would be good for me, too."

"Can you tell me about it?" I want to know more about Ethan Fraser. I want to get in his head, in his heart, see more of what made him who he is.

"I was ten. She was sober for the first time in my memory. Told me we were starting over. Things would be different. She held my hand as we climbed, and when I got to the top—alone, because she'd gotten too tired—I truly believed things would change."

He looks down, his face falling.

"But things didn't change."

"No. They didn't."

The room is quiet for a heavy moment.

"I'm so glad we're going to Skye. Thank you."

Ethan looks destitute in the dark memories of his childhood.

"Hey," I say, and he looks up at me. "I emailed that classmate of mine who owns the moving and packing company. He said he'd be happy to help with your mom's flat."

"I . . ." Ethan's face crinkles, and I can't tell if he's upset or mad or just going through a whole spectrum of emotions.

"He offered to take care of it next Wednesday. They have an early move in the area, then he can head to your mom's flat. You can go to Skye right from there for the shoot."

"I don't know. I don't think I can . . ." Ethan moves his head from side to side.

"I meant *we* can go to Skye for the shoot from there. I'll come to Newcastle, too, okay? I'll help you get through it."

"Stella . . ."

I bite my lip and smile. "And since when do you call me Stella?" The world lazily exists around us, and it doesn't feel like we're at the Pepper Me Marketing offices.

Ethan blinks a hundred times, as if he's just realizing he'd started calling me by my first name. He shuts his laptop and leans forward. There's a whole damn conference table between us, and I wish it would disappear.

Actually, we should get out of here. I need air, space . . . Ethan.

"Can I come see Nessie again?" I blurt. There's something between us. I need to find out what's going on, no interruptions, no running away.

Ethan half-laughs and looks back at me, raising his eyebrows. "You're considering adopting her?"

"Woah, woah." I wave my hands and smile, the absurdity of it all instantly diffusing some of the tension in the air. "I didn't say adopt. You mentioned I could take her home and foster her?"

"Mmm, yes."

"Well, I'm not sure I even want to do that. Remember last time?" I lift my thumb and tilt my head.

"I do remember last time. She might be a bit protective of me."

"Hmm. You're saying the kitten might have a thing for you?" I shake my head. "This might be a terrible idea. I'm not committing to it. Just considering."

On so many levels.

"Agreed. It might be a terrible idea. But the only way to find out is to try."

I can't help but think that he's talking about more than the kitten.

"Should we go now?"

"It's two o'clock in the afternoon. Don't you have to work?"

"Sure, but I can move things around."

I have a call at four o'clock with a client on retainer who wants to kick off a new project next month. Just another thing to add to my overflowing plate, plus I'm flying out tomorrow afternoon for another client shoot, this one in Switzerland.

But this thing with Ethan? Figuring it out? It can't wait. *I* can't wait.

"Are you sure?"

"Give me one minute." I click through to my email inbox and send a quick reschedule request to the client. "Done."

Ethan stands and swoops up his laptop and phone, those eyes locked on mine.

I think we're going down a one-way road, and I have no idea what's at the end of it. But no part of me wants to—or is able to—turn around.

ETHAN DROPS NESSIE onto my lap.

"Hi sweet kitty." I stroke her soft fur. "No biting me today, okay?"

Ethan eases himself down next to me, his body turned in my direction, his inked arm laying across the back of the couch. Even though we're in the same positions as last week, the feeling in the room is so much different. But just like last week, I want to kiss him. I distract myself with the bundle of cuteness in my lap.

"Are you mad about me going over your head for Skye?"

I glance up sharply. Ethan's staring at me intensely. How can he think I'm mad at him right now? He must have dated some awful women. *Because this?* I mentally wave my hands around my entire body. *This is not mad. This is a woman overwhelmed. Aching. Confused. Not mad.*

"No. Normally, yeah, I would be. But not this time."

"How about for making you not cheat on your great-aunt's list?"

"I never wanted to cheat." I shut my eyes and sigh. "Aunt Evelyn meant the world to me. I hate the idea that I'm taking shortcuts with her last wishes, but I've been too overwhelmed to figure out how to do it all in a month."

And now, the only item left is *Find the One that Got Away.* Ben messaged me back over the weekend—this time via text, not Facebook Messenger—with a short: *I'd love to meet up and talk. How about next Saturday night?* I need to follow up about exactly when and where, but now it's confirmed I have to face him in person.

"So no, I'm not mad." I study Ethan's face—slight bump to his nose, wavy, dark hair, beard still giving him a wilder edge. His mouth is wide and lips are thick, and . . . dammit. I shift on the couch, causing Nessie to jump and land claws first on my thigh. "Ouch!"

But I don't look down at the cat.

"Maybe I should put her away." A corner of his mouth turns up.

I nod, and Ethan swoops Nessie up and leaves me on the couch while he returns her to the kitten room. When he gets back, he sits closer to me, our thighs touching, but leans forward facing the coffee table, closing his eyes and pressing his elbows into his knees.

I let out a breath I didn't know I was holding. I function better when we're not staring at each other, but I can't look away from his broad shoulders, biceps thick through his button-down shirt, head hanging.

I need this man's help. And . . . I want it. Maybe I've been thinking about Evelyn's bucket list wrong all along. Maybe it's not that she's projecting her own regrets on me, but truly trying to help me avoid my own, in the only way she knows possible. Through the lens of her own life.

And maybe it's easier to write a list for someone else than it is for yourself.

OH.

"Hey." I bolt up straight on the couch and Ethan opens his eyes and turns his head. "I have a thought."

"Is it about how you could do the Reese one better? Because planning a hen do isn't exactly an impressive way to help your sister, Hart."

"What? You don't like that?" I roll my eyes. "I legitimately think it's fine."

The corners of his eyes crinkle with a smile right under the surface.

"We could do better."

"Hush now." I bite back a grin. "Here's my idea. Why don't we write a bucket list for *you* and pretend it's from your mom?"

His jaw tightens and the smile lines smooth out. My stomach squeezes like an over-tightened screw splitting wood. Maybe this was exactly the wrong thing to suggest.

"Stella," he says, but doesn't continue. I could live forever hearing him say my name.

"Hear me out. I was thinking that a few of the items on my list were predictable. Aunt Evelyn loved her cat, Simba. And volunteering at the hospital."

His continued silence is killing me. I keep talking.

"I think we could do this. We could start with an easy one. Like, I dunno, at some point your mom thought it was a good idea to take you to Skye to hike. We could make one of them something like: *Hike the Highest Peaks in the UK as a Tribute to Your Mom.* It'll be a way to remember the good parts of her."

I cannot read Ethan's blank expression, but if I had to guess, I'd say I'm completely striking out.

Finally, thankfully, he speaks, saving me from continuing to overstep.

"She wasn't a thoughtful person," he says, face stony. "At least, when it came to me. She probably got lost that day and ended up with me on Skye."

I tilt my head. "From what I've seen online, I'm not sure that's how getting to Skye works. But even if that is true . . . it could be *your* list, with the best parts of your mom as inspiration. Or who you wanted your mom to be, I guess."

I'm grasping at straws. Rambling. Digging a hole for myself. I should just leave. I glance at the door and keep my eyes locked on the escape route. What did I even come here for? To kiss Ethan again? Because I'm so easily enamored by a man who changed an entire commercial shoot location so that I could check off a bucket list item from my beloved late great-aunt?

That sounds pretty amazing, actually.

And now I'm babbling like some kind of idiot, and he's not impressed. Not into it. Not into *me*. I can't even bring myself to look at him again. But I also can't leave. I can't walk out of here and away from the man who is forcing me to be true to myself. Not yet. Not like I did last week. Not until I know what's going on in his gorgeous head.

"Stella, look at me, please." Ethan's voice is scratchy, full of some kind of emotion. It's too much. The name again. How is it that hearing Ethan say my name has such an effect on me? Am I that easy?

I don't look at him. I can't. But a second later, his fingers brush my chin and gently turn it in his direction. He's so close now, sweet baby Jesus, and now my heart's taken off like it's starting a hundred-meter race, and he must be able to hear it beating from the center of my chest.

Our eyes meet. I don't know what he's thinking or feeling, but it's something. It's something big. I focus on the sensation of his fingers on my chin, fingers that haven't broken contact. Breath gone, there's a pulse in my core that matches my pounding heart.

"Can I kiss you, Stella?"

23

—————

STELLA

I hate myself for not kissing him immediately, but before I let myself fall into him, I need to know about Helen. His ex, or maybe not ex, the one who has gotten in the way of us twice already.

"Ethan?" We're inches away, and his finger drops from under my chin.

"Yes?"

"Are you . . . Last week, when we kissed, you had a call from Helen."

He pulls back so he can look into my eyes, then nods.

"Are you dating her? Or anyone?" I hope he doesn't realize it's through the slightest bit of online stalking that I know to ask this question.

"No." He shakes his head slowly. "Helen's a friend. Someone I used to date. I think . . . she wants to get back together. But I don't. We won't. And there's no one else."

"Okay." I want to ask for more details on that last time they dated, when he and I first kissed, but the information he's given me is good enough to kiss him today. "You can kiss me now."

He doesn't hesitate, leaning in to connect our mouths. There's a fire sparking inside me, and our lips meeting—again—fans the flames. Ethan's beard tickles my chin as our mouths press together, gently, with closed lips. This is what I've been waiting for. To kiss him. To do it slowly. To savor how it feels. The connection between us is unending, infinite, burning forever.

Then he pulls away, but slides his hand behind my head, burying it in my hair.

"What?" I whisper, opening my eyes reluctantly, immediately lost in his shadowed dark eyes. I want him in a raw way. Desperate, aching need courses in my veins.

And he wants me, too.

It's so unbelievable. How did we get here?

"I'm sorry last week was awkward." His voice is raspy. "When you kissed me."

I try to pull away further, squirmy at the memory, but he doesn't let me.

"Wait. Listen. You surprised me. I wanted it so badly. Fuck, Stella, the way your lips felt on mine . . . and when Nessie interrupted us, I got in my head about things. And you left, and I didn't know what to do."

I still don't really understand why he didn't run after me and pull me back into his arms, but for now, it's enough to know he wanted me.

That he *wants* me.

"You should've done this." I kiss him again, and he's ready for me, parting my lips with his tongue, shallow at first, then deeper. A growing ache between my legs blurs all my thinking. I should respond to him properly, say something, but it turns out that kissing Ethan does *not* help me think straight.

"I wanted to know what it's like to kiss you." I barely stop kissing him to say the words.

"But you already knew that," Ethan growls at me, sucking my bottom lip and pulling me closer.

I want more than just to kiss him. So much more.

"I know, but that night was different." I breathe against him, opening my mouth against his. I slip my heels off and tuck a leg under my body, raising myself up to him.

These kisses. They're making me desperate. My chin is going to be sore from his beard, but I don't give a fuck. No more talking. I just want to kiss him, and maybe—

He pulls away.

I groan.

"How was it different?"

I swallow. "I don't know. Lower stakes? Seemed like just a bit of fun? We . . . didn't know each other."

He's quiet. "Yeah. It was fun. Then what is this? Do we know each other now?"

"We know more." I feel like I know more about who he is deep inside than I ever did about Ben after a year of dating. "It feels like a lot more. But not enough."

"Not enough," he whispers, running a thumb along my jawline. I swallow and his eyes dart down to my throat.

"But I really want to keep going."

"With what, Stella?"

"Getting to know you. And . . . this."

"Then let's keep going." Ethan grabs me around the waist and pulls me on top of him so I'm straddling him with legs on either side.

An involuntary moan escapes my throat when I settle on him, mouth still locked on his, feeling how hard he is, even through my jeans and his. I can't stop myself from wiggling on top of him. Fuck, but I want to get closer. His shoulders lift and lower and he groans, as if he's struggling to control himself.

I don't want him to control himself. I want to see him exactly as he really is.

He moves his hips up to meet mine and I breathe in sharply, perched on top of him, cupping his head in my hands. I lean back as we lock eyes. There's so much there. I can't define it. I can't figure it out. My heart races as Ethan runs his hands from my waist to the edges of my sleeveless shirt, pulling it over my head in one smooth motion until I'm just in my bra, one strap falling off my shoulder. I kiss him again, moving my body against his.

While keeping our lips locked, I unhook my own bra, shake it off my body, and rock gently on him, feeling his cock rock-hard beneath me. I'm feral, like some kind of hyped-up version of myself. This is not how I ever act with men. By this point, I'm usually going through the motions.

But right now? I want to rip off the rest of our clothes and feel him inside me. I don't understand why it feels this way with Ethan, while it didn't feel this way with anyone else in my thirty-four years on earth.

"Christ, Stella." Ethan runs his hands up my bare back, fingers digging into my spine, hurting just a bit, just enough. He moves his hands to my front and takes both my breasts in his hands, his breath speeding up.

I undo his shirt buttons as fast as my fingers will let me, fumbling, going too slow, unable to speak. His shirt finally falls open and I help him shrug it off his body, gaping at his impressive muscles and surprisingly tattoo-less chest, but he distracts me by pressing one of his hands on my ass and putting his lips on my right breast, circling it with his tongue.

"Stella, you're perfect." He sucks my nipple so hard, I'm afraid I'm going to come right here on his couch, half dressed, dry humping Ethan Fraser.

I arch my back and let myself enjoy it. It's gotta be his rawness that is driving me crazy. His grumpy, insanely hot persona, something I blocked out while dating his best friend.

"Bedroom?" Ethan pushes forward on the couch, wrapping his arms around my ass and standing, returning his mouth to one of my aching nipples, balancing my body against his.

"God, yes."

He moves his mouth up my chest and neck to my mouth and

takes slow steps toward the hallway, my legs now wrapped tightly around his waist, stopping against the hallway wall to put pressure against me from mouth to groin, thrusting up a few times and sliding his tongue in my mouth, wrapping around mine, deeper, deeper.

Groaning, I slip down him until my feet are on the ground and tug at the button on his jeans, sliding my hand in as soon as I get the zipper down and fumbling my way into his boxers, finally finding what I'm looking for. I run my hand up and down, squeezing slightly, loving the moans coming out of his throat.

I haven't been remotely interested in anyone since my breakup six months ago. Only Ethan. Damn. I need this man inside me. Forget what a mess I'm currently making of my life, I don't give a shit right now. He's so hot . . . and just what I need.

But what if it's more than just about him being hot?

I don't need to sleep with my client if I only want some random hot guy. The truth: I don't want a random guy.

I want this. Him.

"Stella." He pulls away and lays his hand on mine, stopping the up and down movement. "You need to stop."

"But you saying my name is so hot."

"Do you prefer Hart?"

"Nah. Say my name."

"Stella."

I remove my hand and take his, unbuttoning my own jeans and guiding his fingers down my abdomen and under the elastic of my underwear. "So do this instead."

He moans as his fingers find my core—I'm so wet already—and I shove his hand down further, already on the brink of coming. But I want to come with him inside of me. I want to be as close to him as possible.

Breathing harder and harder, our mouths inches apart but not touching, I yank his hand out and pull his pelvis against mine.

"Ethan. Take me to your room."

He breathes out and leans his forehead against mine. "I was trying to," he murmurs. He spins around and pulls me just another few feet down the hallway and I bounce after him, a half-giggle escaping as I slam the door shut behind us.

Ethan's on me in a second, his hands around my waist, his mouth on my neck. I wiggle out of my jeans, and Ethan slides his hands down my waist and around back to massage my ass and press against me.

"Why are you still wearing pants?" All I know is neither of us is drunk, not like That Night, and I want him. So bad.

He pushes down his jeans and boxers, and at the speed of light, darts to his nightstand to grab a condom from the drawer and slides it on. I have just enough time to appreciate how fucking beautiful he is naked, the thick thighs of a rugby player, abs that reflect countless hours in the gym, and his tattoo sleeves the most gorgeous graffiti on his arms.

And for right now, he is mine.

In seconds, his hands are all over me again, my back still pressed against the door to his bedroom, then his fingers are inside me and I'm rocking against them, not even trying to stop moaning.

"Fuck, Ethan. Please."

In a move I never imagined taking part in, he lifts me up against the door and removes his fingers from inside me a heartbeat before lowering me onto his cock. No hesitation, no more permission asked. I grip his forearms and my vision goes blurry as he thrusts inside me, feeling like he's so deep, he'll be able to see my soul. Who I really am.

Will he hate that person? He knows so much about me. These days I seem to be holding nothing back from him. And he likes me. A lot.

"Harder, Ethan, harder," I breathe into his ear.

He growls again and thrusts so hard he needs to hold me in place, one hand on my back, one hand holding a thigh wrapped around his waist. This isn't gentle, or sweet, or romantic, but god, it's wild and feral and exactly what I need from him.

I scream as I come, and he moans and screams *fuck* as he does right after. We rise together like a tsunami after an earthquake. After, he lowers me gently until my feet are on the floor, keeping our bodies connected, a hand still on my ass, the other remaining on my back. He pulls out and places his hands on either side of me against the door, our foreheads touching, both breathing hard.

Oh, shit. Did I really just have sex with Ethan against his bedroom door?

"Fuck. That was incredible," he rasps.

I agree, but I'm suddenly terrified. Our bodies are still touching, and as long as that keeps going, the spell won't be broken, but as soon as we break the contact, I'll need to face what I just did. What I'm feeling right now. And it's not what I thought it'd be. I don't regret it, not even for a second. I want to do what we just did again. And again.

Ethan steps back and turns away to deal with the condom. While his back is still turned—his glorious, rippling back—I splay my hands against the door behind me, hoping for some kind of stability or strength.

I'm stark naked in Ethan Fraser's bedroom.

"Shit," I whisper, and Ethan turns around, his eyes drinking in my naked body on display for him.

"You're gorgeous."

I would say he's undressing me with his eyes, but I have nothing left to expose to him, as my bra and shirt were tossed aside somewhere in the living room, and my underwear and jeans are tangled by my feet.

"I should go." I have no idea what else to say. Spots of panic appear in my vision.

"The fuck you should." He closes the gap between us, stopping right in front of me. He tips my chin up with his finger and brings our lips together, slipping his tongue inside my mouth and slowly pressing his naked body against mine. I can feel him getting hard. Again.

Jesus. I already want him.

He kisses me deeply, tongue down my throat, and I run my hands up his chest and around his neck, arching my back to press my body against his.

"Stay. For a while."

I don't even answer. I can't. But I'll stay. At least for now.

I feel out of control. It feels awful. It feels amazing. I never want sex twice in a row. Ever. But now . . .

"I want to fuck you in so many ways," he murmurs in my ear and slips his fingers inside me again, deeply and rhythmically until I can't think. I can only moan.

Ethan walks me backward until we're at the edge of his bed, then lowers me down, keeping his fingers moving and adjusting his cock so it's rubbing against my most sensitive parts. In a haze of pleasure, I hear his nightstand drawer slam shut, and he removes his fingers to rip open the second condom.

A second later, he plunges himself inside me and I yell out. He's crushing me and I'm so full of him, I'm on the verge of a complete meltdown. I scream his name as my body comes in waves just a few seconds later. I'm blinded by pleasure. Am I still on this earth? I'm not conscious. I'm floating. In a dream.

"Stella," he says between grunts, coming after I've finished.

He collapses on top of me, keeping his body slightly raised so as not to crush me.

"I'm never letting you leave my bedroom," he growls.

"I don't *want* to ever leave your bedroom," I respond. I'm not sure I can even walk at this point, and definitely not with him still inside me. "But should I go? Don't you have things to do?"

"No rugby this afternoon." He rolls to his side, head resting on his elbow, abs and tattoos on display.

"Other plans?"

"No. You shouldn't go, Stella Hart. You should stay. Please stay with me."

I bite my lip, desperately attempting to ignore the fiery trail his finger is leaving as it slowly moves up my leg. I should want to bolt. Get out of here. We had sex—twice—so that should hold me over for the next six months, shouldn't it? Why do I want to stay? Why does *he* want me to stay?

"Thank you for today," I blurt out.

He quirks a smile. "I usually don't get thanked for sex like that."

I roll my eyes and push him in the shoulder. He doesn't move, just lets out a half laugh.

"For Skye, not for sex." Although I'm thanking *someone* for those orgasms, even if not out loud.

His face settles into a serious expression. "It's no problem," he says, and I wait for him to say more, because I know something's brewing there. But he doesn't, so I don't push.

I LEAVE the next morning after a long kiss at Ethan's flat door.

The smile on my face refuses to dissipate, and when I glance back, Ethan's leaning against his doorframe, hands in his pockets, looking every bit the hot romantic lead. And when I push out his building door into the warm, glorious London summer day, my lips still swollen from our goodbye kisses, I'm already doubting what just happened inside those walls. I can't believe I stayed the night with him.

I was already worried about the feelings I'm developing for Ethan, but that sex? It literally sends waves through my body thinking about it. Was that a one-night stand? There was no follow-up, no next steps, no *I'll text you later*.

I push back doubt and stride down the street, sliding into the Uber waiting to take me to my flat. None of that matters right now. The only next step I need to be thinking of is finishing the bucket list. I'm out of the country for a shoot for two nights starting tomorrow, so I need to make sure I have everything covered with the list.

And that means talking to Ben for real. Time to respond to his text. If I'm honest, I really want to get that over with.

After that, I can let myself fall into Ethan Fraser.

24

———

ETHAN

Wednesday, 24 July

I cannot think about anything but Stella, which is a problem as I'm two blocks away from The Boar and The Bear, the pub near Ben's flat where I'm meeting him for a drink.

I can't get her soft moans out of my head. Her naked body wrapped in my sheets. The way her bare arse felt under my hands. I don't remember the last time I had a woman stay at my flat. I never want them to. I'd rather send them on their way rather than see the regret in the morning light. Or just go to their place so I can make an escape on my terms.

But waking up with Stella yesterday morning? Kissing her shoulder, pressing up against her back . . . I could get used to that.

She booked movers for the flat and will be in Newcastle to help me through it. I was going to pretend it's not happening, block the landlord's number, and try to never think about Mum's flat again. But Stella's helping me through it.

And that look in her eyes as she suggested we write a bucket list from my mum? I had to shut that down as fast as possible because it was too much for me to handle. The woman sees me. Or at least, she's trying to.

I almost stumble stepping off a curb to cross the wet London street. I pull my hoodie down over my forehead and slow my pace, needing more time to work through this.

No one ever thinks that much about me. Women I've dated and slept with only see me as some dark, troubled bloke. Even Helen.

I finally responded to her persistent messages and calls, which I hadn't done since I saw her in Newcastle two and a half weeks ago. I chickened out of calling her, but I texted her that we were only going to be friends. My interest in being anything other than that to her has disappeared completely. I can't pretend with her while this thing I have for Stella is raging.

But Stella and Helen have one thing in common: at some point in their lives, both chose Ben after they'd already chosen me. I'd best remember that. So why does it feel different with Stella this time? I wanted to see her so badly last night, but she was leaving early this morning to go out of town for a two-day meeting with a client in Switzerland.

Bloody hell. I'm losing complete control of this situation. I've *lost* control. I duck under the pub awning and push back my hood before entering the sparsely crowded bar and scanning the room for my best friend.

Ben's at a table in the corner, glancing between his mobile and a pair of giggling women at the bar. He's my opposite. We're both tall, but he's got light hair, blue eyes that I've personally heard women gush over, and a chiseled, clean-shaven face. He never broke his nose in rugby; his is perfectly straight. He's every woman's dream, and the ones at the bar are no exception, stealing glances back at him and whispering to each other. Meanwhile, I'm bearded, tattooed, and gruff.

Stella doesn't seem to mind. I shake my head to get the shattering image of her pressed naked against my bedroom door out of my head.

"Hey, mate," I call out when I'm a meter away. "Another pint?" Ben smiles, revealing bright white teeth.

"Absolutely." He eyes his half-empty glass.

I head to the bar and order two pints, which the bartender immediately begins pouring.

I could tell Ben.

I could tell him I have a thing for Stella. That I'm hanging out with her. My stomach tightens at the idea of it. I sneak a look back over my shoulder as the bartender swipes my card. Yeah, he'd been upset about their split. I got plenty of texts and met him for pints more than usual. But one week after they broke up, we went out on a Friday night, and he'd taken a woman home that very night. Shortly after that, he started dating the German girl. He bounced back really fast.

Ben's not a wallower. It shouldn't matter to him that I've hung out with Stella a few times. I don't have to confess that I've slept with her, or the feeling I get when she locks her dark-blue eyes on mine, or gets that look where she's trying to pay attention to what I'm saying but I'm sure she's thinking of kissing me.

That I might be falling for her.

Fuck. No. I can't tell him that. I barely want to admit it myself. Is it even true? Have I *already* fallen for her? Yes. Of course I have. If I'm honest with myself, I fell for her a year and a half ago. It's always been Stella Hart for me, and I'm only now letting that beast out of its cage.

Oh, fuck.

Isn't the whole thing a betrayal, though? Don't I owe Ben and his family basically everything? Or . . . is it possible I don't owe him my entire life and one hundred percent blind loyalty?

Beer sloshes over my hands as I stutter in my steps to the table with the full pints.

Ben and his family were my personal Sporting UK Foundation. Even more. But this is worth a try. I can bring up Stella again. See how he reacts this time. Work it in that we've had a drink, and she's . . . friendly. I flash back to her screaming my fucking name on Monday night. Christ.

"How's life, mate?" Ben reaches out for the pint, draining his first one with the other hand.

Life is Stella. She's the only thing I think of right now. She's in every part of it. Work. Mum's flat. The bucket list. It's all Stella. Everything's changed in the almost two weeks since I last had a drink with Ben. Longer than usual for us . . . I can't deny that I've been partially avoiding him.

I need to ease into this conversation, not just throw it all at him at once.

"Still on that project for Sporting UK Foundation. A few more weeks and it'll be done." I clink his raised pint. We drink deeply.

"How's Stella?" Ben raises his eyebrows.

I practically spit out my mouthful of beer, but I hold up a finger and chug half my pint to delay answering.

"I heard from her, you know." He returns his drink to the table.

Once again, I have to concentrate on not spewing my pint all over the table. *The fuck?*

"Which was a wild coincidence, as I was thinking about sending her a text after you and I met up the week before last. But she messaged me first."

"Yeah?" I feel like I just took a hard hit in the stomach on the pitch. Ben lazily wipes the condensation off his pint glass. "What did she have to say?"

Why is Stella talking to Ben again? Not that she needs to tell me everything about her life. But we've been sharing a lot lately, like a fucking bed for twelve hours, and this is a big deal. What's she hiding from me?

"We're getting together this Saturday night. She wants to talk about our relationship, apparently."

The breath disappears from my lungs, and I remain completely frozen. It's like I've been transported from my body to a spot above us, watching some terrible rugby play where someone's getting their ear ripped to shreds.

"She said she wants to figure out what went wrong. If she made the wrong decision leaving. I don't know, something like that." Ben shakes his head with a tentative smile. "Something about a bucket list."

"A bucket list?" Her aunt Evelyn's bucket list? What's this have to do with—

The fifth bucket list item.

Ben leans forward and slides his elbows on the table. "Has she said anything to you about me? Or a bucket list? Or are you keeping it purely work? I know you and her never quite got on when we were dating."

The blood drains from my face. Apparently, *everyone* thought I hated Stella. And since Ben never knew she and I had kissed before they got together . . . he had no reason to question it. To doubt my loyalty. But I never hated her. I was protecting myself. Protecting myself from all of this. I'm in deep and it feels too late to save myself. This was the danger if I talked to her while she was with Ben.

Would her great-aunt dictate that she get back together with him? It's possible. The woman seems like she was delightfully unhinged. Or maybe she only asked for Stella to reconnect with him.

Either way, I can't compete with Ben. I won't. Hope crumbles off me like the rotten soles of old boots, my plans to bring up hanging out with Stella gone.

"No," I lie to my best friend. "Not sure what bucket list she's talking about." Prickles of sweat sting my forehead and armpits. I shift in my chair, suddenly uncomfortable in my own skin. I hate lying to Ben. And how I feel about Stella is the only thing I've ever lied to him about. What was I supposed to say when he first started dating her? *Hey, mate, you know I made out with her a few days ago, right?*

Maybe. Maybe if I had told him right away, they wouldn't have gone out.

"Well, I guess I'll find out what it's all about Saturday night. I'm thinking I'll have her meet me here at eight. How's it been working with her?"

Ben's watching me carefully. I can only imagine what he's seeing. Hopefully not someone losing their shit.

"Fine, I guess." I shrug and drink, knowing I'm trying too hard to be casual. Is there a sheen of sweat on my forehead? I hear her scream *harder*. I taste her on my lips. Feel her rub herself on me in the middle of the night.

"You're being weird, mate."

I finish the pint and drop it down on the table with a too-aggressive sound. "Nope. All good. She's fine," I repeat myself. Damn. I need some other detail. "Um, let's see. Her aunt Evelyn just died. So I think she's been bummed about that." Across the room, the bartender mixes a cocktail for the two women, and I watch so I don't have to meet Ben's curious gaze.

"Right. She said that in her message. What else? It'd be good to have information for when I see her."

What else can I tell him? Details, but not too personal?

"She's been mentoring a teenage girl. Her name is Izzy." I swallow. Stella loves talking about Izzy, and her face lights up when she does, even though she doesn't realize it. I shouldn't tell Ben this. It's not my story to tell. "You could ask her about that."

But I'm loyal to Ben, not Stella. I need to remember that.

"You seem to know a lot about her outside of the commercial, huh. Aunt Edith dying, her mentoring . . ."

"Evelyn."

"Huh?"

"It was her aunt *Evelyn*."

"Isn't that what I said?"

"Oh, maybe." I shrug. "And I don't know. She babbles a lot to her coworkers. I overhear sometimes." It feels like a betrayal to blow off our conversations.

"Yeah, she can be like that, I guess." But Ben gives me a funny look, and the air between us tenses. Or maybe I'm imagining it.

The thing is, Stella's *not* like that. She doesn't babble. She doesn't throw her personal information out into the world for anyone to hear. I had to practically force her to accept my help on the bucket list, and that was only because her great-aunt literally put it in the will.

"Enough about Stella Hart. Besides hearing from her, I also sent Ulrike a text. And she actually texted me back."

"No way. You're on fire."

"I know. I'm trying to get her to meet up with me. What about you and Helen? Any progress there?"

I could let him believe there's something going on with Helen, and then he won't be suspicious about Stella. *Is* he suspicious? My head's all messed up.

"Maybe. I might head up to Newcastle again soon." That part's true. Except it'll be with Stella. Not Helen.

"How's her kid?"

"He's cute. Kids aren't really my thing though."

"Yeah, I know. So . . . will you get back together with her?"

Christ, no. But I can't bring myself to come clean to Ben.

"Right. You're not one to kiss and tell."

I raise my eyebrows like I'm holding something back about Helen. What am I doing? I need to get off the subject of our love lives.

"And how are Robin and Simon's plans to trek across England?"

My attempt to change the subject is successful as Ben laughs and tells me about his parents' plan to post about their whole journey on Facebook. I've totally chickened out of telling him about hanging out with Stella. How can I, now that I know they're getting together on Saturday?

After another pint, I fist-bump Ben and stride out of the pub, pulling out my mobile as soon as I clear the pub's awning. I send Stella a text.

ME

When can I see you again?

Three little dots immediately dance on my screen. I stop on the corner of the street and stare down at them, transfixed with the idea that Stella dropped whatever she was doing on her trip to respond to me.

STELLA

When you ask nicely

ME

Please, may I see you again?

STELLA

Yes. I've been thinking about Monday night
(and Tuesday morning) more than I'd like to
admit

ME

Want to do it again?

STELLA

When and where?

I grin, forgetting for a split second about my conversation with Ben. Then it comes crashing back.

ME

Can I make you dinner on Saturday night?

It's not a trap. I'm giving her a chance to tell me about meeting up with Ben. But I feel awful as soon as I press send.

There's a delay, then she responds.

STELLA

I've got plans with Gemma on Saturday night.
She's been out of town, and we need to catch
up. How about Friday?

The air whooshes out of me. She's lying to me. *Dammit.* She's hiding her plans with Ben. Maybe she's going to see what he says first. See if he'll take her back, then make a decision about us. If there even is an *us* for her.

Maybe what's been happening is all in my head, and she's just going to choose Ben. Nausea washes over me. I groan and head toward the tube station.

Again.

25

STELLA

Thursday, July 25
BUCKET LIST DAY 18

I wiggle under a cozy fleece blanket on my couch, so glad to be back from Switzerland.

This month has been exhausting. But I feel different than I did in the beginning, when I first got Evelyn's bucket list. The idea of cheating was distressing, but what else was I going to do?

Now, I'm nearing the finish line, with only ten days to go. And there has been no cheating. Well, not really.

I stare down at the text chain with my ex-boyfriend. I hadn't heard from Ben since last weekend when he suggested meeting, so I reached back out.

ME

Hi. What's the plan for Saturday?

BEN

Hey! Let's do The Boar and The Bear at eight

I groan. Going to the pub by his flat feels too familiar. We always hung out there. Our relationship was about me joining his life, not us making a new one together.

I give his text a thumbs up and go to drop my phone back on the couch when it lights up again.

> **BEN**
>
> I heard you've been spending time with Ethan
> at work. I know you two never much got along.
> Is it better now?

Oh, sweet baby Jesus. The very last thing I want—or expected—is comments from Ben about Ethan. The other way around? Yeah, once I tell Ethan about the Ben item, after it's done, I'm sure we'll discuss. But for now, I should not engage with Ben on this topic. I should ignore any questions about Ethan—

> **ME**
>
> Yes. It's better

> **BEN**
>
> We had a pint earlier this week and talked
> about how you're working together

Ah. That sounds innocent enough. They're best friends, of course they had drinks and talked about their jobs.

> **BEN**
>
> He talked about his ex-girlfriend, who he's been
> hanging out with again

What the hell? But no. I know about Helen this time. I can't stop from responding, even though I absolutely shouldn't.

> **ME**
>
> He said they're friends

I *definitely* know more than Ben about Ethan's love life. Ben doesn't have all the information. Ethan and Helen aren't a thing.

He told me so. But I hate that the text came off defensive. I shouldn't be continuing this conversation.

> **BEN**
>
> He dated her ages ago, then I dated her, then when you and I first got together, they had a thing. She's got a little boy now, who Ethan loves. He spends a lot of time with them when he's in Newcastle

The life drains out of me, oozing from my head and down my body, spilling onto the hardwood floors.

> **BEN**
>
> Anyway. I don't want to waste time talking about Ethan when we meet up this weekend. I want to talk about us x

I throw my phone across the couch. *Oh, Evelyn, why are you making me talk to Ben?* I don't want to deal with him, and it's making me lie to Ethan. Until now, not being transparent about the Ben bucket list item has been more like a hidden truth. Not a deception. But telling him I'm seeing Gemma instead of what I'm really doing—meeting up with Ben? That was a full-on lie.

It's like when I asked him not to tell Ben that we'd kissed. He was a part of that lie, but it just goes to show that I keep asking him to hide the truth. *Dammit.*

My shoulders clench and my jaw starts to ache. I'm not sure what part of that whole chain of texts is most disturbing. That Ben thinks Ethan is dating Helen, that Helen is Ben's ex-girlfriend, which means they *both* dated her, or, and it really might be this one, that Ethan loves her son. But I should calm down. Ethan can both not want children of his own and also enjoy spending time with them. I mean, I love my niece and would do absolutely anything for her.

But I know where I stand with having kids. Pushing me on

that was as much of a betrayal as if Ben had cheated. When Ben and I broke up, I promised I wouldn't compromise myself again. I wouldn't be with someone who doesn't love me just as I am. Someone who wants to change me.

I don't want to see Ben on Saturday. I want to figure out what's happening between me and Ethan. I want to be in his arms again. Was it as fantastic as I remember? My breath catches in my throat, and I lift my hand to my mouth. I shut my eyes and can feel his beard rough against my chin, running down my neck, tickling my ribs as his mouth covers my breast.

I'll tell him everything when it's all over. It'll be better then. By the end of this weekend, the only bucket list item left will be climbing the Old Man of Storr in the Isle of Skye, which I'll do next week after the shoot.

With Ethan.

It'll be after his mom's flat is taken care of. Then we can celebrate together. We can laugh over the stupid list Evelyn wrote for me, and how it was the best thing ever because it brought us together. He helped me, I helped him, it all will have worked out.

I'm pretty sure what I want after all that is Ethan.

My phone lights up from across the coach and I dive for it.

"Fuck!" I whisper as I grab the phone. "Go away!"

But it's not Ben.

> **ETHAN**
>
> I'm coming into the office tomorrow morning for the final run-through meeting. Come over for dinner (and other activities) after work?

Anticipation washes over me, sending tingles up my spine. That's exactly what I need. Maybe it'll be a distraction from the lies and the omissions, the holes we're already digging for each other in our relationship, or whatever it is that's happening between us. When we're together, when we touch . . . everything else falls away. Soon, it will all be done.

ME

I can't wait to see you

I type out a quick text to Gemma. I need someone to document Saturday night, and there's no way I'm asking Ethan, advisor or not.

ME

I need you Saturday night to, like, document
me and Ben talking

GEMMA

Are you serious?

ME

Yeah. For the bucket list

GEMMA

I thought you had the advisor thing covered
with Mr. Ethan Fraser?

She adds about a thousand winking smiley faces, an eggplant emoji, and a bottle of champagne. I totally shouldn't have told her about what happened with him, but she has a way of getting things out of me, and she did exactly that during an epic text chain earlier this afternoon when I was at the airport.

ME

I do, and hush. But for this one . . . I don't think
I want it to be Ethan

GEMMA

Why ever not? That feels totally not horrifically
awkward

ME

Shut up. You'll finally be back in town after
abandoning me during my time of need, so you
gotta do this one thing for me

GEMMA

I'll be there, bestie

I just gotta get through these last days and hope everything doesn't fall apart.

26

STELLA

Friday, July 26
BUCKET LIST DAY 19

I'm so damn nervous to face Ethan again. When I last saw him, he had me pinned against his front door, giving me a goodbye kiss that lasted five minutes and almost had us heading back inside.

I picked up drinks from the coffee shop on the way into the office—black for Ethan, vanilla latte for me—but his sits untouched on his desk, which is still vacant at ten o'clock. The final meeting before the shoot next week isn't until ten-thirty. He doesn't have to come in for it. He can call in, like the director will.

If he doesn't show, does that mean he's changed his mind about us? Whatever we are? Because I wouldn't blame him. I wouldn't want to be with a filthy liar, either. Part of me knows I should just tell him about meeting up with Ben. But the other— much louder—part of me knows it would make everything so much more complicated.

I flip over my phone and tap it awake. No new notifications. My computer's asleep, which emphasizes the fact that I've gotten exactly no work done since I arrived an hour and a half ago, despite being even more overwhelmed than I was three weeks ago. Why did I even get him coffee? Now it's ice-cold on his desk. I drop my head in my hands and breathe deeply. I should go pour it out.

"Hey."

I whip my head up to drink in Ethan, standing at his desk next to mine, a concerned expression on his face, the space between his eyes crinkled together.

The sight of him is even better than the fantasies I've had over the past three days. Probably because I know what's under that untucked, checkered button-down shirt, sleeves rolled up to his elbows, exposing tattoos and waves of muscles on his forearms. The bottom half of his body is covered by the cubicle barrier, but I can imagine his hip-hugging jeans, maybe the ones that were crumpled on his floor Monday night. His beard is now neatly trimmed, but still a good three inches from his chin, and his lips are slightly parted. I know what those lips can do. My cheeks turn to fire.

And he's holding two coffees.

"Hi," I squeak out.

"I got us triple mochas with whipped cream and an extra shot of espresso." He moves one hand toward me. "It's still disgusting, by the way."

I bite my lip and stand. "Thank you."

He nods. "I'm not sure there's any coffee in there, even though I specifically asked for extra."

"Well, you don't have to drink it, because I got you a black coffee. It's probably cold."

I reach for the drink he's holding, letting my fingers gently layer on top of his, not touching the coffee cup at all. The touch, which sends tingles up my arm and through my body, makes every doubt disappear. This must be right—he and I touching each other. A brush of fingers isn't enough. Who cares about Ben? Helen? I just want this man's hands on my bare skin. Nothing else matters.

"Sorry I was late," Ethan says, his face expressing even more. What's going on in that gorgeous head of his? God, but I want to know.

"Ethan!" Tessa's voice singsongs down the hallway.

Ethan's nostrils flare dramatically, and I pull my hand away, careful to take the mocha with me.

"Good morning." She pauses at our desks and looks back and forth between us. "We've got a few minutes, but do you want to head to the room together?"

"I have something to get done quickly. I need Stella's help. Can we meet you in there?"

"Of course." Tessa disappears past the cubicles.

The way he says my name . . . it's like a whisper. A naughty word. Two reverent syllables. After weeks of calling me by my last name, or not at all, *Stella* sounds sacred coming out of his mouth.

Ethan deposits his mocha next to the cold black coffee and nods toward the nearest small huddle room, dark with the door shut.

I follow him—because obviously—and as soon as I clear the door, he pushes it shut roughly until we're alone in the dark. In a smooth motion, he steps forward until our bodies are almost flush against each other, but not touching yet. A hand rests above my head on the closed door, and he moves the other to the side of my hip, finding the belt loop of my jeans and pulling me firmly against him. Once our hips are pressed together and the core of my body pulses, his fingers find the space in between my jeans and my silk shirt, making skin-on-skin contact with my lower back. I wrap my arms around his waist, and he leans down to my ear.

"I fucking missed you, Stella."

His words are a jolt that goes from my head to between my legs. So honest and open. Raw. The way he growls my name? My *god*. I'm aching for him.

He hasn't changed his mind. He still wants me.

"I missed you, too," I whisper, pulling back to lock eyes with him. He only breaks eye contact to glance down at my lips.

There's more than raw hunger there. It's not just lust. It can't be. I can feel his body pounding where our chests are pressed together. And it hurts—right there—where our hearts are only inches apart.

"Kiss me, Ethan."

He leans in and touches our lips together. It's not a ravishing, but instead the sweetest kiss. His right hand moves up and cups my chin.

"Stella . . ."

"You go for weeks without saying my name, and now you can't seem to stop." My insides are fluttery, like the wings of my tattooed butterfly.

But that text conversation with Ben. The things he said about Ethan. They float in the very back of my mind.

He chuckles and kisses me again, this time more insistently, a gentle swipe of his tongue in my mouth.

I should tell him about meeting up with Ben on Saturday. Damn! Every time I think I'm doing the right thing not telling him until after it's done, I question myself. I don't want to overcomplicate my drink with Ben. But maybe I should just come clean now.

Unless it's the wrong thing to do . . . and by telling him I'll ruin everything, he'll never look at me like this again, and he'll realize he can't be with me.

Unless I should just keep kissing him and not overthink everything in my life.

Voices drift from down the hallway through the huddle room door.

I gasp and my body goes rigid. Good god, what am I doing right now? I'm at actual work, at my actual job, and instead of working, I'm rubbing myself against a client in a conference room?

Ethan pulls back and presses a finger to his lips, not taking his eyes off me. But instead of staying quiet and still, he presses his mouth to mine again, gently, reverently, and only after the voices grow louder and then fade as the people—Graham and Luke, probably looking for me—pass by, does he go deeper, grinding my hips against his, absolutely turning my lower half to Jell-O. Now one large palm is on my ass, the other teasing the bottom of my breast, and I can't do anything but moan into his mouth.

When I'm about to drag him out of the office and immediately to one of our flats, he slows his kisses and pulls back, rubbing my bottom lip with his thumb, then smoothing my hair down tenderly.

"I've been waiting to do that for days."

"Ravage me in a conference room?" My insides squeeze and I run my hands down my shirt.

"Yeah. I like ravaging you in a conference room." His eyes burn into mine. "Or anywhere."

"Me too, I guess."

"Later," he says. "Later, we don't have to stop."

And with that, I'm pretty sure I'll get nothing done the rest of the workday.

27

ETHAN

'm not sure I'll ever be enough for Stella, but tonight I'll at least try to impress her with the one dish I know I can do well: shepherd's pie. I put the final mashed potato layer on top of the meat and vegetables, then a sprinkling of shredded fresh parmesan. The flat already smells delicious from searing the minced lamb and vegetables. I probably should've made some kind of side dish, but it's too late now, so I slide the baking dish into the oven.

Colin's out, staying at his girlfriend's for the night. He took care of the kittens and asked me to check on them later. My insides swirl with thoughts of a night alone with Stella. Maybe she'll tell me about her plans with Ben tomorrow night.

But what if she doesn't? With Stella—with any woman—I'll always suspect she's about to cast me aside for a bloke like my best friend. A golden boy. Bright and happy, oozing success and stability.

I will always wonder if she's going to choose Ben.

Fuck. I shake my head, dispersing the cloud of darkness that's always resting on my shoulders. Seeing her at the office this morning proved that when I'm around her, nothing else matters. I wanted to do more than grope her arse in that conference room, and had it not been for those voices . . . she might've let me. Heat washes over me and my cock presses against my jeans. I lean against the counter, head down, trying to calm my body.

A knock startles me. I yank the door open and drink in the sight of Stella Hart. She changed after work, keeping the heels and jeans but throwing on a low-cut cotton tank top, and my eyes linger on the swell of her breasts. She bites her bottom lip, shifts her passenger bag on her shoulder, and blinks her beautiful eyes, smiling. At me.

"Hey." She lifts her nose in the air and sniffs. "Smells amazing."

"Dinner will be ready in twenty. Come in." I step back so she can enter my flat, and as soon as she shakes the bag off, I close the gap between us and slide my hands around her waist. But unlike this morning, we aren't at the office, and we don't have a potential audience. I shove the door shut and push her arms up and around my neck. I savor her body pressed up against mine.

"We can do a lot in twenty minutes." Stella caresses the back of my neck.

"Now it's more like nineteen."

"I have faith in us." Stella pulls my head down toward hers, crashing our lips together, like two writhing snakes desperate for each other. The room spins, and her hands are fumbling with the button on my jeans. I push down one of the straps of her bra and tank top, releasing her soft breast which I immediately cup in my hand, rubbing her nipple in circles with my thumb. She's managed to unzip my jeans and free my cock, already engorged with need for her, and she slips a hand around me.

"Fuck, Stella," I growl.

Stella pulls back and looks at me with wide, hooded eyes, biting her lip. "Now we have seventeen minutes, so let's move it along."

"Easily doable." I nod my head to the family room. "Couch.

Now. Take off your jeans, because god knows I can't peel those off you."

Stella grins and backs slowly toward the couch, unbuttoning her jeans and wiggling out of them a little with each step. By the time she's there, her legs are bare and her underwear askew on her hips, her one breast still exposed, and damn, I could stare at her all day. She's perfect. She slips her underwear down her body, and I stalk toward her, easily lifting her up. She knows exactly what to do and wraps her legs around my waist, wiggling against me.

"Fuck me," I whisper. Stella fits exactly just right, and I lower us onto the couch, pausing just above her.

Her lips are parted and her eyes closed, but she opens them when I remain still.

"What's wrong, rugby dude? I'm sure we only have fourteen minutes now. Maybe twelve."

I actively block out all the reasons I shouldn't be here with Stella. And without those reasons, the emotions I feel are over-whelming.

I'm falling, falling, falling.

I don't know where I'm going to land, but there's no going back.

I'm in too deep now.

"Your phone," Stella calls from the couch.

"Ignore it." I walk back from the kitchen with Stella's refilled wine glass and another beer for me, ignoring the dishes piled in the sink. That's tomorrow's problem. As is any phone call—there's literally no one in the world I need to hear from more than I need to be present with Stella.

When I sink down next to her, she's got a funny look on her face.

"It was Helen."

I nod. "She didn't react particularly well when I told her I just wanted to be friends." I pull on Stella's legs, sliding them onto my lap as she lounges, gently massaging her right foot.

Helen had responded to my text saying we could be casual, that she could come visit me down in London, that maybe we could just see where this goes. I told her no firmly one time, then again, then stopped responding two days ago. She told me she'd convince me I'm wrong. But there is no chance Helen is going to win my heart. Now I need to give her time to come to terms with that.

"Did I ever tell you she's the reason I even agreed to go out with Ben?"

"What?" I freeze my hands on Stella's foot.

"Gemma told me you were getting back together with a girl from Newcastle. Helen. So when Ben asked me out that weekend, after you and I had . . . you know." She gives an adorable shrug. "I thought it'd be best. That you'd just had a slip-up with me."

Everything from back then starts to become clearer. I shake my head.

"Helen and I were just talking. Yes, we were considering getting back together. But she had a baby at home, and that's way too complicated for me."

"Well, shit."

"I wish you'd talked to me. Maybe . . . things could've been different." Because after Stella and I kissed, I knew I didn't want to be with Helen.

"I think I tried, actually, the night Ben asked me out. But you wouldn't even look at me."

"Yeah. I was raging after I found out you agreed to go out with him." Dammit. "I'm sorry."

We sit in silence. Stella stares at me, sipping her wine, her forehead crinkled.

"What are you thinking?" I ask.

"You said before you don't want to have kids. Is that really true?"

"I'm sure, Stella." Helen's son appears in my head. Henry's adorable, and sweet, and I wish the best for him, but I don't want one of my own. I'd decided that years ago.

"Well, sometimes people say that. And then don't really mean it."

"I know." I reach over and grab her free hand. And wait. Wait for her to tell me about tomorrow night, and why she's meeting up with Ben. That it's about a bucket list item she hasn't told me about.

But Stella says nothing, just chews on her lip. I take her wine glass from her hand and put it with my bottle on the coffee table, then climb on top of her, gently easing between her legs, not putting my weight down, just feeling us touch.

I support myself with my hands on the cushion and bury my head in her neck, placing gentle kisses in a trail from the crook of her neck to her collarbone. She breathes loudly and arches her chest toward me.

"That's not going to happen with me," I say, pausing the kisses. "What you see is what you get. I'm just a grumpy arse who can't stand being away from you."

"I can't stand it either," she says, then wraps her legs around my waist, pulling me down against her. We fit perfectly together, like the two final shapes in a thousand-piece puzzle. Warmth cascades throughout my whole body, not just my groin. There's no other place in the entire universe I would rather be than on this couch, with Stella smiling beneath me.

I love this woman. Fuck.

That's about the most inconvenient thought that's ever entered my mind.

28

ETHAN

Saturday, 27 July

The knock on my door comes twenty minutes after Stella leaves.

She must be coming back to tell me about meeting up with Ben. That must be it. After last night, this morning, after this week . . . It's hard to believe we have secrets left between us.

Except there *are* secrets.

Like the secret where I love her. The one where my traitorous heart fucking went and fell for my best friend's ex-girlfriend. But if I'm honest with myself, that happened the first night we met, before she even met Ben. I was a goner the moment she played her Unless Game with me.

And the secret where she's meeting up with my best friend. Tonight.

I stride to the front door, running my hands through my hair, ready to pull her into my arms.

What other secrets are there? I might always worry that she's deciding between me and Ben, but she explained what happened last time. That it was because Gemma told her about Helen and me getting back together, which didn't even end up happening.

My hand pauses on the doorknob. She'll tell me.

I pull the door open, but it's not Stella.

It's Helen.

All five feet of her, long dark hair in waves on her shoulders, her smooth and delicate face smiling up at me, a backpack on her shoulder.

"Helen. W-what are you doing here?" I stutter and blink a few times quickly to clear my vision and make sure I haven't conjured her from nothing.

"Can I come in?"

"Of course."

Helen steps into my flat, eyes scanning the living room, the hallway to the bedrooms, and pausing in the kitchen, where dirty dishes from last night are piled in the sink, next to Stella's empty wine glass and my beer bottles on the counter.

She wiggles out of her backpack and turns back to me, posing in the middle of my flat in wide-legged ripped jeans and a cropped yellow t-shirt with Nirvana on the front. She's adorable. Objectively good looking.

But she's my friend. And that's all.

"Is everything okay? Your mum? Henry?"

She nods, and I have déjà vu from the time she showed up at Ben's and my flat years ago, when she told me she wanted him, not me.

I'm frozen at the front door, hand still on the handle, so she steps to me and puts her hand over mine, pulling it away and shoving the door shut with a click. She puts my hands on her waist. First one, then the other, like a girl teaching a boy how to dance, then she gazes up at me with adoring eyes, her hands splayed gently on my chest.

If it weren't for Stella showing up back in my life three weeks ago, I might have been into this. I might have kissed Helen. But now . . . touching her feels wrong. Being with her in my flat feels wrong.

She's the wrong girl.

"I'm sorry for the dumb shite I've done in the past." Helen stares up at me intensely. "But you have been such a good friend to me these past few years, and Henry loves you so much. So does Mum—"

"Hey," I try to interrupt. We *have* been good friends, especially after she told me she had a baby at home. After that, it was purely friendship—on my end, at least. Maybe I'd let that slip these last months, after Mum died. I'd let my guard down, and she took that as an invitation.

"Shh, let me finish. I know we could be happy together." She reaches up and runs her hand along my shoulder, reaching for my face, but not quite tall enough to get there. I lean back.

"Helen . . . I can't do this." I move my head from side to side and take half a step back, removing my hands from her waist and gently pulling her hands from my chest.

"I know last time it was too soon after Henry was born." She closes the space between us again, more hesitation in her voice. "And I'm sorry about the time before that. When I chose Ben. You were always the one I should have stayed with. But I'm making it right now. You can trust me, I swear to it."

I search Helen's face. Trust is a terrifying thing. Without it, love can't exist, can it? Only lust and obsession. But I'm also terrified of what I'm feeling for Stella.

If I want to be with Stella, I need to trust her. Really trust her.

I need to let her and Ben meet up without freaking out. I need to trust that she'll choose me.

And once she does, I can tell her I love her.

"There's someone else." I wrap Helen's hands in mine.

"Oh, bugger." She deflates before me, and the intense look fades off her face, replaced by a frown and creased forehead. "I came all this way to get another *just friends* speech?"

"We're best as friends. I love you . . . but only as a friend."

Her face falls. "It *is* a friends speech."

"Helen, you'll find the right bloke, one who will worship you and Henry."

She tilts her head and hides a small smile, pulling her hands from mine and crossing her arms. "I was hoping it'd be you."

I pull her in for a hug and kiss the top of her head. She keeps her arms against her body but otherwise melts into me.

"Who's this girl then? And where is she?"

"Come sit, Helen. Want a cuppa?" I know my old friend, and she'll want tea.

"Yeah, sure, I guess." Helen kicks off her sandals and skips over to my couch. I guess we're still friends. Good. I need more friends.

"I don't know what I'm doing." I fish the kettle out of the low cabinet next to my stove and fill it with water from the sink. "We work together. She's—" I freeze and stare miserably at the kettle, heating up next to Stella's empty wine glass.

"She's what?"

I almost said *Ben's ex-girlfriend*.

"Out of my league," I say instead.

Helen scoffs. "Unlikely. You're a fucking snack, Ethan."

I grin and grab two mugs from the cabinet. I'm more of a coffee guy, but I'll have tea to bond with Helen.

An hour later, Helen gathers her things, claiming she has a friend she's going to visit and stay with tonight. Her mum's watching Henry, and Helen had a backup plan in case she didn't end up here.

"Come see us sometime again, yeah?" She stands at my door, mobile in hand, tapping away.

"Absolutely." Guess she's over me already. She spent the last hour trying to convince me I'm worthy of love and should go after Stella. I never named her—that felt too weird—especially with the connection Helen has to Ben.

I let the door click shut behind her. I know what I need to do.

I'm going to go to Stella tonight. I know where and when she's meeting Ben, and as this is bucket list related, she'll need to document it for the lawyer's approval. I trust her. I'll be there for her, getting what she needs from a distance, and then I'll slip out and text her to come meet me.

And when it's over? No more secrets, no more holding back. I'll tell her I'm hers, completely and absolutely.

29

STELLA

BUCKET LIST DAY 20

I'm meeting Ben in an hour. I need to make sure I get this right, so I open the bucket list document on my phone and scroll to the last one.

5. Find the One that Got Away

Nausea rolls over me as I read, just like it did the first time I saw it. Evelyn wasn't messing around when she made this list. She must've known I'd hate this one. But the difference is, she wanted to tell her own *one that got away* about how wrong she had been, how she shouldn't have held back, how she should have accepted his proposal, no matter how scared.

But I don't feel that way about Ben. Was it my fault for not opening myself up to him more when we were together? Did I not give our relationship the chance it deserved? Shit, I don't know. Maybe. Am I sure having broken up with Ben isn't a mistake I'll regret in fifty years?

Well, yeah. Probably.

I keep scrolling, reading the requirements for number five again: *talk to someone else about it. Get it straight in your head.* That, plus the evidence requirement. I saved the email I sent Gemma about why Ben and I didn't work together, and the evidence requirement is why I asked her to come along and document me with Ben. She just got back from her trip with Cercei yesterday, and we have *so* much to catch up on once this is all done.

Even though I'm close to walking out the door, I consider texting Ethan. It's my last chance to come clean before everything happens tonight. Instead, one pops up from Gemma.

GEMMA

Ready for this?

ME

No, definitely not

GEMMA

Fantastic. One question: do you think Ethan
knows about you meeting up with Ben,
anyway? Think Ben told him?

I squirm in my soft spot on the couch as cold tingles of fear shoot up from my feet. It's possible.

ME

I hope not

GEMMA

lol. Hope is a fair strategy. See you in a bit

When it's over, I'll call Ethan. I'll go see him. Tonight. I can tell him what happened. See Nessie. And maybe his bedroom door again.

I got this.

WALKING into The Boar and The Bear brings back an avalanche of memories. Ben's flat is only a block away, and we'd always come here for drinks and then spend the night at his place. Sure, his flat was bigger and nicer than mine. Still. I always felt like I was in his territory.

It's a crowded night at the pub, but Ben's waiting for me at the table we'd always claim in the corner. A bench on one side and a pair of wooden chairs on the other, far enough away from the door to not get distracted every time someone walks into the pub, but close enough to the center of the action that we could people watch.

I played the Unless Game countless times in my head while sitting at that table.

I haven't seen Ben for six months. His handsomeness strikes me and a tiny, dull ache forms in my chest. Tall and slender, with blond hair and charming blue eyes. Before he spots me, I glance at the busy bar, but don't see Gemma. She'll be here.

Ben looks up from his pint and waves, standing when I get to the table, smiling so wide I think his face will crack in two.

"Stella, it's so good to see you." He opens his arms and pulls my body against his, saying my name in an easy-breezy way, unlike Ethan, from whom it comes out like a declaration.

Ben's cologne engulfs me, cinnamon and bergamot, and I'm sucked right back to the year we spent together. He keeps his arms wrapped around me and I let my cheek rest against his shirt for a few seconds. Was this so bad? Sure, his polo shirt is kind of scratchy, not like the smooth button-ups Ethan always wears. And he's hugging me a bit too tight, and I try to take a deep breath but can't, because the air has left my body . . .

We broke up because I didn't feel like *me* around him.

Suddenly I'm imagining pressing my face against Ethan's chest, not Ben's, and I pull back sharply, narrowing my eyes at him.

"You okay?" Ben looks down at me with surprise, crinkling his forehead.

"Yeah." I stare at the contours of his face, my eyes skimming over his smooth chin and cheeks, such a contrast to Ethan's mountain-man beard. "Good to see you, too, Ben."

He puts his hands on my arms and grins. "Come. Sit. I got you a drink."

I settle in the seat across from him, leaving my small purse linked over my shoulder, and sip the full pint. I prefer red wine, but he always forgets and gets me beer. When I do drink beer, I like an IPA, not lager, but any alcohol will do right now.

"I'm sorry about your aunt."

"Great-aunt. Thank you." I drink again. He waits for me to say something, but instead I slurp another few inches off the top of the pint, like the lady that I am.

"So, she left you a bucket list? And said we shouldn't have broken up?" Ben leans back and crosses one leg over the other, his hands folded on his lap, eyes steady on mine.

Choking on the amber liquid, I hold up a finger while I catch my breath.

He grins at me and leans forward, reaching over the table to pat my back, his hand resting on my body for too long, again.

I wish Ethan was here. He doesn't make crazy assumptions, or put words in my mouth, or try to make me drink things I don't want to drink or convince me to have *children*, for fuck's sake. The thought slams into me as my throat relaxes and I can use my vocal cords again. Jesus, where did that come from?

And no, I don't want Ethan to be here to witness this.

"Stella?" Ben looks worried again. "Sorry, I said that to get a rise out of you."

Suddenly I realize how complicated having any kind of relationship with Ethan would be. Ben will always be around. He'll always be Ethan's best friend. Would Ben approve of me and Ethan dating? If he knew what I was doing with Ethan last night, would he be here smiling at me like this, just so I can check my bucket list item off? I doubt it.

Gemma's words ring in my head. Do these two best friends tell each other everything? But the man across from me does not know about Ethan's bedroom door, or the couch, or the kitchen . . . Nope. No way.

"That's not what I said, I don't think." I attempt a casual smile. "And it's definitely not what Aunt Evelyn said."

"Yeah, I know. I read your messages again when I first got here. Sorry to have freaked you out." Ben rubs his clean-shaven face, a sheepish grin on his face. "But I want to say right away, I don't think breaking up was the right thing to do."

"You don't?" The breath whooshes out of my belly.

"No." He leans forward, resting his elbows on the table, his expression as serious as it could be. "It was my fault. I know that. I scared you by asking you to move in. I brought up marriage and kids. I moved too fast. You panicked and bailed."

"I don't think it happened exactly like that." Nerves rumble in my belly and an uncomfortable giggle escapes my throat. But didn't it? There's more to the story, sure, but that's the heart of it.

Ben cocks his head at me and raises his eyebrows. "Really?"

"I did feel things were moving too fast. I wasn't ready to move in. And you said I wasn't girlfriend material. Or wife material." I go over it in my head. Yeah, it happened that way.

"Stella, I'm so sorry." Ben reaches over and takes both of my hands in his, intertwining our fingers together, keeping his eyes locked with mine. He rubs his thumbs over my palms, and I focus on the touch.

Nothing happens.

No tingling, no bursts of energy, no desire running up my arm. His thumb drifts to the butterfly tattoo on my right wrist and I jerk my hands away. He grunts softly and glances down at his empty hands.

There's more I need to say.

"It wasn't just the moving in thing, Ben, or you telling me I'm not girlfriend material. I'd told you I didn't want to have kids, and you brought it up. Again and again. Don't you remember?" Sitting here across from him, the memories come flooding back. He'd said we could live in his flat for a while, and he'd kick his roommate out, and then we could move somewhere bigger if we ever needed a nursery. The way my soul flew out of my body when he said the word *nursery* to me. I felt like a terrible person for not wanting that. I love it for other people . . . but not for me.

Ben sighs, his mouth turning down to a frown.

"I was serious about not wanting to be a mother. And you told me I wasn't mother material . . . which is okay, but still made me feel like shit. And that's just not something I'm going to change my mind on."

A shadow flickers over his face.

"I'm sorry about that. I was going through a hard time and felt you pulling away from me. A bunch of people around me— friends from back home, from university—have been settling down and starting families. I got distracted for a bit and thought it's what I wanted. What *we* would want. And sometimes people change their minds. But you're more important to me."

I'm frozen. I'm not going to change my mind. In the background, I'm vaguely aware of groups of people coming in and out of the bar, which is getting more crowded, the noise level rising.

"It's so loud in here, can you come sit next to me?" Ben pats the space next to him, and I move around the table to sit next to him. There was a lot of me following his directions when we were together. It was nice in one way. To be told what to do.

Unless I lost myself in his baby blue eyes and his well-planned life.

Unless it wasn't nice at all, and it was all a trick, a way to hypnotize me into wanting what he wants.

Unless I found myself living *his* life, not mine.

I face him, our legs almost touching, thighs just inches away from each other.

"I was thinking that maybe I don't have to have kids to be

happy. Maybe we can try again, and I promise not to bring it up ever again."

God, the forlorn look on Ben's face right now. I feel for him.

At this point, I'd normally clam up, stop talking, and push him away. But maybe I can be honest with him. Really honest. Maybe I can do this differently.

"Ben, you can't compromise your wants and desires like that. Listen, you told me I wasn't girlfriend material. That hurt, but you were right. I wasn't. At least not for you. Maybe we're simply not right for each other."

But wait.

Ben ignores that last part. "I never meant to say you aren't girlfriend material. I don't even remember that. I was lashing out." His face crinkles and his eyes fill with concern, tenderness, affection.

Still, a shadow of a thought is forming in my brain, even as his proximity distracts me and chases the revelation—so close—away.

I examine his handsome face, noticing the slight crow's feet forming in the corners of his eyes that make him look more charming than ever. He will marry someone beautiful and have delightful children and the exact life he's dreaming of. I know it.

"I think we had something special." Ben touches my thigh gently. I hardly register he's done it. "I've learned a lot in the six months we've been apart. I dated a few girls . . . but they weren't you, Stella."

The fleeting thought from before comes back, landing firmly in my mind. *Find the One That Got Away.*

"Can I kiss you, Stella?"

I'm so wrapped up in my almost-revelation that I barely hear the words, and by the time they process, it's too late.

My eyes widen, locked with his, and then he's leaning forward and cupping my cheek with one of his hands, pulling me gently into a kiss. It's so surprising that I'm unable to pull away instantly.

I have just enough time to think about how it feels, the sensation of our mouths locked.

Like when our hands touched, I feel nothing. Absolutely nothing at all.

And now I know for sure: Ben's not the one that got away.

Ethan is.

30

———

ETHAN

I can't breathe.

There's nothing inside me. No heart beating, no lungs pumping, nothing to prove I'm alive. It's like the feeling right after getting slammed to the ground from a tackle, when the life is pushed out of my body.

"Are they *kissing*?" Gemma says, bouncing lightly next to me.

Out of the corner of my eye, I see Gemma swing her head toward mine, then glance back at Stella and Ben, who are, indeed, kissing.

Now I might understand the look on Gemma's face when I walked in ten minutes ago and stationed myself next to her in the nook of the bar by the restrooms, mostly hidden by groups of people, but with a clear enough view of Ben and Stella. Her face was part-horrified, part-delighted.

I'd explained to Gemma that I was here to help. No, Stella doesn't know I know. Ben told me. I'm here as her advisor to document the bucket list item completion.

I didn't tell Gemma the real reason I'm here, which is that I'm madly in love with Stella and always have been.

But now I know. Gemma thought it was a mistake for me to

show up uninvited. Because what feels like a lifetime later, Ben and Stella are still connected by their lips. Ben's got his hand on her face, cupping her jaw just like I did last night.

I finally breathe, then growl and close my eyes, lowering my mobile, with which I was recording them. It's on video. I've got the betrayal on video.

I need to ground myself, then get the fuck out of here. But at this moment, I'm afraid if I move toward the door, I'll mow people down like a raging hulk.

I was an arsehole to let myself fall for Stella.

I knew why I shouldn't do it. It's the same reason I avoided her when she dated Ben—except for that one night I helped her into her flat after he abandoned her. I'd wanted to curl up next to her that night, or even sleep on her couch, to make sure she knew she was safe and cared for. But it wasn't appropriate.

Because Stella is Ben's. Even though I *saw* her first, and *kissed* her first, she was Ben's even before they met.

"Ethan, I don't think that is what you think it is." Gemma places her hand on my forearm. I open my eyes and look down at her.

"I think it's exactly what I think it is."

Gemma swears softly, keeping eye contact with me, and says under her breath, "I should have told her you were here right away."

It's better this way. Now I know. There's a reason why she didn't tell me about meeting Ben tonight. Because she wasn't sure what would happen. She wasn't sure who she'd choose. She was so unsure about me that she needed to kiss him to figure it out. Or maybe she was sure, and I was just some loser she'd string along until we've checked everything off the list.

"Stella," Gemma says, her hand moving off my arm.

Stella's right in front of us, her jaw dropping open, eyes wide.

"Hey . . ." Stella flits her gaze from Gemma to mine and

freezing there. "Ethan." She whispers my name. "What are you doing here?"

"Ethan's here to help, uh, document this for the bucket list," Gemma says in a voice that's too high.

"Damn." Stella unfreezes and grabs one of my forearms, attempting to slide a hand down to mine, but I'm locked with my arms against my sides, ungiving. She doesn't let go, her hand frozen at the crook of my elbow. "That wasn't what it looked like. I promise you. I swear to you."

She steps closer to me, and Gemma melts backward, attempting to give us privacy in Ben's crowded fucking local. More people have arrived, and the view of Ben's table is completely obstructed.

"You lied to me about tonight." It's a statement. A fact.

She shakes her head, her blond hair swishing with the movement. "No. I mean, yes. Fuck."

"You kissed him." Another fact. My voice is colder than I mean it to be, colder than it's been in weeks with her. Not since I opened myself up, left myself vulnerable—too vulnerable. A helpless child, or a teenager in love. So naive.

"*He* kissed *me*. I didn't tell you about tonight because it was too awkward, too weird, after everything that's happened . . ."

"It was all a mistake." I wish I could get more out. Say more. Express how I'm feeling, but that part of my body has shut down, doors locked, the key dropped in a sewer drain.

"No. It wasn't a mistake. Ethan." She steps closer to me, her second hand on my other elbow. "Please. Let's go somewhere quiet and talk."

This is too much. I shake my head, not answering.

"I just wanted to finish this, and then go tell you about it afterwards. I didn't want you to have to deal with it. Not when it had to do with Ben. But I figured it all out."

We're so close. It would only take a slight movement to open my embrace to her, let her into my arms. Into me.

But I can't. Because now I really understand.

My heart squeezes to life and emotions burst free, bleeding out all around me. Absolute love for her, but also anger. Resentment. Devastation. Regret.

Betrayal.

Not betrayal by Stella. I now see so clearly—like I thought I had before, but hadn't—she was never really mine. She'll never be mine.

It's my betrayal to Ben that's killing me. Here I was, rationalizing falling for Stella, convincing myself that it's okay for me to be with her since they've been broken up for six months and he's dated other people. That a tiny bit of betrayal would be okay, and that Ben would get over it, and our friendship would remain intact.

I can't believe I almost screwed up my relationship with the person who has been the most loyal, the most supportive, the most loving of my entire life. Ben and his parents have done everything for me.

No woman is worth risking that.

No matter what I feel for her. No matter how perfectly she fits in my arms, in my bed, in my heart.

"Ethan. Please. Say something."

I draw every kilo of strength inside me to end this thing between me and Stella.

"Whatever is happening between us—" I try to swallow, but my throat feels too scratchy, too swollen. "It can't continue. It's over. I'm sorry. I have to go." I shake off her hands and rip my eyes from her shocked face, then stride toward the pub exit, knocking into people along the way, just like I thought I would.

Outside, a cold London mist is falling, denying that it's summer, and it fits. The perfect setting to have ended my misguided attempt at loving someone.

"Ethan!" Stella's right behind me. She darts around until she's in front, and I'm forced to stop. She reaches up her arms, touching the sides of my face with her hands, and the lightning that sparks from her body to my center floors me. "Please. Let me explain."

"No," I say softly. "Let *me* explain. I'm not mad at you, Stella." I let myself put my hands on her waist and she moves against me. Fuck, the feeling of our fully clothed bodies touching is too distracting, it's too much. I must end this, once and for all.

I push her gently away with my hands, then tug on her arms until they are no longer touching my face. It'd be easy to lean into a kiss. But that would make it impossible for us to part tonight.

"Then what's going on? I don't want to be with Ben. I know that now, Ethan—"

"Even if that's true, he clearly wants you on some level. And I can't compete with him. I *won't* compete with him. He's my best friend. He's my family."

"But . . . I just came here to finish number five. I really tried to do it like Aunt Evelyn told me to. I searched for the answer to her question. And I found it."

"You found it kissing Ben?"

"Yes," she whispers. "I don't want to be with him." Stella steps forward and her hands lift. She's going to touch me again. I can't let her do that. I hold out my hand, palm first, because this can't happen.

"When I first started dating Helen long ago, she showed up at the flat I shared with Ben." Maybe if I give her more background, she'll understand. She'll let me go. "Helen told me she loved Ben, not me. I pretended like I didn't care, and had to watch them together." My voice breaks.

I hate how pathetic I sound. I won't sound like this ever again, I promise myself.

"She chose *him,* Stella. Just like you did after we first met. And even if I could betray Ben—which I can't—I can't ever be someone's second choice. Never again."

"Oh, fuck, Ethan." Tears shine in her eyes. "You're not, I promise. I told you why I said yes—"

"Stop. Please." I cut her off and shake my head too hard. A dull headache has already formed, pulsing behind my eyes like a drumbeat. This is all too much. I need to walk away. "I can't do this with you, Stella, I told you. I'm so sorry."

She whimpers and moves her head in disagreement, much more subtly than my movement.

I hesitate for a second, then lean forward and press my lips to her forehead, letting myself linger for a second too long. She sighs and touches my chest with her hands.

"Ethan . . ."

"This is over, okay?" I murmur, my lips still against her skin, memorizing the feel of it. "I'll sign off on your bucket list. We'll finish the commercial. Then, no more."

"No!"

I pull back and force myself to turn and walk away, not looking at her again, convincing myself with each step that this is the right decision.

Stella's voice drifts toward me, calling my name.

I can't compete with Ben. And I can't be someone's second choice, the way I have been, over and over.

But *fuck*, the feeling of losing Stella is worse than the other two combined.

I'm making the right decision. I need to go back to the way I was before. I'm the one-night stand bloke. No second dates, no texts the day after. I'll beat my heart into submission until I'm back to being the dark, troubled loner I've always been.

31

STELLA

I stand in the rain for what feels like an eternity before Gemma appears by my side.

"Is he gone?"

I nod, unable to squeak out a word. I keep picturing Ethan's look of utter resolve when he told me it's over. The betrayal was written all over his face. Helen's betrayal, my betrayal, and his own perceived betrayal of Ben.

There'd be no coming back from this—not for us. I know it in my soul.

"Oh, Stella. I'm so sorry."

My purse is still strapped over my shoulder. I shake my head.

"It's all my fault. I totally fucked it up. This is all . . . fucked."

"I'm sorry," she says again, and when I look down at my own best friend, her eyes are wide and filled with tears. "I should've texted you right away when he showed up. He wasn't mad at all, he wanted to be there for you, so I thought . . . But then you and Ben . . ." Gemma bites her lip. "What happened back there, Stella? I really thought the night would end differently than this."

"I made a mistake. More than one." I shake my head and let Gemma hug me, leaning into her supportive touch, but knowing she can't fix this. She didn't mess up. I did. "I gotta go, okay? I need to think. I'm gonna walk to the next tube station." I peel her arms off me and back up a few steps.

"Are you sure? I can come with you. We can get kebabs or disgusting fast food or a bottle of wine and cry over it together?"

"Not tonight, Gemma." I grind my teeth together to stop the tears, backing up another step. *I really screwed things up.* The gravity of it is making my body heavy and tired.

"I'm coming over tomorrow, and we can talk."

"Okay." I turn and stride away.

"Noon!" Gemma calls, and I turn to look at her. "Make sure you're decent." She smiles, but it doesn't penetrate the layers of my misery.

My phone buzzes in my pocket and I fumble for it. Maybe it's Ethan. I turn the corner and glance down at the screen, but it's Ben. Ben, who just kissed me. Ben, who I never said goodbye to.

BEN

Where are you?

In no world do I have the strength for more Ben Hughes right now.

ME

I'm sorry. I need to go home

BEN

What?? We should talk about that kiss. And where we go from here

No, Ben, we shouldn't. I figured it out, and it's Ethan I want. I don't want to hear Ben tell me he wants to be with me. Because I don't want to be with him.

ME

I don't want to talk about it. Not tonight. I'm sorry

BEN

I really think we should. Can I catch up to you?
Come over?

ME

No

BEN

Is this about Ethan? I saw you leave after him.
He's not responding to my texts. Where
are you?

I roar and press ignore when he tries to call, then silence notifications from him.

Ethan truly didn't look angry. He wasn't being irrational. He looked devastated, then resigned. As if he'd uncovered a painful, undeniable truth. Which he had: he can't betray Ben. And because I'd let Ben kiss me, he sees being with me as betraying his best friend. His best friend is his family. I know that now, after getting to know him over the past three weeks.

It's Day 20 of the bucket list.

I walk and walk, dodging the crowds of Saturday night revelers who annoy the shit out of me with their joyous screaming and laughing, hand holding and gentle flirty touches. How dare they giggle and gossip about the night ahead when my life is in shambles?

A twenty-something man has a woman pressed up against the side of a mobile phone storefront, kissing her, one hand on her ass, and he stops to caress her cheek with the back of his other hand. Instead of being disgusted at their very public display of affection, I'm envious. I want to tap them on the shoulder and tell them how lucky they are, and not to fuck it up.

If I had just told him everything. If I had shared the whole damn bucket list from the beginning and not left out the last requirement. This could have been the night that brought us together for real.

As I turn into the station and get assaulted by the warm, distinct, London Tube air, I touch two fingers to my lips. It should be the shadow of Ethan's kiss on them, not Ben's.

Being with Ethan was everything. Not perfect, not a rom-com, but exactly what I need and want.

The escalator takes me down below the streets. I swallow hard. It can't be over. Can it?

TRUE TO HER WORD, Gemma shows up at my basement flat at noon the next day, banging on the door and calling my name.

"Dammit." I groan. I'd hoped she'd forget all about crashing my pity party, even though the multiple texts she sent last night should have clued me in otherwise. Ignoring them probably wasn't the best idea. Maybe she would have let me wallow by myself if I'd assured her I'm okay.

I'd been smart enough not to ignore the texts from my sisters, because that would have guaranteed relentless video calls until I answered. But I know they think something is up. That it might be more than work and Evelyn's bucket list.

I move slowly to a sitting position. I haven't budged from my couch, where I relocated to at seven o'clock this morning. I've got the worst hangover, and it has nothing to do with the pint Ben got me at the pub, and everything to do with how I've completely fucked up my love life.

I'm the worst.

No word from Ethan. No answer to the text I sent when I got home last night:

ME

Can we talk tomorrow? I'm so sorry

He read it, but didn't answer.

It's over between us. I know this is the truth. Ethan doesn't fuck around. There's no way I can change his mind.

"Stella! I can literally see you through the window. Open your damn door." Now Gemma's banging on the window. Better let her in before she throws a metal chair from my patio through the glass.

As soon as the door's open, Gemma throws her arms around me and hugs tightly, a food bag crinkling in her hand.

"Can't breathe. Can you let go?" I squeak out.

"You're talking, so you can breathe." She releases me from her embrace and pushes her way past into the flat to assess the situation. "How are you? Have you showered today? Eaten? Changed your underwear?"

I tilt my head and raise my eyebrows. "No. It's noon on a Sunday. And I'm offended you think I'd completely fall apart in, like, fourteen hours."

"You're kind of a disaster, so I was worried." She looks me up and down, probably considering whether I'll ever shower again. Maybe I won't. Maybe I will let myself devolve into some kind of secluded hermit-rat who never leaves her flat. Why not?

Right. Because I have a job to go to.

"Let's sit." Gemma pulls me to the couch and pushes aside the crumpled blanket, then turns to me with an intense stare. "I brought almond croissants." She holds up the paper bag before ripping it open and shaking a pair of pastries onto the table, flaky crumbs scattering.

"Oh, you're amazing." The smell is heavenly. One of my favorite London delicacies is train-station almond croissants.

"Now you like me, huh?" She sinks to the couch and rips into one of the croissants, the sweet almond insides squeezing out from the middle. "No word from Ethan?"

I turn my face to avoid answering.

"And how are we feeling about that today?" Her wide eyes look as serious as I've seen them.

I chew as slowly as possible, but she waits patiently for my response, and eventually I have to swallow.

"Awful. Like my heart's been ripped out and thrown to a bunch of vicious foxes."

"The foxes in London are not vicious, and you know that." Gemma shoves the rest of her croissant in her mouth. "You got coffee?" Crumbs tumble out and I can't help but giggle.

"You're gonna make me get up again and be productive?" But I stand anyway.

"Making coffee on a Sunday afternoon is hardly being productive," she says after swallowing.

I roll my eyes and head down the short hallway to my kitchen and the coffeemaker. Maybe lack of caffeine is part of the reason I feel like such garbage. Gemma follows me and leans against the doorframe.

"You gotta get him to talk to you, girl."

I roll my eyes. "Gee, thanks for the great advice."

"Maybe you should call him?"

I ignore her. "How was your vacation with Cercei?"

"Fantastic, and now we're probably breaking up. But this visit is about you, not me."

"Whoa! Wait, what? Spill." I crinkle my forehead and finish scooping ground coffee into the appliance. She thinks *I'm* a disaster in love? I press start and cross my arms. Now it's my turn to patiently wait for her to respond.

Gemma groans. "Okay, quick download and then it's back to your problems. We had a lovely two-week holiday in Greece. Hotter than hell, but lovely. Then on the way back on Friday, she started saying crazy things to me."

"Such as?"

"That she loves me? And wants to move in with me?" Gemma flails her hands around, fingers splayed out dramatically.

"Truly awful behavior."

"Right? And then, when I suggested *I* move in with *her* for a bit, just to see how it works, she called me out for doing the whole moving-in-with-someone-while-also-keeping-a-backup-flat thing that I like to do." Gemma uses air quotes.

I stifle a laugh. "She knows about that?"

"Yeah, well, I guess I tell her a lot."

"Maybe it's different with her." The coffee finishes brewing. I pour Gemma a generous mug and grab the creamer from my fridge, handing it over before I fill my own mug.

"I find it harder to date women because I just think of them as a close friend, who I also happen to want to make out with. Men are easier to compartmentalize."

"Dating a friend who you also want to make out with sounds really healthy, actually." We wander back to my couch.

"Hmm. I don't think so." Gemma snuggles back against the side of the couch, kicks her slides off and crosses her ankles next to my legs, sipping from her steaming coffee. "It's too much. Too fast. I don't think I can do it." She closes her eyes and rests the back of her hand on her forehead, all drama.

"She said she loves you, but do you love *her*?"

"What?" Gemma's eyes fly open.

"Do. You. Love. Her." Delighted to not be talking about Ethan, I'm enjoying torturing my friend. My friend who claims she's never been in love, is a serial dater, moves in with people after a month of dating while also keeping a backup flat, and hardly hesitates to ghost said people without a second thought.

"How dare you."

I laugh and make a motion for her to go on.

Gemma sighs. "Fine. She's sweet. And hot. And really gets me. I dunno. I suppose it's possible. Maybe." She spins a ring on her finger.

"Really? Wow."

"Wow what? I said maybe. Not yes. It's probably a no, actually. Definitely a no. I detest her."

I roll my eyes. "She get that ring for you?"

"Yeah." Gemma stares into her coffee, then shakes her head violently. "Girl, this is not why I'm here. I'm here to comfort you. Be there for my best friend. Help you figure out how to fix things with Ethan."

"Thank you, but I don't think there's any fixing this." I swallow hard, and now it's my turn to throw my head back against the couch and close my eyes. "And for what it's worth, I think you're pushing Cercei away because you're feeling something real for her, and it scares the shit out of you."

Gemma makes a grunting sound. "Well. I could say the same for you."

I sit up straight. "I am not pushing Ethan away. I want to be with him. I . . ."

". . . want to ride his bones?" Gemma stares at me innocently and we both dissolve into giggles.

"Yes," I say when I get a breath. "I definitely want to do that again." But Gemma's words echo in my head. Have I not been letting Ethan close to me, like I've done with all the men I've dated since Hunter? I thought I was getting better at that. I made progress last night, telling Ben how I felt about us, that he shouldn't give up on his dream of marriage and kids.

"So, what's the problem? Ben?"

I nod, focusing on Gemma again. "Ben. But not for me. For Ethan. He's, like, fiercely, stupidly loyal to that guy."

"You found the one man who is so committed to a friend that he'd say no to shagging you?"

I groan, but she's totally right. I messed it up with the right one. The one who listens to me. The one who actually sees me. But I didn't let him close enough.

"You have it bad, Stella."

"I do." I can't stand the idea that I can never be with Ethan, just because I dated his best friend. Ethan. He's the one I should have stuck with. He's the one who really sees me. Who cares. Who, with hardly a hesitation, wanted to help me with the bucket list.

To do it better, the right way, the way Evelyn wanted me to. He acts like he actually knew her, or wanted to, anyway.

I fucking love that guy.

Wait, what?

"Shit!" I sit up straight and lukewarm coffee splashes onto my hand and Gemma's bare foot.

"Hey!" She pulls away from me but laughs. "What's going on in your pretty little brain right now, bestie?"

"I should have chosen him to begin with," I whisper. "Back when I first met them."

"Yeah, probably." Gemma runs her hand through her chin-length hair.

"But someone told me to choose Ben. Remember that, *bestie*?" I point a finger at Gemma. "It's all your fault."

"Oh, fuck off." She whacks my finger down and laughs. "Ethan was legit getting together with that girl from back home. And Ben was perfect for you on paper. How was I supposed to know you would prefer Mr. Damaged, Bearded, Dark, and Extremely Hot?" She cocks her head. "Actually, he sounds like everyone would prefer him."

Oh, god, I'm in love with Ethan Fraser.

"Is it hopeless, then?" I whisper and look at Gemma. "Because I might be really into him."

"Like, love him?"

I nod.

"You absolute sap. Pull it together." She kicks me in the thigh and pulls her feet under her body. "You say I've not been letting Cercei close. But have you told Ethan how much you like him? That you love him?" She draws out the word love.

"What? No. I literally figured that out thirty seconds ago." I thought I'd been letting him in. I was wrong.

"You got to tell him how you feel." She makes a *carry on* motion with her free hand. "For real. Not just some stupid text.

Go and tell him you love him. Make it good. Romantic. Try hard. Try harder than you think you need to. And that way . . ."

". . . if I fail, I'll at least have done all I could?" But I'm just not sure I can do it. If what I've done so far is not enough, and there's a whole other layer that I need to peel off myself and let him see, I don't know if I'm capable.

"Good. Now go do it."

I squirm on the couch, picturing confessing my love to Ethan. Pricks of sweat stab my armpits.

"Well, I'm not going to do it, like, now."

Gemma rolls her eyes. "Whatever. Do it soon. You saw his face last night. He's got one and a half feet out the door. He thinks he's got them both out, but he really doesn't. Cause I think he kinda likes you, too."

But not enough. There's no way it's enough. His loyalty to Ben is eternal.

"Maybe you could open yourself up to Cercei as well."

"Hush right now, girl." Gemma throws the blanket at me.

After I pour us more coffee and Gemma tells me every detail of her trip to Greece, she leaves me alone in the flat, where I collapse back on the couch.

I'm gonna tell him that I love him.

And if doesn't work . . . fine. But Gemma's right. I have to try.

I tap out a text to him. *Another* text to him.

ME

Can I come with you to Newcastle on Wednesday like we planned? To help with your mom's flat?

Immediately, three dancing dots. Finally, he's responding! I keep my eyes fixed on the text chain.

ETHAN

No. Best I do it alone

ME

> I really want to help you

I really want *you*, is what I want to say, but I can't say that with a text. Gemma forbade it.

ETHAN

> You already have. It's enough. More than
> enough. Thank you

It's not enough. He deserves more than he's gotten out of life. The people around him have disappointed him again and again. But someone needs to be there for him.

ME

> Can you still do Old Man of Storr with me on
> Friday? After the shoot is done Thursday?

ETHAN

> Stella . . . that's just not a good idea

After the shoot on Thursday, after next weekend when the bucket list's twenty-eight days will officially be over, he has an excuse to never speak to me again. I've gotta change his mind. I've gotta find a way to convince him to give me a chance. Give *us* a chance.

ME

> I need your help with this last bucket list item. A
> picture on top of the mountain. Please?

No response for what feels like forever, then a one-word answer that makes my heart soar.

ETHAN

> Fine

My insides swirl and I lay back on the couch, eyes closed,

thankful I have the chance to try. I hope he'll listen to me on top of that mountain.

But I'm also gonna show up for him at his mom's flat in Newcastle. There's no way I'm letting him go through that by himself, no matter what he says.

32

———

ETHAN

Wednesday, 31 July

I stand in the hallway leading to Mum's flat. But this time, I'm not frozen with the key burning a hole in my pocket, hovering pathetically outside the door. This time, the flat door is propped wide open and a whole crew of people are hard at work inside. I can't bring myself to enter.

Thanks to Stella, I don't have to.

The head bloke in expensive-looking jeans and a polo shirt emerges from the flat, where he's been packing items up in the kitchen. Twenty minutes ago, five of them walked in with arms full of collapsed boxes and other supplies. The sounds of tape dispensing and cardboard being assembled drift out into the hallway, and three of the men have moved further back into the flat to Mum's bedroom and the small room that used to be mine.

"Should take us two or three hours, max."

I nod. I should thank him, say something, say anything, but it turns out I'm not okay, even though I don't have to be in there.

"I'm Scott. Friends with Gemma and Stella, so they let me know what you've gone through. Sorry for your loss, mate."

"Thank you," I finally manage to say. I ignore the squeeze at my center at the mention of her name.

Stella. I wish she were here with me right now. I know all the reasons why I didn't let her come, but I've had to remind myself of them again and again since I walked away from her on Saturday night. Since I dismissed her on Sunday.

No, I'd said. *Best I do it alone.*

Fuck Sunday me. Alone is the worst way to be. Alone is how I felt growing up in this damn flat.

A dozen times, I'd picked up my mobile to text her. Wanted to show up at her flat. Wanted her to show up at mine.

But because of Ben, I can't do any of that. I clench my fists at my sides. First, because I owe him and his parents everything. And second, because she'd chosen me second once before. And she did it again on Saturday night. If I let down my guard, it would happen again. I can't let someone close to me like that. It was almost disastrous.

Scott stares, probably waiting for me to say more. "Well. We're planning to donate most things and dispose of what the charities won't take." He pauses and I attempt to relax my shoulders, unclench my jaw.

"Great."

"Do you want to come in at all? Or is there anything you want us to set aside?" He says it kindly, but with curiosity. I wonder what Stella told him about this situation.

But come in? Christ, no. I'm not sure my feet would listen to me if I commanded them to move forward. I take a step backward, away from Scott, away from the flat.

"Ethan," a woman's voice calls from behind me.

I spin around.

Stella stands in the hallway.

My heart pounds, and I already feel more alive, less like a wordless statue. *What is she doing here?* But the vision of her—in a black hoodie and worn jeans, blond hair standing out against the dark top, looking like she belongs cuddled into my side on a couch, not in this godforsaken hallway—awakens something inside me. Something that has felt dead since Saturday night when I watched her kiss Ben.

"Hey, Scott," she says.

"Hi, Stella." Scott brushes past me and gives Stella a friendly hug. "Good to see you. How've you been?"

"Fine. I'm just here to make sure things go smoothly."

Scott laughs. "I'll leave you to it, but I promise we're not going to bugger it up." He steps into the flat and turns back to me for a beat. "Let me know if there's anything you want us to grab for you."

Once he's gone, Stella takes a cautious step toward me.

My tongue is tied in knots and all I can do is stare at her.

"I know you told me not to come. But I couldn't let you face this alone. You're a good person, and you deserve to have people in your life who support you during shit times. Like these."

Oh. Fuck me. I lift my shoulders and bury my hands in the front pocket of my England Rugby hoodie.

"Thank you," is all I manage to say.

"Come on, want to go in?"

I nod, even though my body's screaming against it, and will my feet to follow Stella as she enters Mum's flat. I take one step inside. Scott and one other man are wrapping mugs and dishes in paper before tucking them in a medium-sized brown box. I have a vision of Mum in the kitchen, standing on the chipped black-and-white tiled floor, smoking, drinking instant coffee, draping her arms around one of her many boyfriends, ignoring me.

What would I possibly want to save? There are no good memories in this flat. Nothing I want. I should probably sign up for a decade of therapy to work through all these issues.

"They should get rid of it all."

"You sure?" Stella touches my arm lightly, and I nod. "Okay. Hear that, Scott?"

"Sure did. All donate or trash." He pauses his wrapping and looks at me. "If we see anything sentimental, we'll put it aside for you to look at, okay? Just in case."

"I guess."

"What about all the books? Your mum was quite the voracious romance reader, huh?"

Stella spins her head to the bookcase. One of the shelves is almost identical to the one in my flat with the books I'd given Mum.

My stomach twists in shame, for trying so hard all those years, trying to connect with her by reading her smutty romance novels. Fine. It wasn't torture. Some of them had actual plot, and the love stories? Top-notch. Maybe I kept reading them even when I realized it wouldn't be something for us to bond over. Maybe I'm a true romantic at heart. Fuck if I know.

But Mum never acknowledged my attempts. Those desperate olive branches I offered to my own mother, which always splintered and stabbed me.

"Donate them." I don't need her castoffs. The bloke nods.

"You want to go peek in the bedrooms?" Stella asks.

"No." I'm done.

"Then let's get out of here for a bit."

I stride out of the flat, down the stairs, and out the front door of Mum's building, Stella on my heels. There's a wooden bench a few buildings down and I collapse onto it, head in my hands. A gentle breeze waves past, caressing my neck. It's beautiful out, cooler here than in London, but sunny. How dare the sun show up in Newcastle on this day, this miserable bookend of my childhood?

Stella doesn't say a word, just drops down next to me on the splintered bench and puts her hand on my back, rubbing comforting circles. I should tell her to stop, to leave me alone, to leave in general, but her presence here means more than I can handle admitting.

I can't wait until this day is over. Until all of this is done, and I can put it behind me.

Thanks to Stella. She is the only reason why I am here today, with a few days to spare from the landlord's thirty-day deadline. And it's not about Mum's belongings. It's more that I'm taking care of what I'm supposed to, unlike how my mum managed her life.

"You okay?" Stella asks.

I nod, but involuntarily picture Stella and Ben kissing at the pub. My stomach turns and I contract my abs to make the nausea go away. I'm not okay.

This might be the woman I love, but Stella and I have no future. Not with the past she has with Ben. Not with the past I have with him, either, and the future in which I literally have no biological family left. Just Ben, Robin, and Simon.

I fell in love with Stella. But just before I hit the bottom of that seemingly endless pit of butterflies and soft touches and pleasure and joy, I grabbed the ladder and started climbing back up. I'm still working to escape. Out of necessity. Now I just have to move on and bury whatever it is that's there. I don't want to face her tomorrow for the shoot or Friday in Skye. I'm sure I'm not strong enough.

But she deserves it. And I need to.

After these things are done, this will be over. I'll sign off on her bucket list and we can go our separate ways.

I have to hold it together long enough to get through all of that. I have to not let myself fall further into her.

I twist my hair in my fingers, my head bowed on the bench, elbows digging into my thighs. The problem is, I'm having a hard time separating what I'm feeling about Mum and her flat, with what I'm feeling about Stella, with what I'm feeling about Ben and his parents. It's all twisted together like some mass of feral vines climbing up my body, and I don't know what's causing the grim feeling in the pit of my stomach.

We sit on that bench in Borinwick for almost two hours, only moving to take a walk around the rundown neighborhood. Stella doesn't try to make small talk, and for that I'm thankful. The movers stream in and out of the flat, carrying boxes and furniture and lamps and loading the truck, its back gate gaping open like a monster gobbling up memories. I watch them feed my childhood into the truck, and feel nothing but desolation and loneliness, much like I did growing up.

Scott emerges and gestures to us. I stand and head back in his direction, with Stella striding next to me.

"We found this." He nods to his feet, where there's a beat-up old box covered with peeling brown tape. The top is labeled *Ethan's Memories* in faded black marker.

A breath catches in my throat. *Mum had a memory box for me?*

"I'm guessing you might want to keep it?"

"Yes," I say, my voice too loud as I attempt to project casual confidence.

"We're all done." Scott looks at Stella first, then at me.

"Thank you, Scott."

"What do you want to do with the keys?"

"Give them to me," Stella says before I can jump in, then turns to me, a darting glance at the box. "I'll drop them off with the landlord. He lives around here, right?"

I nod and pull up the address in my mobile. I should fight her on this, insist I can do it on my own, but the truth is, I'm not sure I can. She's pulling me through this flaming forest of pain and nightmares, not leaving me behind to burn. For that, I'll be forever grateful.

"Thank you," I manage to mumble, looking at Scott, then Stella. I wish I could say more. I want to say more, but there are no words. Scott heads back inside.

"Want to open the box together?" Stella slips her mobile in her back pocket and clutches the keys.

"No," I say, and she nods once.

Five silent minutes later, a car pulls up behind the moving truck.

"That's my Uber," Stella says to me. "See you tomorrow, okay?"

I can't manage a word or a gesture, and then she's gone. The movers leave, and I'm by myself in front of the building of flats, done with it forever.

I eye the box at my feet like it might be full of spiders or sharp knives. I bend to grab it—it's heavier than it looks—and shove it in the backseat of my rental car.

I have a feeling it might be like Mum's flat: something I never have the nerve to open.

33

STELLA

Thursday, August 1
BUCKET LIST DAY 25

"The shoot's gone amazing so far," I say to Tessa.

"Lovely!" Her voice projects through the speaker on my phone.

We're at the base of a rocky mountain on the Isle of Skye, large boulders strewn on either side of a bumpy trail, bright green moss and ground cover everywhere it can grow. There are mountains and lakes and beautiful views. It's vast and feels like the wild west of Scotland.

Ethan stands twenty feet away from me with the director, Gerald, who gave me a ride from Inverness to Skye yesterday after I took multiple trains to get there from Newcastle. I'm assuming Ethan drove from Newcastle—which is a seven- or eight-hour drive—and stopped to spend the night somewhere along the way.

I was not kidding when I said it's impossible to get to this gorgeous little nook of Scotland.

And Izzy is here, which warms my heart. She's so happy, bouncing around and joking with the other girl and the pair of rugby boys. They are laughing and taking selfies and generally having the time of their lives.

She told me today that she is in the final three for the scholarship competition.

"We just have a few more shots to get," I say to Tessa. "Rugby scenes went smoothly, Izzy's interview was perfect, and they are about to start a quick hike up to the best viewpoints for the group scene."

My chest constricts, thinking of why we're even shooting this here. Why I'll be able to check Skye off the bucket list, knowing I did it the way Evelyn wanted me to.

Ethan.

Tessa asks a few more questions before letting me go.

Letting me go to panic about the bed-and-breakfast situation. When we got to the accommodations in Skye last night, I realized I'd never tried to update the reservation I'd originally made for the second night.

I should've gotten two rooms to begin with, even if Ethan and I were already sleeping together at the time I booked. I let my professionalism slip at the worst time.

I asked the nice, older Scottish lady at the front desk—er, her kitchen table—if there was space for tonight, but she said she's booked solid. No availability. It's a small, quaint B&B, and the crew plus me filled up the handful of rooms last night. I did some quick searches online and we're basically in the middle of nowhere, so there's not a lot of convenient options.

Ethan and I are stuck in one room tonight. *Shit.*

I don't know how he'll react when I explain to him there's just one bed. One bed followed by a hike and a confession of my love to someone who's already decided we can never be together.

Am I really going to do that? Like, tell him I love him?

I blame the stupid bucket list. I blame his gorgeous brown eyes. His painful kindness when he finally stopped glaring at me. His beard. All of it. And especially my great-aunt.

However it turns out, I'm so glad I met up with him in Newcastle yesterday. No one should have to do that alone.

There's a ringing in my ears, and I wonder about the magic of this place. Of Skye. I was reading about mystical fairy pools somewhere on the island. One day, I need to come back and visit them. Seeing Izzy's beaming face and hearing the news about the scholarship contest? That's pretty magical, too. My throat is tight, and I can hardly swallow. Ethan's why she's here.

As if he senses me thinking about him, Ethan looks right at me.

Damn. He looks like something straight out of a dark romance. He's wearing a different hoodie from the one in Newcastle yesterday, this one blue with the logo of his old rugby team on the front instead of England Rugby. There are dark circles underneath his eyes that I can see from here, but it takes nothing away from his feral, tortured good looks.

How could I ever have overlooked him? Chosen Ben? Regardless of what Gemma had told me, how the fuck had I not found him after that night and made him talk to me?

Ethan's not smiling at me with his mouth, but his eyes are intent and locked on mine. I want to throw my arms around his neck and press my body against his. Ask how he is. Touch his face. Tell him I want to be there for him, even if his mother wasn't. I want his hands wrapped around my waist, finding the skin, pulling me closer. His lips on mine. His rough beard scratching me.

I slide my phone into my back pocket. Even though it's July, the biting Scottish island wind whooshes around the rocky mountains and lifts my hair.

The problem of just one room hangs over me like a thick gray cloud about to dump its contents on the earth. Just one bed. Disaster. But . . . surely, he'll talk to me when we have to share a room?

"DID you pay for tonight's room, or is it on hold on your credit card?" Ethan slams his driver's side door shut and heads around to the back of his rental car in the parking lot of the B&B.

The crew was finishing packing up and the bus with the kids had left the mountain, so Ethan gave me a ride from the shoot site back here.

We drove in complete silence, and he didn't look at me, not once.

But now he is.

"So, here's the thing." I bite my bottom lip and wait for him by the trunk. *Here we go.*

"What?" Ethan's voice is gruff as he reaches for the back door handle and pulls out his bag, pausing for a second. Then he slams the door shut.

His rough demeanor, his attitude . . . it's a protective measure, I know. I'm just glad he agreed to climb the Old Man of Storr tomorrow. He's too good a guy to back out on something he said he'd do.

"When I went to book your room yesterday, they were sold out."

"What?" He takes a step toward me and then freezes as my words sink in. "Sold out?"

"Yeah." I cringe. "I . . . I'd booked one room for us, as soon as the shoot was scheduled . . ." I trail off. "That was before last week-end. But . . ."

Ethan's staring at me, eyes wide, begging me not to say what I'm about to.

"You can stay with me. In my room."

His jaw tightens. "Are there two beds?"

"No. Just one bed. A big one, though."

"I'll talk to the crew. Maybe one of them has two beds."

"The crew?" I crinkle my face in confusion. Why would they be coming back here? But I think back to the morning and try to remember them hauling bags at the lovely Scottish breakfast we were served . . . and I don't.

Ethan nods, his eyes turned downward. "After we confirmed plans to climb tomorrow, I texted Gerald. Some of the crew decided to stay and tag along."

"On the hike?" The bottom of my stomach drops. He's doing everything he can to avoid being alone with me. To make sure nothing happens with us. My plans shatter, as if I'd dropped my favorite mug —the one from the local coffee shop in Reese's hometown that says *I'm not yelling, I'm from New Jersey*—and watched it break to pieces.

"Yes." His face is a blank canvas. He's wiped all emotion. He's probably working on wiping away any feelings for me as well.

"Oh. *That's* probably why there were no rooms left." I take a few cleansing breaths. "Well, I feel a little less bad about not being able to get you a room."

"Fair point." Almost a twitch of a grin crosses his face.

"Just come look." I sigh and cross my arms. "You can at least leave your stuff there for now, since the crew isn't back."

He tightens his face, as if even being in a room with me is the worst idea. And it might be.

"Come on." I wave my hand at him. Suddenly, I'm exhausted. It's been a long week. A long month. "I'm tired. Then we can get a drink while we, uh, wait for the others, I guess."

I spin around and head toward the giant house, and after a second, there's a crunch of gravel as Ethan follows me.

"This is the smallest room I've ever seen. There's not even room to sleep on the floor." Ethan drops his bag right inside the door and crosses his arms. I'm standing in front of the bathroom door and had to dodge the bed to get here.

There's a tiny desk with a chair in one corner, and a pair of nightstands on either side of the bed. Ethan's eyes linger on the romance novel on my nightstand. I'm still reading *Love to Hate You*, the enemies-to-lovers book. I have a suspicion that the romance novels at Ethan's flat are his, not his roommate's. The thought of Ethan reading them makes me love him even more. The matching shelf at his mom's flat? That wasn't a coincidence.

"I know." I also cross my arms. "But the bed is big."

We both look at it. Is he imagining sleeping next to me? Scooting to the very edge of the bed to avoid brushing against my thigh in the middle of the night? Or maybe not avoiding me at all?

"I read that one," Ethan says, eyes back on my nightstand. "I believe there's a scene where there's only one bed. It's entirely unrealistic. How could that even happen?"

I snort. Ethan Fraser, cracking a joke. "It does seem very unlikely. I haven't gotten to that part."

A smile forms on his face, then melts away.

"I used to buy matching romance novels for me and my mum. I'd give one to her and suggest we read them at the same time. Like a little book club." His face darkens. "But she always blew me off. I think she did actually read them—they were all on the shelf in her flat yesterday—but that only makes it worse. They were good enough to read, but not to talk to me about."

I stride over to him and slip my hands on his forearms, expecting him to flinch. But he doesn't. His muscles pulse beneath my hands. This man. He tried so hard. I wish I could make it hurt less for him.

"Ethan. That was a sweet thing to do."

"No. It was stupid."

"Not stupid. You were an amazing kid, and you're an amazing adult, and you've done your best with a really shit situation." I step even closer until our bodies are practically pressed against each other, then run my hands down his forearms.

He relaxes and lets me weave my fingers with his.

"How are you? After yesterday? Have you opened the box?"

Ethan shakes his head aggressively. "No." His voice cracks on the one syllable word. "It's rubbish. I'm going to toss it."

"Come on." I tug Ethan through the door.

"What?" He pulls against my hand and stops after two steps. A look of panic crosses his face, his eyes wide, throat bobbing.

"Let's open it and get it over with." It's gotta still be in the car. That's what he was looking at in the back seat.

He doesn't respond, but eases his resistance and follows me down the hallway, through the living area, and out the door to the still-empty parking lot.

I open the passenger side back door and slide in next to the box. When he doesn't get in from the other side, I peek my head out and over the roof.

"Get in. Sit." I duck back inside the car, hoping he follows direction. When the car door clicks open and he slides in, I'm already messing with the old, peeling tape. With a loud rip, I free the flaps of the box and they spring open, his mom's handwriting no longer visible.

Ethan doesn't move, so I reach in. A blue baby onesie is at the very top, with a big train on the front and the words *Choo Choo*. I pick it up and show it to Ethan.

"Aw. Sweet." Hope surges in me. Please, let the box be filled with thoughtful moments from Ethan's childhood. *Give him this, at least.* Give him some peace with the memory of his mother.

He looks at the onesie, then back down at the box. Clearly, the man isn't going to touch it, so I lay the tiny clothing on my lap and reach back in.

The next item is a single piece of paper, stiff with age. It's a child's colorful drawing of a mountain, with a woman holding the hand of a small boy at the very top. The clouds are shaped like puffy hearts and the mountain is gray and green and rocky. It's quite good, actually. The corner says *Ethan, 10,* in cute, loopy handwriting.

I smile at him. "Your artwork, Leonardo?"

Ethan makes a murmuring sound, staring at the drawing, but not touching it.

"That was after Mum took me to Skye. I can't believe she saved it. I can't believe she saved anything."

"Well, she did." I carefully place the paper on top of the onesie and pull out an old picture with bent edges. It's of a baby sitting on a young woman's lap. I hand it to Ethan, and this time, he takes it.

He draws in a shaky breath, and I imagine he's overcome with emotion. Thank the universe that his mother is pulling through for him.

But next in the box is a layer of yellowing paperback novels, the kind sold in grocery stores with old-school romance covers. Long-haired, shirtless men holding half-dressed women with their heads thrown back.

"Books. Did you read these together?" I pile a few on my lap, briefly showing him the covers. But I think I already know the answer.

"No." Ethan's one-word answer comes out like a bark. "They're just trashy old books."

Well, shit.

"What else is in there?"

I peer into the box, pushing aside a few more books, furrowing my brows at what I see. I fish out a pile of t-shirts and drop them in my lap, holding them up one-by-one.

"Queen." Another. "Kiss." One more. "Def Leppard. That's it. Mean anything to you?"

"They belong to one of her exes. She dated a guy for two or three years when I was little. He was a total arsehole and would yell at her all the time. Then he left her, thank fuck."

"I'm sorry, Ethan." My heart pulses for him. For what he had to endure.

"It was after that we went to Skye. She wanted to change, but she failed, and things went back to our shite normal."

"Why would she put them in this box? Did they mean something more?"

"They mean *nothing* to me. Just a reminder of how she chose her loser boyfriends over me."

Ethan lunges and turns the entire box over, dumping the few items left onto the seat and dropping the box on the floor of the car. He doesn't reach for anything, just stares like it's a bomb about to detonate.

I touch a few loose papers with handwritten scribbles and move them around. With a jolt of hope, I pick up one of the pages and skim. When I catch the phrases *your heavenly body* and *the most beautiful woman in the world* and *we should run away from everything together*, I stop reading.

"Oh," I say. "I think they're letters from one of your mom's boyfriends."

He snarls and looks out the window. "Of course they are."

"There's one more thing. Looks like a journal?" I pick up the gray bound notebook from the floor by my feet, where it landed when he dumped the box. I open the journal and there's writing on the first two pages, and then it's blank.

Ethan looks over at me.

"It's mostly blank. There's a few—"

"Toss it. Please."

The words on the first page say *I'm better off without that man. I've made the best decision of my life to have this baby . . .*

"Are you sure? I think you might want to read it."

"I can't. This is all rubbish." Ethan waves his arms around at the contents of the box.

"I'm so sorry." It's like his mother didn't think of him at all. I want to reach out to him, to grab his hand and comfort him, but at that moment, multiple cars pull into the parking lot. I look over at the new arrivals, and Ethan takes that opportunity to slide out of his rental car and walk toward the crew.

34

ETHAN

I'm absolutely sloshed. To be fair, so is the rest of the crew. The B&B has a covered, expansive porch with four rocking chairs, two loveseats with outdoor cushions, and a few single chairs. A bottle of Scottish whisky sits on the table in the middle—I believe it's the second bottle of the night—but it doesn't stay put for long as glasses are constantly getting topped off.

Stella's curled up on one of the loveseats by herself, covered in a fleece blanket, nursing a glass, quiet and not taking part in the loud shenanigans. I'm doing my best to ignore her existence. Because that way lies painful truths. She's seen too much. She knows too much about me, my pain, my life.

Dave, the cameraman, is telling some kind of meandering story, his drunken Scottish accent even thicker with the influence of alcohol. I laugh along with the rest of the men, even though I'm not following. No matter who I'm looking at, no matter how many swallows of the burning liquid I take, Stella's always in the peripheral of my vision. Can she tell my laugh is fake? Can she sense the pain swirling inside me like a tornado?

Of course she can.

I don't make eye contact with her. Drinking has dulled the

sharp hurt of the past week, but it hasn't lessened the feelings I have for Stella, the ache in my chest. I want to collapse in her arms. In her bed. I want to be with her in every way possible.

The one fucking bed. I can't go back to that room. There's no way I can lie next to her all night and not reach for her. Not when I know how it feels to entangle my limbs with hers and listen to her soft breathing as she falls asleep, or the sounds she makes when I stroke her body with nothing at all between us. I squeeze my eyes shut and the noise of everyone dims for a few seconds as I disappear into my thoughts.

I shouldn't have left my bag in her tiny room.

Shouldn't have let her lead me to my car to open that box.

Shouldn't have opened my heart to someone who isn't mine. Who *can't* be mine. When I open my eyes again to the clink of the bottle against my glass, Stella's gone.

An hour or two later, I stumble back into the house, leaving the crew to continue to drink. I'll just go grab my bag and come back down to crash on the couch. We're the only guests here tonight, so what's the harm? The owner of the B&B probably won't like it, but she's long since gone to bed and I'll get up at the first creak of a floorboard.

But standing in front of Stella's room, my hand rests on the door handle and my thoughts swirl with indecision. She wants me. I want her. But it can't be. What bad fucking luck. I shake my head hard to clear it, but only manage to make myself dizzy. I squeak open the door and stand in the entrance, dim light streaming in from the hallway over the bed.

Stella's curled on her side, blond hair splayed out on the pillow, one arm resting on her side, the other on the bedsheet with her mobile lying next to it. The sheet's down to her waist, revealing a tight white tank top that's ridden up to reveal her waist and belly. The curves of her breasts cast a shadow on the bedsheet. A small moan escapes my throat.

It's then I notice a notebook on the empty side of the bed. The journal from Mum's box. She read it?

I step inside the room and carefully pick up the journal, then lean against the wall inside the door, sliding down to read the bloody notebook by the hallway light.

There's one entry, dated from just before I was born.

I'm better off without that man. I've made the best decision of my life, to have this baby, to change my life, to clean up and make things right. No more drinking. No more drugs. No more bad men. It'll be me and my baby against the world. Me and Ethan.

She must be talking about my biological father, who left before I was born, whose name she never even shared with me. Eventually I realized she wasn't protecting me from hurt, she was protecting herself from having to face who she had a baby with, from having to think about him ever again. It was about her, not me.

I swallow and grind my teeth to keep the tears from filling my eyes. She doesn't deserve my tears, even though she's gone. How long did that last? Putting me first? I let out an angry breath. Until the next drink, the next boyfriend? And then she managed to pull it together once more, years later, for our hike to Skye? Only to get distracted again.

I turn the page.

I have dreams for him. Dreams for my baby. Dreams I won't ever accomplish for myself, but I can hope for Ethan. I hope he travels the world. To America. To even farther places, like Australia or New Zealand.

I hope he falls in love. Finds his soulmate. I hope I do that one day myself.

But he's my priority. My son.

This will be where I record my thoughts and dreams for him, and one day, I'll give this journal to Ethan as a record of how much I loved him. How he saved me.

Then the writing stops, and the rest of the journal is empty. Tears slide down my cheeks.

Stella shifts in the bed and I watch her settle, waiting for her to wake up. Maybe if she does, I'll talk to her, even though I shouldn't, and confess how confusing this journal is. Mum had the right intentions but couldn't follow through. I wish she'd have talked to me. I wish I'd known the mum who wrote this journal entry, the mum who took me to Skye. Not the mum I had the rest of the time. The mum who ignored me, neglected me, disparaged me. The mum who lost herself in a bottle and a never-ending string of loser men.

I study the curve of Stella's cheeks. The lids of her closed eyes, covering the dark-blue irises I could get lost in, like a thick mist on the sharp mountains of the Scottish Highlands.

But I *have* fallen in love. I found my soulmate. She's right there.

And I'm going to spend one last night sleeping beside her.

35

STELLA

Friday, August 2
BUCKET LIST DAY 26

After I left the men last night, I stayed up another hour to work on what I would say to Ethan today. This morning, I woke up to the pillow wall between us. The man slept in the bed with me, but built an actual wall of pillows.

He *does* read romance novels.

It's heartbreaking, but I'm also still cracking up about it inside as our group gathers in the parking lot of the Old Man of Storr.

"Come on," I say to the men behind me, who do not move an inch. It's the director, Gerald, two members of the crew, Joe and Dave, and Ethan. They're all a little slow this morning, which is not surprising, given how trashed they were when I snuck away last night.

Ethan's standing in front of one of the cars, posed with his arms crossed and one leg loosely linked over the other, looking out over the gorgeous expanse of horizon and water. I memorize the width of his shoulders, the curve of his arms through the hoodie, and his profile, waiting for him to make eye contact. It doesn't happen, but he follows the others as they head toward me.

The gravel path is well worn, rocky, and lined with tall grasses that sway in the cool island breeze. The views from here are absolutely magical, with the impressively large Loch Leathan sprawled out in front of us, pulling on something in my soul. I breathe in through my nose and close my eyes for a few beats. This is the last item on Evelyn's bucket list, as well as where I'll tell Ethan how I feel.

Am I going to have to do it in front of the crew? Maybe.

I shift my backpack and lead the group, trailing a couple probably around my age. They're dressed in woolen hats, rain slickers, and hiking boots. Probably the right choice, as the vast sky is covered with a mixture of white fluffy clouds and menacing darker ones. The couple is holding hands, reaching over to kiss as I watch. I pull up my hood and lift my shoulders. I could use another layer.

This place is special. It's where Evelyn's true love asked her to marry him. Where she hesitated, said no, and later regretted it. The Old Man—a towering, skinny rock, so tall it's basically reaching into the heavens—looms ahead of us and I tilt my head to take it in. I picture Evelyn and her love walking up this very path fifty years ago, about to take a hike that would change their lives. He'd be thinking about how he was going to ask her to marry him, ask her to uproot her life by moving to Scotland so they could be together.

What was she thinking at that very moment? I don't know. But I know what she thought about it later, thanks to the letter she left me.

Hers is exactly the type of story I used to fear, and before this month, I would have thought it was a close call, almost getting sucked into changing her life completely for a man. Giving it all up for love? No way. I've never felt that close to someone. Even Hunter was an illusion, and everyone since then—including Ben

—has felt just fake. Evelyn must've agreed with the sentiment, at least when she was on her way up the Old Man of Storr.

But now, that just looks like choosing loneliness, and I don't want to do that.

I want to stay who I am, but also live my life with Ethan. I can do both things, can't I? It's all clear now. To me, anyway.

The internet tells me it should take about an hour and fifteen minutes round trip: forty-five minutes up to the top, then around thirty back down. So that's how long I have with Ethan. And a bunch of other dudes.

I glance behind me. Gerald and Joe are trailing about ten feet behind, chatting and laughing. Ethan and Dave take up the rear, and Dave's telling a story about his teenaged son getting into trouble at school. Behind our crew is another group of people. A family. Two men walking closely together and two middle-school aged boys ahead of them, laughing and fighting over who is better at rugby versus soccer.

Ethan's quiet. Thinking about his mom? Thinking about me? He makes eye contact and quickly looks away. My heart squeezes. I'm not sure how he's wormed his way this close to me over the past month, when on the first day, that meeting in the conference room, he seemed to hate me.

And now . . . this. It was never really hate.

I get to a wooden gate and push through, leading the group between rolling, green, moss-covered hills. The gravel part of the path ends, turning into a dirt-packed trail that gets gradually steeper and rockier, with muddy patches to traverse, my sneakers not having ideal traction. The chattering behind me dies down and my own breathing gets heavier.

Rounding a corner, the view is breathtaking over another large expanse of land and water. I gasp quietly and pause to take it in. It's a view of a million miles, the ocean in the distance, Loch Leathan in front of me, the rolling, rocky Skye landscape between here and there. Looking out, anything seems possible. Everything, really.

It's magical.

The men approach behind me and Gerald whistles.

"Gorgeous. I'd say this is about good enough for me."

"Aye," Dave agrees.

"What?" I spin around.

"We're going to have a seat on these comfortable-looking rocks and enjoy this view." Joe nods just ahead of us at a wide viewing area. "And maybe some of the beers we brought along."

"Hair of the dog." Gerald nods solemnly.

"Gross, but okay." I bite my lip and my heartbeat accelerates. I find Ethan's eyes on me. I need to get to the top. Even if I was going to tell him how I feel right here—and every bit of my being screams no to that—I need to find Evelyn at the peak. Not here.

The family of four treks past us at a quick clip, nodding a greeting and beginning the even-steeper part of the hike, at least according to the internet.

Ethan's eyes are narrowed, his face scrunched. He's not looking at the view or the men. He's looking at me. *What's he thinking?* Probably wondering how to get out of this. I wait and let him sort it out.

Finally, his face softens, and he nods his head in the direction of the trail.

"Let's go."

I nod and start walking immediately, not giving him another second to change his mind. Evelyn's bucket list dictates I need someone to come with me, and I'm not cheating on the list. Not now, when I've come so far.

Ethan pulls up next to me. The silence between us is heavy, but I pretend that the last week went differently, that it was the beginning of something, not the beginning of the end.

I wish it was a misunderstanding. I wish I could've simply

explained that the kiss with Ben didn't mean anything. It was a test, and the test showed that I am meant to be with Ethan. But it's not that clear. The layers of neglect and of craving love and belonging from his desolate upbringing won't allow him to let me in. They won't allow him to adjust his loyalty to Ben and give us a chance.

Hopefully, what I worked on last night will be enough to convince him that we deserve to try.

At a fork in the trail, we take the path to the left. The mid-thirties couple from earlier passes us on their way back down, and the family of four is camped out drinking water and eating granola bars.

It'll be just us at the top, then.

The trail becomes skinny, narrow, and steep, and I concentrate on not tripping as I climb the natural stone steps that lead to the base of the giant rock. When we get there, a sheen of sweat covers my forehead and my heart races.

I look around. "Oh my god."

Ethan stops next to me and follows my gaze. The view is breathtaking, higher than the viewpoint where we left the men. Several islands dot the ocean in the distance. The rolling, jagged hills around us are covered in bright green, scattered with large boulders and giant rocks, not quite as big as the Old Man, but still impressive.

"That's the mainland," Ethan says, his voice soft and reverent. "And those islands are Raasay and Rona."

"It's beautiful." This is where Evelyn's proposal happened. Her man must've been the ultimate romantic to plan such a thing. *How could she have said no? At a place like this?* I close my eyes. Evelyn said in her letter she'd try to talk to me when I got here. Reach for me through the heavens. I breathe in through my nose, out through my mouth. Again. The cool Scottish breeze lifts my hair and I run my hands along the sides of my exposed neck.

Are you there, Aunt Evelyn?

She doesn't speak, but I feel her. She's in the whisper of the wind through the surrounding grass. The rays of the sun warming my shoulders. The memory of her alive—a life lived so fully and well—all around me. The love she gave me, from when I was growing up in New Jersey to the last years of her life, when I was across the ocean.

She's here. She's all around me. She *is* me.

Stel-La! Her voice rings clearly in my mind. *You made it!*

She's saying hello, and goodbye, and that she'll always be with me.

Peace blankets me. A smile crosses my face and I open my eyes.

I'm not alone on top of this mountain. And there is one more thing I have to do here, something besides checking off Evelyn's bucket list.

36

ETHAN

Tears run down Stella's cheeks, but she looks peaceful. I clench my fists to stop from reaching over and swiping the moisture from under her eyes.

Vivid memories of when I was here last flood my brain. My mum stopped at the halfway point, down where the crew sits right now, and I stumbled up the rest of the climb by myself, a ten-year-old boy who probably shouldn't have been allowed to do it on his own. I was still hopeful then that she'd turned a corner, that she was going to be the mum I'd needed. I thought maybe if I was really nice to her and studied extra hard, she'd be that person.

But it wasn't meant to be. I struggled to focus. She struggled to mother.

Could I have done something differently? Been less of a disappointment? Achieved more to capture her attention earlier? Even when I went to university and had success with rugby—which impressed most people—she was completely uninterested.

Staring at Stella's face on top of this breathtaking mountain, clarity descends on me.

It wasn't my fault. I was a kid.

Just like Stella's mentee, Izzy, and my rugby boys, Leo and

Callum. I would never blame them for their parents' failing. I would never even *hint* that they should be doing anything different. That would be toxic, damaging, and simply not true.

Mum made her own decisions about how she lived her life, and nothing I did caused that. At some point, she had the right intentions—the journal entry from that abandoned notebook showed it—but she wasn't the kind of person who could pull it off. Nothing I could've done would've changed her.

I'm lucky I had Ben and his parents to step in when she frequently stepped out. But maybe, just maybe, I don't owe them everything. I was just a kid. I owe them *something*, but what if it's okay for me to live my life the way I want it? What if I don't need to carry a lifelong debt because my mum was awful, and another family helped me survive?

Stella turns to me and reaches out her hand. I take it after a heartbeat of hesitation.

What if I can have Stella?

"Ethan." Her voice is like a gentle breeze, wrapping itself around me. "I have a few things to say." She holds up her other hand as if I'm going to cut her off, but I haven't even opened my mouth. "Please, let me get through this."

I nod and swallow, my shoulders rising and falling like I'm out of breath, the warmth in my chest vibrating.

"That night. A year and a half ago."

I clench my jaw.

"I made a huge mistake." She reaches for my other hand, the one dangling by my side. I don't resist, and now we're connected in a circle, the energy flowing effortlessly between our bodies. It would take no effort at all to pull her close against me, feel her warmth, dip down to kiss her.

"I had the most fun I'd had in years with you."

"You were drunk." A shadow of a smile quirks across my face.

"A little." She bites her lip, and oh, bloody hell, I want to be doing that. "But that wasn't it. We clicked, as if we'd been best friends all our lives. And kissing you?"

My breath catches in my throat, and I glance down at her lips, left slightly parted. I could never kiss them enough.

"What about kissing me?" My voice is raspy.

"We were a perfect fit."

I nod, remembering that night, remembering last weekend, knowing how fucking good we are together.

"I started your bucket list," she says simply. "And I want to tell you about it." Stella drops one of my hands and pulls out her mobile, unlocking it with her face and tapping a few times with her thumb.

"My bucket list?" The warmth ebbing from my heart spreads out, like sweet, spilled molasses.

"Yeah."

"I told you not to," I say, but my protest is weak. She lifts her chin, and her blue eyes meet mine.

"I didn't listen." Her lips turn up into a smile. "Obviously."

"Get on with it, then." I swallow the suspicious lump in my throat and squeeze the hand I'm still holding.

"There are four items. Number one: *Travel to America*. Have a local show you around." She has her mobile in her hand, but hasn't broken our gaze.

From Mum's journal. I bite my cheek to keep unwanted tears from springing up in my eyes.

"I thought that since your mom put that in her journal entry . . . and you happen to know an American who could show you around . . . this would be a good start." Her face is open and anxious, and she studies mine, waiting for a response.

I squeeze her hand. "Who wants to go to America? It's full of . . . Americans."

"Right. We're the worst."

"You said it."

She stifles a grin. "Ready for the next one?"

"Yes, Hart."

"*Join—or Start—a Romance Novel Book Club.*"

I can't help but chuckle. "Seriously?"

"Yeah, seriously. A hot man who reads contemporary romance novels? That's amazing. You'd have a hundred women signing up for your book club."

"What if I just ask one person to be in it?"

Stella tilts her head. "If they are the right person . . . then okay. But we might have to check with your advisor on that one."

I throw back my head and laugh.

"Number three: *Climb the Highest Mountains in the United Kingdom.* You know, like we talked about before. Oh, and bring someone with you." Stella drops my other hand and runs it through her hair, leaving a chunk out of place. I reach over and gently push it behind her ear, grazing her cheek with my fingers, leaving them there for an extra few seconds.

"That's ambitious. How long do I have to do this?"

"Negotiable." She grins at me, then it fades and Stella stares intently. "There's truly magic here. And even if you're not trying to connect with someone, it's worth it to be up here and connect with yourself."

"You're right." The silence descends on us for a moment, and we keep our eyes locked as the mountain wind moves Stella's hair around her face. "But, you know, this isn't actually a mountain, more like a big rock, and it's much, much less of a climb than the highest one, which is Ben Nevis."

"Yeah, I know, I did, like, thirty seconds of research. This is roughly half the elevation." She shrugs, and I can tell she has no idea how hard it will be to climb Ben Nevis. I let it go. For now.

"You'll need to buy some actual hiking boots to wear, not trainers."

"Who said *I'm* coming with you?" She bites her lip, and my eyes are drawn to her gorgeous fucking mouth, her plump lips. I know what they can do. The tension between us is a live wire.

"Can I kiss you yet?"

Stella's breath hitches and I see it all over her face. Hope. Happiness.

"No, not yet. There's one more."

"Go on."

"Number four: *Release Yourself from the Debt to Ben and His Family*. Talk to them about it. Thank them for all they did, then let it go."

Now it's my turn for a breath to hitch.

"That's going to be hard." But releasing myself from that debt? Wasn't it what I was just mulling over?

She slips her mobile back into her pocket. "Do you honestly believe that they think you owe them? I doubt it. And they would never let you pay them anything back, monetary or otherwise. That's not what good people expect when they help a child. Maybe you can continue to give back in some way, and that would be what you need to let yourself off the hook. You're already coaching those rugby boys. And you've been doing it for years."

"You're right." She is. And I love her so much for it. Stella Hart is on my side, wholly and completely, and I know it. I feel it.

"I'm sorry for choosing Ben eighteen months ago. I didn't think I had a chance with you back then. If I did, I would never have agreed to go out with Ben."

"Stella . . ." Fuck, can I kiss her yet?

"Wait. Not done quite yet. And I'm sorry for letting Ben kiss me last weekend. I didn't know he was going to, and then it just proved—as if I needed it—that my lips belong on yours, not his or anyone else's." She reaches up and touches my cheek, then rests her hand on my chest. "But it's you. It's always been you. I didn't know it when we first met, and I let myself get distracted. *You* are my person. *You* are the man I'm in love with."

Her face is so open and vulnerable. She's waiting for my response. She's laid herself bare for me.

"There's one more item I want to add to my bucket list, but

it's kind of cheating," I say, closing the remaining space between us and sliding my hands to the sides of her face, tilting it up to mine.

She blinks at me, her eyes wide and dark.

"I want to fall in love. To find my soulmate."

"You read your mom's journal," she whispers.

I nod. "And it's cheating because I've already done it. I found my soulmate. I love you, Stella Hart. Fuck, I've loved you since we first kissed a year and a half ago. I loved you while you were with Ben, when it was torture to be around you two. I've never stopped loving you."

Stella grabs my waist and pulls me against her, breaking my hold on her face and crashing us together. Our mouths kiss in desperation, tongues wrapping together, and I move my hands to her waist and let her wrap her arms around my neck until our bodies are pressed together.

After a minute, we pull away.

"I love you, too," she whispers, and tugs my jumper until I lower my head back to hers. Centimeters from our lips touching, she keeps talking. "I realized it after last weekend. And today, on this ridiculously beautiful mountain, I'm actually completing two bucket list items."

"Two?" Our hot breath mingles, our lips a beat away.

"The one from Aunt Evelyn that had me messaging Ben. She said to *Find the One that Got Away*. That's you."

The hardy thistle of hope growing in my belly blooms, and I'm filled with a happiness I didn't know possible.

Time freezes on top of the Scottish mountain as our lips meet again, slower this time, softly, gently pressing. The scent of the mossy ground cover creeps into my nose. This is exactly right. Being here, with Stella, there's no doubt in my mind that kissing this woman on top of this mountain on a Scottish island is perfect.

I part her lips with my tongue, and she leans farther into our kiss. There's a stirring in my groin and I can't wait to get her back to a room with a bed and . . . wait, what room?

"Hey." She pulls back, her arms still wrapped around my neck, her brow slightly furrowed. "What's wrong?"

"What happens next?"

She grins. "Well, I think we live happily ever after. That's what happens when you find your soulmate."

There are still things I need to deal with. Like telling Ben what's going on.

But living happily ever after with Stella? That's exactly what I want to do. I slide my hands down from her waist to her arse and lift her up against me.

"Perfect. Now let's go find a bed. We just need the one."

She laughs and nestles into my neck.

37

STELLA

Saturday, August 3
BUCKET LIST DAY 27

"We should be at Eilean Donan Castle in a few minutes." I track our movement on the map app and sigh contentedly. "I love castles."

Our destination is only about an hour's drive from where we were on Skye. Instead of heading off the island yesterday after our hike to the top of the Old Man, we snagged a room back at the same B&B. After spending a bit of time inside the room, we drove to the main town on Skye, Portree, for dinner and a wander around the gorgeous, rainbow-house-lined main drag, set on a scenic harbor where any good romance novel could take place.

Now we're driving to Edinburgh, where we'll drop off the rental car and fly back down to London, arriving late afternoon.

With a stop at an ancient castle along the way.

I feel like I'm in my own romance novel. Ethan left the ones his mom packed in that box at the B&B, where the owner has a *Take One, Leave One* bookshelf. He tossed the band t-shirts and the onesie—even though I protested at the last one—and kept the journal, the picture of his mom and him as a baby, and the drawing he'd made as a ten-year-old.

"Love castles? That's because you haven't got any of your own in America."

"Yeah, Americans live deprived lives." I stare at his profile, the side of my head against the headrest of the car. "Anyway, going to castles—with you—makes me happy."

But what I mean is: *You make me happy. Not castles.*

"Good. That's the goal." He glances over at me, his expression soft.

Still in my hand, my phone buzzes. It's the group text chain with Reese and Maddie, and they're confirming our video call date for tonight. Today is day twenty-seven, after all, and I can't wait to hear what was on their lists. We agreed we could talk tonight about the lists without breaking Evelyn's rules, since we've all finished our tasks a day early.

I haven't quite finished revising number two, *Adopt an Animal*, but I have a plan. And I don't love number four, *Help Reese*. Planning my sister's bachelorette party should be good enough but feels not as impactful as it could be. I'd plan that, anyway. It *almost* feels like cheating. Which I don't do.

"What's wrong?" Ethan glances briefly away from the road.

"Huh?"

"You just made some weird sigh. You're desperately in love and happy, remember?" He stares at me, completely serious. "No unhappy sighing allowed."

"It wasn't an unhappy sigh, I promise."

"Want to add castles to our highest mountain peak adventure?"

I gasp. "Yes, let's absolutely do that!" I imagine traveling the country with this man, visiting the most romantic and inspiring places in the United Kingdom. *Sign me up.*

"Well, maybe not all the castles. There's a lot here."

"Maybe half of them?"

He chuckles. "Yes, half sounds good. We better do it in the summer, at least up here. It's cold and dark in Scotland in the winter." He pauses. "Spill. What were you thinking about?"

Ethan waits patiently for me to say something. I love that he already knows when I'm holding something back, probably because we've done that too much.

"Number four. I think it could be better."

"*Help Reese?*"

"Yeah." I nod. "Oh, the turn is right up there."

"Got it. I don't think I need directions anymore, Hart." Ethan follows the obvious signs for Eilean Donan Castle.

"I saw on their website that they do weddings," I murmur. The pictures were breathtaking, with the rough Scottish mountains in the background and the craggy castle reaching toward the heavens. Some of the images had miles of blue skies, and others dark, angry ones. Those were my favorite. The gorgeous couples popped against the gray Highlands backdrop.

We turn a corner, and the castle appears ahead of us, set on a small piece of land on a loch, a narrow stone pedestrian bridge over the water the only way to reach it.

Ethan parks in the gravel lot next to the visitor center and we get out and walk across the cobbled bridge connecting the tiny island to the mainland. Halfway to the castle, I spin in a circle, overwhelmed by the sense of wonder I feel as we approach the castle. When I stop spinning, Ethan comes up behind me and wraps his arms around my waist, nuzzling his chin into my hair. I will never get used to this feeling, the tingling up my spine, the warmth blooming inside my body, the knowing that we belong together.

"They're not sure where to get married, but they know they want to do it here in Scotland," I continue. "He's not close to his parents. Maybe . . ." I trail off and my heart beats a bit faster. *Yes. This is the answer.*

"Maybe what, Hart?"

I spin around to face Ethan, his hands remaining on my waist. "Maybe we can take some pictures of this place today." The wheels in my brain turn faster. "And maybe I—we—can visit some other wedding venues in Scotland. I can give her a list with pictures and an assessment, so they can easily choose one."

"I think that's an amazing idea."

"Along with the tour of the highest mountain peaks and the complete castle itinerary?"

He sniffs. "There will be some overlap, but yes. Obviously."

I reach up and wrap my arms around his neck, leaning in for a kiss. I can't wait to talk to Reese.

We wander through the castle grounds and the historic old stone structures. We're early so it's quiet, the summer tourist crowds yet to arrive. I take in the historic cannonballs and tea sets and seriously old-looking wooden furniture in the Billeting Room, a stone room deep inside the castle.

"The outer walls are fourteen feet thick," I read from a sign on the wall. "Guess this room was ready for battle, huh."

Behind me, Ethan buries his head in my neck, pressing his lips against my skin and making me sigh.

"Christ, but I love you all to myself in a thick stone room."

I laugh and turn to him. "We are not alone."

But he looks pointedly around the room, then back down to me. "Aren't we?"

"I'm sure there's people here . . . somewhere." But my stomach flutters at the hooded look in his eyes, and when he slides his hands down and grips my ass, I let him pull me up his body, slowly, until the only thing to do is wrap my legs around his waist.

"No one's around, Hart."

I shrug my jacket off and let it fall to the floor. "Ethan . . ." I should protest harder as he rakes his tongue down my neck and nuzzles my nipple through my shirt, causing it to immediately harden.

"You can't scream my name in here. You'll need to keep quiet. A whisper-scream, maybe."

I choke out a laugh. Ethan backs me up until I'm against the stone wall, where he moves his pelvis against me in a way that makes the room fade away.

"Fuck, Ethan."

"I said no screaming." But he pauses and looks around.

"I wasn't." I shut my eyes and concentrate on the ache in between my legs.

"There."

"Where?" I open my eyes as he backs away, letting my feet gently touch the floor before grabbing my hand. My knees are wobbly, but I let him pull me to the far corner of the room next to an old glass-encased bookshelf, beside which there's a closed door that almost blends into the wall. He jiggles the doorknob, and it opens without much effort.

Ethan steps inside and turns to me. "Get your smoking-hot arse in here. And shut that door behind you."

"My god, what? This is wildly inappropriate." But I follow him into the tiny room. It's got a small round window, ancient desk, wooden chair, and metal filing cabinet with papers stacked on top. I shut the door, and he yanks me against him again, fumbling with the button on my jeans and breathing into my mouth.

"Let's make it quick, before whoever works in here finds us."

"There's no way we're having sex in this little office." But I unzip my jeans and wiggle them to my ankles, underwear tangled with them. Ethan runs his hands on my bare ass and groans.

"You don't want to?" He nibbles my ear, making words difficult.

"We might as well, since you've already taken off half my clothing."

"Better than a conference room at your office, right?"

"Yeah, but we didn't . . . oh." I must've missed him pushing his own jeans down, because now he's rubbing his cock against my stomach. He reaches between my legs and slides his fingers over my entrance, wet with need for him. His hand feels electric against my clit, rubbing circles in my most sensitive part.

Ethan groans and backs up two steps to drop onto the office chair. I take a second to admire how gorgeous he looks waiting for me there, his need for me on full display. He reaches for my hips and yanks me to him. Last night we'd established that I'm on birth control and he hasn't been with someone in six months and got all the testing, so we're ditching condoms.

"Ride me, Stella."

I obey, lowering myself onto Ethan, letting the length of him slide inside me, filling me, completing me. My breath ragged, I rock back and forth on his lap. "We shouldn't be doing this here."

"Better hurry up and come, then."

The pressure builds inside me, and I press my body down harder on him, desperate for the release that's just about cresting. He thrusts up and I come in waves, with him following a few seconds later.

We press our foreheads together, breathing heavily.

"Was that fast enough?"

"Christ, Stella, have I told you how much I love you?"

"You have, rugby dude."

A voice rings out from beyond the door in the Billeting Room.

"Someone dropped their jacket." A man's voice sounds.

"Shit." I lean back with my eyes wide, Ethan still inside me.

"Let's grab it for the lost and found," a woman says. "I bet it belongs to that couple we sold tickets to. They're the only ones here."

Ethan holds a finger to my lips, but he's silently laughing, shoulders rocking.

I dismount from my boyfriend and silently apologize to the person who works in this room.

"Get dressed!" I whisper-scream at Ethan.

"Unless you want to go again?" He winks at me.

I tilt my head and consider it, then point to his pile of clothing.

The voices are gone, so we sneak back out of the little room and pull the door shut.

"That was close." I let Ethan grab my hand and entwine our fingers. "And fun."

"We could add that activity to our castle, mountain peak, and wedding venue itinerary?"

"Again—wildly inappropriate, but sure." I follow him out of the room.

AFTER WE RETRIEVE my jacket from the ticket office, me desperately hoping I don't look too flushed and disheveled, I send Reese a text offering to scope out wedding venues, plus a link to the wedding page for Eilean Donan Castle. I throw in a selfie of Ethan and I standing in front of the castle with the loch in the background. She responds back right away.

> **REESE**
>
> Yes, please! And who on earth is that gorgeous, bearded man? Tell me everything!

> **ME**
>
> My boyfriend

> **REESE**
>
> Your WHAT

> **ME**
>
> Tell you more later

"She's psyched about it!" I turn to Ethan, beaming.

Her reaction was exactly what I hoped for. I let out a big, satisfied sigh and shut my eyes for a second, imagining how perfect Reese and Oliver's wedding would be here. Anywhere.

And I can't wait to tell her and Maddie the Ethan story on our video call, or at least an abridged version of it.

"But I haven't quite finished with the bucket list. Number two."

"I thought you'd adopted that polar bear?"

"Shut up." I open my eyes to glare at Ethan, which he doesn't see as he's driving, but smirks in response anyway.

Could I really kick ass in four of Evelyn's bucket list items, then have *I donated fifty quid to London Zoo* for number two?

There's only one solution to this, and my cheeks scrunch up in a broad smile.

"What are you thinking about?" Ethan asks.

"Nessie."

Ethan risks our lives for just a second to turn to me. "Really?"

I nod. "I'm not promising to adopt her. But I can foster her for now."

He turns back to the road, a sweet smile on his face. "I think we'll have enough time to get her over to your flat tonight."

That'll finish the list off just perfectly.

38

ETHAN

After sending Stella to her flat from Heathrow Airport, I'm back at The Boar and The Bear, my backpack strewn over my shoulder, still filled with things from the past three nights. I head to the table in the corner with two full pints.

I'm nervous. Nervous to talk to Ben, to tell him everything. Well, maybe not everything, but about me and Stella. It must be done, because if I'm not honest with him, it'll throw a shadow over my new relationship with Stella.

"Here you go, mate."

"Thanks, mate," Ben says, gratefully gulping down the pint. He's got no idea what's about to hit him.

"How are things?" I slide down into the cushioned chair, gulping half my pint.

"I had quite the night last night." Ben raises his eyebrows suggestively.

"Did you?"

"Guess who agreed to meet up?"

Um, this is an unexpected twist. I know it's not Stella, because she was in my arms at the B&B in Skye.

"Ulrike?"

"Yes! Ulrike."

"No way."

"Since I reached out to her two weeks ago, we've texted nonstop. I asked her out for a proper date."

"Really?"

"Took her to dinner at a nice restaurant, then we had a drink after, then walked along the Thames."

Honestly, this is not how I imagined this conversation starting, but there's a spark of hope that maybe it'll make my news less dramatic.

"Did you take her home?"

He shakes his head. "I was a gentleman and got her home, then left her at her flat. We're going to see each other again for a lunch date tomorrow."

"Lunch date, hey? That's not exactly your style?"

"And then we're going to the British Museum."

"Have you ever even been to a museum?"

"Shut up, mate, of course I have. I just want to start things right with her this time."

Starting things right. Yeah, I can relate to that. I gather up all the nerve I can.

"Ben, I wanted to talk to you about Stella."

He freezes for a beat with his pint mid-sip, eyes trained on me, then downs half the glass. I guess we'll need refills soon.

"Go ahead." He nods.

"I've . . . I've fallen for her."

Ben's eyes widen and he lets out a shocked guffaw.

"What?" He blinks and then his eyes narrow. After a long pause, he speaks. "Oh. That's why you were here last Saturday night. At my disastrous meetup with her."

I nod.

"And you never responded to my texts after that, when I saw

you run out of the pub." Ben's face is a blank slate. For once, I can't read him.

"Yes. I'm sorry I didn't respond." I didn't, because I couldn't. I'd screwed everything up. Handled it wrong with Stella, risked my lifelong friendship with Ben. I avoided the whole situation.

"I thought you couldn't stand her?"

"Turns out, I can."

There's a silence between us. Our eyes remain locked, and it looks like he's pondering the situation. Going over his possible responses. It's a lot more processing than he normally does, my easygoing, no-stress best friend.

My gut twists at the idea he could hate me for this. Push me out of his life.

"I'm sorry if you think it's inappropriate. We started working together and got close."

A slide show of our moments flips in my brain. That first meeting, the time I caught her as she fell in the office kitchen, when I offered to be her advisor, when I told her about my mum at the zoo, that first kiss . . .

"I want to be with her. I . . . I'm in love with her, mate."

Ben blinks and continues his quiet, disconcerting assessment of me. I wait for his response, like a prisoner awaiting sentencing.

"How could you?"

Oh, fuck.

I swallow hard. What the hell am I going to do if Ben doesn't support this? I can't not be with Stella. That's off the table. But I can't lose my best friend.

"Mate . . ."

"You didn't trust to tell me earlier, so you lied about it? Because you don't just fall in love after one meeting." Ben clenches his jaw, and color rises to his cheeks.

I hesitate. "I've had feelings for her for a long time."

"When I was dating her?"

I nod once. I don't need to tell him I think I've been in love with her all along.

"I'm sorry you're angry. But I can't take it back. I love her. And I hope you can accept that."

"I'm not mad you love her, mate." He raises his eyebrows.

"You're . . . not?"

"No. I'm mad you lied. I'm mad you didn't think you could be honest with me." Ben gulps his pint, then sighs deeply. "Aren't we best mates?"

"We are."

"Then treat me like it. Always."

Relief courses through my veins.

"I will. I promise." I pause. "So . . . this is okay?"

"I'm still mad as hell you lied. But yeah, it's okay." He shakes his head. "It's a good thing that when I kissed her last weekend, it was kind of like kissing a dead fish. I tried to get her to talk to me after she ran out—after you, I guess it was—but she cut me off. I wanted to tell her that we *don't* belong together."

His words wash over me, relief in every drop. He doesn't think they belong together. He is dating Ulrike again. This is all going to be okay.

"How about to make it up to me, you buy the next dozen rounds of drinks?"

"Done." I laugh.

Ben studies me. "It might get a little awkward. But honestly, I've never heard you say you loved a girl. You barely tolerate the women you hook up with. Even Helen. The look on your face right now is ridiculous."

I reflexively reach up and touch my jaw, as if the answer is under my beard, and Ben laughs. I crack a grin.

"You deserve happiness with someone, Ethan. And if it happens to be with Stella? Alright then."

I nod, my throat tight, my chest warm.

"Thanks, mate."

"Let's have one more before you go off to shag my exgirlfriend."

My eyes widen. "Um . . ."

"Right, as soon as it came out, I heard how inappropriate that sounded, and I promise I won't call her that again."

We both laugh, and I go to get the pints. One more pint with my best friend, then I need to make two more stops before heading to Stella's flat.

My body hums with the thought of being with Stella. Especially now that the Ben part is sorted, there's nothing holding us back. I was honest with him, and it didn't backfire, like I'd so dreaded.

We'll just keep That Night—the one before she and Ben got together—as our little secret.

39

STELLA

To: Richard Ramsey
From: Stella Hart
CC: Ethan Fraser
Date: 03 August 2024
Subject: Re: Re: Stella's Final Bucket List Update for Approval

Dear Richard,

I've now completed Aunt Evelyn's bucket list in the true spirit of my late great-aunt. I know she'd love how I finished each item. I know it because I felt her all around me when I was on top of the Old Man of Storr in Skye just yesterday morning.

Copied to this email is my advisor, Ethan Fraser. He can confirm I've completed the list, as he's been there every step of the way.

1. Volunteer

For this item, I changed my focus to helping a specific teenager, Izzy. I mentor her already, but this month I helped her through an application for a university scholarship, and she has since made the finals. She's so excited, and I'm hoping she gets that scholarship. She deserves it. For documentation, I attached Izzy's final submission, plus several screen shots of the texts and feedback I've given her. Ethan has also helped with the submission.

2. Adopt an Animal
Instead of adopting a polar bear from London Zoo, I'm fostering a shelter kitten, Nessie, but I am not promising to adopt her. I'm testing it out first. I'm sure Aunt Evelyn would appreciate that. Attached is a picture of Nessie, who is arriving at my flat tonight.

3. Adventure to the Isle of Skye in Scotland
I climbed the Old Man of Storr yesterday with Ethan. That place is magical, just like Aunt Evelyn said it would be, and I felt like she spoke to me on top of that rocky mountain on Skye. Her spirit was everywhere. I felt her peace, and her love, and her hope for my future. Attached is a picture of me on top of Old Man of Storr, taken by Ethan.

4. Help Reese
Being in the Scottish Highlands was so inspiring, and as we drove to Edinburgh from Skye, we visited a gorgeous castle. They have weddings there, and then it came to me: I will help Reese and her fiancé find the perfect Scottish wedding venue. Eilean Donan Castle is one option, but I'll visit a few more so she can choose. For evidence, attached is a picture of the castle I'm suggesting she consider, plus a screenshot of her acceptance of my offer to help her find a venue.

__5. Find the One that Got Away__
I was right to break up with my ex-boyfriend, Ben. In the process of talking to him via text and in person, I confirmed we do not belong together. And I found the one who really got away—Ben's best friend, Ethan, who has helped me fulfill Aunt Evelyn's bucket list. He's the one I would regret not taking a chance on, and I don't want to make the same mistake Aunt Evelyn did just because I am scared. He's already changed me, but I'm still me, just a better version. As evidence, here are two attachments. One is a picture of me with Ethan in front of Eilean Donan Castle. The second is a picture of me meeting with Ben last weekend. I almost ruined things right after this picture was taken . . . but luckily, it all worked out.

Please let me know if you need anything else.

Best,
Stella Hart

L uckily, Gemma had gotten one picture of Ben and I talking before Ethan started filming and captured that ill-fated kiss.

I've deleted that video from all our devices.

Ethan will be here with Nessie in a bit, but in the meantime, I have a video call date with my sisters. I click the *Join* button and Reese and Maddie's faces jump onto the screen.

"Hi!" they both scream at once.

I grin.

"Stella, did you submit your final list to Richard?" Reese's dark hair hangs around her face as she leans forward.

"Sure did."

"Thank god!" Maddie squeaks. "We were a bit worried about you."

"You better not have been talking about your lists behind my back."

"We didn't!" they chorus together, and we all laugh.

"Stella, why don't you go first?" Reese says.

I tell them about my five bucket list items, summarizing as quickly as I can, but there are so many squeals and questions, especially when I tell them all about my advisor and how things turned out with Ethan.

"Stella, thank you so much for your help planning the wedding. I can't imagine a greater gift." Reese has tears in her eyes, clear even through my laptop screen.

"And we need more information about Ethan!" Maddie sips from a steaming mug, eyes wide. "Immediately. I need to live vicariously through you."

"I told you a lot already! And if I can find love, you can too, Maddie. Your time will come."

Maddie dropped out of college and has gone from one restaurant job to another for the past decade, always employed, but never truly happy. I hope this inheritance gives her a chance to really figure things out for herself. She's also the most disastrous in love. She falls fast and hard, and constantly makes bad decisions, like always dating or hooking up with people she works with. Never a good idea. It messes with her jobs as well as her emotional stability.

I silently cackle as I recognize the irony in me criticizing dating coworkers, as I just had a whirlwind romance with a client.

Maddie shrugs and her face falls. "Whatever. Who needs love?"

"Mads, tell us about your list," Reese prompts.

Our youngest sister brightens. "I'm basically changing my entire life because of Aunt Evelyn." She laughs, and my eyes widen. "The first item was to make a plan on how the inheritance would build my future. So . . . I quit my job."

Reese and I both gasp.

"I'm going to enroll in a hospitality course that starts in October. I'll figure out what to do from there."

"October? What will you do between now and then?" I'm thrilled she quit her restaurant job. Shitty benefits, shitty hours, and no chance for a real social life besides dating waiters or cooks or bartenders, and, at least once, her manager.

"The second and third items are kind of connected and explain what I'll be doing. Aunt Evelyn said I needed to book a vacation, a real one, and also volunteer for something. So, I'm leaving in a few weeks for a month in Saint Lucia, where I'm going to volunteer for Helping Build Homes. They're a nonprofit. You guys have heard of them, I'm sure."

My jaw drops open, and a quick glance at Reese shows a similar expression.

"Holy shit, Maddie, I'm impressed," Reese says.

Maddie blushes and continues. "Two more. I had to go to Aunt Evelyn's favorite spot in New York City—the top of the Empire State Building—and see if I could find her. I did. Just like you, Stella."

"I don't want to butt in, but I might as well add that I had a similar item," Reese says. "I went hiking in the Ramapo Mountains in Jersey to find her. It worked for me, too."

We all sit in silence for a few seconds, feeling Evelyn's love and connection flow through us.

"Last one," Maddie continues. "I needed to do something significant for Stella, so I set up a shared bucket list and photo sharing site. It's really for all of us to keep more in touch. There's a great app for it."

"That's awesome, I love it," I say.

"Agree. That will be wonderful," Reese says. "My turn. You already heard one, and the next was to do something significant for Maddie. It was my offer to have you live with us, Mads, although you didn't tell me why you needed a place to stay temporarily. I would've been happy to have you no matter what."

"Our great-aunt was so sneaky." Maddie has a big smile on her face. "And staying with you will let me travel and do the hospitality program without wasting money on rent."

"It's perfect. I'm glad it works out." Reese smiles. "I had to volunteer as well, so I not only took Aunt Evelyn's cat, Simba—Peanut Butter is not impressed so far—but I signed up to volunteer at the animal shelter she loved so much. You know, the one she was going to donate all her money to if we screwed up."

We laugh.

"Another item was to do something only for me. I took the next step to opening my own website design side hustle by setting up the website, the LLC, and put a basic marketing plan together. A little bit of cheating, as I was already going to do that. But it'll work."

"I won't judge you for a little cheating." I shake my head. "Sometimes that's just necessary."

"Finally, she wanted me to schedule a trip in the future with the two of you."

"Ohhh," I say, loving the glint in her eye.

"I've decided that next summer, before the wedding, I want to do a road trip through Ireland."

Maddie gasps.

"Ireland? Amazing," I say.

"Yup. Oliver's best friend and old soccer teammate, Patrick, lives in Dingle, which is in the south of Ireland, a gorgeous seaside town, apparently. And I've always wanted to go. Get ready for it, ladies."

"I am ready." I nod enthusiastically. "Maddie?"

"Sure, why not? Can I help plan it?"

"Of course," Reese says. "I'll be swamped with wedding stuff, so I'd love if you can help."

"And by then, it won't matter if Stuffy Richard doesn't like you helping with Reese's bucket list item," I say. But internally, I raise my eyebrows at Maddie's offer to help plan the trip. Maddie is not the most organized of the three of us, so I can't wait to see how this goes.

"Hooray! Just . . . remind me where Ireland is?" Maddie deadpans.

Reese snorts, then Maddie starts giggling, then I join in, and soon the three of us are laughing so hard tears flow down my cheeks. It's joyful and sincere and sad at the same time. When the laughter dies down, Reese speaks.

"I can't believe Aunt Evelyn's gone. I wish she was here to see all this."

"Me too, but this is what she wanted," I say. "To encourage us to live our best lives, like she did."

I think about her lost love on the Isle of Skye. She had regrets, too. Maybe we all will, eventually, but I guess it's a worthy goal to minimize those regrets as much as possible.

We all say goodbye with promises to let each other know when we hear back from Richard. I disconnect the call with a wide smile on my face. When I minimize my video call screen, there's a new email in my inbox.

To: Richard Ramsey
From: Ethan Fraser
CC: Stella Hart
Date: 03 August 2024
Subject: Re: Re: Re: Stella's Final Bucket List Update for Approval

As her advisor, I can confirm Stella has completed all the tasks as she stated.

-Ethan Fraser

There's a knock at my door.

I rush over and swing it open. Ethan's standing there, gorgeous as always, holding a giant bag in one hand and a cardboard cat carrier in the other.

"Kitten delivery service," he says. "Did you order an angry black kitten?"

"Hmm, nope, sorry, wrong flat." I fake close the door, then open it and step back so he can come in.

Nessie is desperately mewing in the box.

"She can wait just a minute." Ethan places the bag and box on the floor.

"Got everything I need?"

"Yes." He steps forward and closes the distance between us, pulling me against him. I slide my hands up his chest and around his neck.

"It went okay with Ben?"

"Mmm-hmm." He dips his face down to mine and kisses me, gently at first, then with more intensity. My heart pounds so hard in my chest, I feel like I just might explode.

This man is mine. He loves me. I love him.

Nessie mews with increasing intensity and we both freeze mid-kiss.

"Let's get that kitten out so I can officially finish Aunt Evelyn's bucket list."

And after one more kiss, we do just that.

February (six months later)

"How many kids are signed up?" Ethan drops next to me on the couch in our new flat, a glass of red wine for me in one hand. After his sabbatical ended in the fall, Ethan went back to work at his brand management job. We got a bigger place in St John's Wood, sticking close to the Pepper Me Marketing office and Regent's Park, where Ethan continues to coach the boys a few times a week. Even in the winter. It's not like a New Jersey winter, but it's wet and cold and dark in London.

"We've got ten, so we're all full for the first trip." I click through the website for Evelyn's Magical Skye Tours, admiring Reese's design. It looks amazing.

"Congratulations."

"To us." I take the wine glass from him, and he clinks it gently with his own drink.

The new charity has been a labor of love and determination over the past six months. I took some of Evelyn's inheritance and started Evelyn's Magical Skye Tours as a side project. We plan to take groups of kids from the newly established Sporting UK Foundation—and other charities that serve underprivileged teenagers—to Skye for an outdoor adventure trip. They'll ride a bus up from London, stay one night in Edinburgh, then continue on to the adorable town of Portree, where Ethan and I visited after our hike up the Old Man of Storr. They will do some hiking of their own, go see the famous fairy pools, and absorb the magic of the island.

The same magic I felt when we were there in August.

I've been working on getting a few corporate sponsors to support the trips, which we'd like to do three times a year—June, July, and August—but will start with just one this summer. We're partnering with tour operators that are already there to make it easy, and sending mentors to supervise the trip. Ethan and I will be going on the first one, right after Reese's wedding this summer.

Ethan's been amazing, using his brand management experience to help with messaging and communication with some of the sponsors. We're a great team, and between the two of us, we can handle the charity plus our regular day jobs. He even got promoted just after the new year.

And the Sporting UK Foundation commercial brought in significant donations, helping to establish the merged charity and ensure it can continue to serve kids in London.

Nessie springs up from the floor and settles on Ethan's lap. He's definitely her favorite, and I still get some *somewhat* gentle nips from her if she catches us kissing and wants his attention.

Ethan's a man transformed. He went to see Ben's parents in the fall, and talked to them about his childhood and what they meant to him. And as expected, they didn't think he owed them one single thing. We've even gotten drinks with Ben and his girlfriend, Ulrike, a bunch of times. It was a bit weird at first, but now it's almost normal.

I think Evelyn would be happy with what I've chosen to do with her money. Besides starting the charity, I finished paying off all my loans, and had a bit leftover to get a few things for the new flat. I saved some as well, because you never know what'll come up.

I appreciate what she forced me to face last summer. Sure, the bucket list was a reflection of herself and her own regrets, not how she needed me to live my life. But I figured a lot of stuff out. Things that will ensure I don't end up with a life full of regrets like her or my father. How I choose to live my life is all about me.

And now, me and Ethan.

I rub the butterfly tattoo on my wrist. When I got it before I moved to London almost eight years ago, I thought it was about freedom. But now? Now I think it's really about transformation. That you can change your life completely, while also keeping who you are at the core.

"I have a surprise for you." Ethan slides his beer bottle onto the coffee table and lays his hand on the back of the couch around me.

"A surprise?" I push my laptop on the cushion next to me and turn to Ethan, giving Nessie a gentle stroke on the head to show her I'm not trying to steal her man.

"I booked us a trip for next weekend. You'd said you wanted to get out of London for a few days, and since our hiking is on hold for the winter . . ."

I laugh. Yeah, it's on hold. When I said I wanted us to climb the highest peaks in the UK, I didn't really know what I was getting us into. This is probably going to be more like a five-year project, as some of these mountain peaks are only reasonably accessible in the summer months, unless you want to bring an ice ax and other hard core hiking tools, which I do not. We got through just one before it got too cold in the fall, and we have another planned for this summer. We're thinking Ben Nevis up in Fort Williams, Scotland. It happens to be the highest of the peaks, so I'm wondering if we're being too ambitious. Probably.

"So it's not climbing a mountain?"

"Hey, that was all *your* idea for my bucket list. I bet you didn't do a lot of research on that one before you suggested it."

"You'd be correct." I picture that one Google search.

He grins. "But fortunately, no, this is a long weekend at a castle."

"Ahhh, that sounds great. But Reese already picked the castle she wants to get married at."

Ethan and I visited five different wedding venues from August through December, including three castles, but Reese went with the first one we sent her, Eilean Donan Castle in the Scottish Highlands. She got super lucky with a June wedding opening.

"So you're done visiting castles?" Ethan quirks an eyebrow.

"God, no." I fake a look of horror. "Where's this one?"

"We're going to stay at Thornbury Castle, a gorgeous old castle in Bristol which is now a fancy hotel. Giant, drafty old rooms made of stone where kings and queens once stayed. Quaint little town."

"You know how I like stone rooms." My cheeks warm at the memory of what we did in Eilean Donan Castle last summer and at two other castles since.

"I do. Unless you don't want to go to a gorgeous, cozy castle for a romantic weekend with your boyfriend-slash-roommate?"

"Hmm, not sure. It's a tough call."

Ethan rolls his eyes and hands me his phone, where pictures of Thornbury Castle are pulled up. I gasp.

"Still a tough call?"

"This is amazing. Unless there's like a foot of snow on the ground and it's too cold to leave the room to appreciate the castle."

"Unless that would make the weekend even better." Ethan waggles his eyebrows, then takes a finger and runs it under my chin, turning my mouth up to him, sending tingles down my spine.

"That would definitely make it better."

I close the short distance between our lips and shut my eyes as we make contact. I'll never get over the way his body feels against mine, the way my heartbeat speeds up when he's near, the way my mood soars just looking at him.

And this happily ever after? I don't think it has an *unless* attached to it.

THE END

Want to read one more chapter with Stella & Ethan? Get the bonus epilogue by subscribing to Chrissy's newsletter on her website: www.ChrissyHopewell.com. Also available only to Chrissy's newsletter subscribers: *One Hundred Lights*, a free novella.

Loved *Unless It's You*? Leave an honest review on Amazon or Goodreads. It helps so much!

Check out *If We Pretend*, Reese & Oliver's love story, out now!

Since We're Here is next, Maddie's happily ever after! Preorder now, and it releases September 2024.

Stay in touch:
Instagram: @ChrissyHopewell
Facebook: ChrissyHopewellAuthor
TikTok: @ChrissyHopewellBooks
Email: Chrissy@ChrissyHopewell.com
Free novella & bonus chapters:
www.ChrissyHopewell.com

ACKNOWLEDGMENTS

I'm beyond excited I got to publish another romance novel. I can't believe I'm lucky enough to do this! Writing a novel based in London felt so good as I lived there for five years and absolutely loved it. I got to hang out in Regent's Park again, even if just in my imagination.

Thank you to everyone who's supported me in this journey, including my Pitch Wars support network and all my beta readers and CPs who made this book so much better: Lillian, Paris, Lisa, Sarah, Cate, Ericka. Thanks to my Discord writing buddies and my high school besties. And thank you from the bottom of my writerly soul to my husband and children, who are just generally confused as to what I'm doing with my life (same same).

Finally, thank you to my editor, Brenda Chin, my cover designer, Stephanie Anderson at Alt 19 Creative, and Lindsey Hinkel, my proofreader. I'm lucky to have you all on my team!

And thank YOU, reader, for giving me your time and attention. I can't wait to share my next story with you!

Love, Chrissy

BOOK CLUB DISCUSSION GUIDE

1. Grief was a key theme in this novel, with Stella mourning her great-aunt and Ethan mourning his mother. How different is it grieving someone you are close to versus a relative you're not close to?
2. Stella was firm in her decision to not have children. What do you think about this decision in this day and age? How do people perceive women who choose not to have children? Is it different from how they perceive men?
3. Sometimes readers don't like fiercely independent women like Stella. They can be called *unlikable*. Why do you think that is?
4. Have you ever had to deal with a parent who was not engaged or involved in your life, like Ethan? Or seen someone close to you deal with it? How do you think that affects adult children of these types of parents?
5. Ethan had a found family in Ben and his parents. Why do we, as readers, love the concept of found family so much? What's the difference between found family and friends?

ABOUT THE AUTHOR

Chrissy Hopewell started her love for romance novels by sneaking her mom's steamy books in middle school. She has spent varying amounts of time overseas, including working at a pub in Dublin, waitressing at a hotel in the Scottish Borders, and studying and living in London. Because of these experiences, international flair and accents often show up in her writing. Chrissy now lives in the suburbs of Cincinnati, Ohio with her family, and she no longer has to sneak what she reads.

instagram.com/chrissyhopewell

tiktok.com/@chrissyhopewellbooks

facebook.com/chrissyhopewellauthor